MAGICAL QUEST

BARBARA DONLON BRADLEY

MAGICAL QUEST
Copyright © 2022 by Barbara Donlon Bradley

ISBN: 979-8-88653-037-7

Published by Satin Romance
An Imprint of Melange Books, LLC
White Bear Lake, MN 55110
www.satinromance.com

Published in the United States of America.

Cover Design by Ashley Redbird Designs

CHAPTER ONE

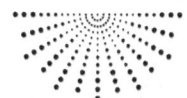

Grinnell sat in the cockpit of his ship and stared out at the stars. The freedom from the tyrant who had control of his home planet was a heady thing. Now he was in charge of the Emori space fleet created to explore as well as protect the planets in the system from another tyrant taking control ever again.

He had run several of the ships through maneuvers and was happy with their performance. Grinnell had a few more tests to run, and then he would be able to approve their latest class of ships. Then maybe he could have a few duras to himself. It would all depend on Astrid and Orla.

Astrid wiped her brow. She stood with Grenta in the ballroom with the massive doors open to the outside. Astrid was born with Barou blood, giving her the ability to create images that looked and felt real to anyone without it. Grenta continued to train her to be a Barou master, something she strived to be good at, but right now she just wanted a cool breeze and a cold drink.

"If I am pushing too hard, you must tell me," said Grenta.

"You're not." Astrid placed her hands against the small of her back and stretched. "I just feel a little uncomfortable."

Grenta didn't believe a word. "Child, you're six lunas along. If you need a break, then let's take a break."

"I would like a drink." Astrid nodded to the young woman who was her personal handmaid. The young lady bowed and went to get refreshments.

Astrid gave her mate, Orla, a bright smile when he was the one who came out with a tray a few microns later.

"How are you feeling?"

"We feel good." Astrid rubbed her protruding womb. "Maybe a little uncomfortable from time to time, but good."

"I am very happy to hear that." He put the tray on a small table against the wall, then placed one hand on top of hers as he placed a soft kiss against the corner of her mouth. "Can you take a break?"

"Of course," said Grenta. "I'll go check on Metan. He's been working a little too hard."

Astrid leaned into Orla's strength as she watched her mentor leave. "What has he been working on?"

"I don't know, but they're both being secretive about it." He wrapped his arms around her. "As much as they dote on you and our unborn child, I think it's something special for the birth."

"It must be, if he's working on it this early." As their hands rested on her abdomen, the baby chose that moment to kick. Astrid laughed. "And I think he's happy about a gift."

"So you think it's a boy? I thought you didn't want to know."

"I don't, but I just get this feeling." The baby moved, and she felt it.

"Are you alright?" he asked.

"Orla, I am fine. Oh." She stopped talking when their baby kicked her hard. "You've had how many doctors watch over me?"

"This is the first time a Barou and a Miran are having a child. I don't want any harm to come to you or our baby." He led her to a chair out on the balcony of the ballroom. The cloth covering the sitting area he had brought out to blocked the sun's rays. "I just want everything to go right."

"You worry too much. There have been no signs of trouble." She took a seat. "I'm…"

"You're what?" He had gone back in to get the tray. Once he set it on the table she sat at, he pulled up a chair. She didn't respond and sat motionless. "Astrid, are you alright?"

She blinked a few times then looked at him.

"Oh, my." He stood up. "I'll be right back."

"Now what was that all about?" Astrid brushed her hair out of her face. She braced her hand to lever herself up but found it a little too hard to do. The tray was next to her, so she picked up the drink and took a sip.

It didn't take long before Grenta followed Orla back outside. She took one look at Astrid and said the same thing Orla did.

"Oh, my." She pressed the back of her hand against Astrid's pulse then moved it behind her ear.

"Have you ever seen this before?"

"Once." Grenta looked at Astrid. "How do you feel?"

"Why does everyone keep asking me that? What is going on?" She created a hand mirror and held it up so she could see her face. "Oh, my."

Orla sat in the chair he had occupied earlier and took her hands.

"So why is one pupil white?" Astrid asked Grenta.

"The one time I saw this was when a child had developed their Barou power in the womb, and not knowing better, the child started draining power from their mother."

"You first said 'a child,' then said 'their.' Why?"

"Because there were two. Twins."

"But I don't think I'm having twins. I haven't felt two moving inside." She gripped Orla's hand. "My stars, are you saying that our child is not only going to be a Miran, but also a very powerful Barou?"

"I don't know, but there is a way to test you and the baby."

"There is?" She felt relief wash over her. "Oh, Good."

"It has to be done by the leader of the Barou." Grenta tried not to show her worry, but Astrid saw it.

Astrid wanted to scream. How was she supposed to be tested when she couldn't leave the planet at her stage of her pregnancy? Grenta had been banned by the council, so any Barou training she received from Grenta didn't count.

"We're talking about the same person who won't recognize me as a Barou because I haven't been tested properly." Astrid tightened her hold

3

on Orla's hand. "And I've been ordered to stay here by the doctors until I give birth."

"Then we must bring the leader of the Barou here," said Orla.

Grinnell stepped into the garden of the palace. He found Orla waiting for him. "You sounded urgent."

Orla gestured for Grinnell to walk with him. "I need you to bring the leader of the Barou here."

"Um, you want me to go to the Barou planet, where no one but a Barou is allowed to step foot on and scoop her off her feet and bring her here?" Grinnell felt like he had walked into the middle of a crazy dream. What was going on?

Orla laughed. "If you pull that off, it will make you famous."

"You mean infamous."

"Grenta will get you clearance."

"The woman who was banned by the same people you want me to steal their leader from?" That didn't make Grinnell feel any better.

"You're not stealing her." Orla gave him a reassuring smile.

"I am if she says no." Grinnell placed a hand on Orla's shoulder. "I know you wouldn't ask me to do this if it wasn't important, and I'm pretty sure it involves Astrid, so you know I'm going to help no matter what. But it sure would make me feel better if I knew what was going on."

"There has been a slight complication with my mate. Grenta has been in contact with the council and made them aware of Astrid. She also let them know she couldn't travel because of her pregnancy." Orla opened one of the doors that allowed them to enter the ballroom. "They will know you're coming and will make sure you come back with the person we need to help my mate."

"Is something wrong with the child?" Grinnell could sense the urgency in Orla's voice. The thought of Astrid or the baby being in danger twisted in his gut. They were family.

"No, we're just being cautious right now." Orla slapped him on the back. "Would you like to join us for midmeal?"

"I do have some time before I can lift off."

"Wonderful," said a soft feminine voice behind him.

"My Queen, you look wonderful." He bowed in front of Astrid. He felt her hands on his shoulders and he stood so they could hug. "You have two different color eyes?"

"Yeah, one of the reasons we're asking for help from the Barou." She stepped back and took Orla's hand. "Grenta says it's unusual and feels the leader of the Barou would be the one who will be able to tell me if there is a problem and how to deal with it."

"I'll get her as quickly as I can." Now he understood.

"Don't race off too quickly," said Astrid. "You did promise to have a meal with us, and I feel wonderful. So you don't have to break the light barrier to retrieve her."

He nodded, then followed them into the family area of the palace. Astrid hadn't wanted to be the queen of Emori after Varal was defeated, but the people had wanted her. When she'd told them she didn't want the power, they'd agreed. So now she was a figurehead. She had the title but not the power, and that made her very happy.

Once he sat in the chair offered to him, he spoke to Orla. "And how is your father?"

"Much better." Orla smiled. "He has destroyed anything my stupid brother created and repaired anything that idiot destroyed."

Astrid nodded to the chef, who stood near the kitchen entrance. He snapped his heels together and headed back into the kitchen.

"There has been a steady flow of items to sell and trade to other planets. They love the unique creations the Draharians make and are clamoring for more."

"That is good to hear," said Orla. "And as time goes on, there will be more. There are many talented artists on Drahar. A lot went into hiding when Varal took control of my brother and imprisoned my father."

Varal had been the general of Emori's army. Astrid's father had trusted him, not knowing that Varal had designs to take control. He'd killed Astrid's father, thinking he could marry Astrid to become the ruler of Emori. When he learned that Astrid had been betrothed to the heir to the throne on Darhar, Varal went to that planet, signed a treaty with Orla's brother and forced Orla's parents into hiding. Orla's stupid brother had seen this as an opportunity to take over. He pretended to be Astrid's intended. Varal had no clue who Astrid's betrothed was, and Orla's brother took advantage of that.

"A lot realized there was something wrong when your mother went to visit family and never returned, Orla," Astrid responded. She looked up as people started to flow in with their food.

"Really?" asked Grinnell.

"Orla's father didn't want Varal to use her to control him. He was also smart enough to make his son believe she was killed in an accident before she could come home," said Astrid. She sat back when her meal was placed in front of her. "When I finally met her, I realized where Orla got his intelligence from."

"You make me sound like some sort of brainiac." Orla nodded as someone placed his meal in front of him as well.

"Oh, my stars, you hacked my father's computer system, then you hacked the general's system when we were on the ship Grinnell stole. You are brilliant, and so is your mother."

"Then I should say thank you. It's not every dura that my mate gives me a compliment in public."

"This isn't public. Grinnell is family, and he would never repeat anything I say here. Neither would the staff." She gave him a sweet smile. "No one heard a thing."

Orla laughed. "I see. Then the next time I do something and you compliment me, I should make sure it is on the main news feed so I will have witnesses."

"You can try sweetheart but remember we women stick together. And there are women who work for the newsfeeds. They're the interviewers, or on the staff. There might be an accident and the information gets deleted."

"And I'd have no evidence?" He grinned as he looked at her.

She just smiled.

Grinnell watched their interaction with rapt attention. Once Varal had been defeated and life went back to normal, Astrid and Orla's relationship changed from protector and victim to a happy couple. Something he was glad to see. "You look wonderful, Astrid."

"You are too kind, Grinnell."

"She doesn't agree, my friend. It seems her womb has knocked over one too many items and now she feels like a warbling grenat."

"Those big, lumbering birds?" Grinnell looked at her like she had lost her mind. "Why do women always feel that way as they get closer to their child's birth? You are beautiful and graceful, and you barely show."

She nodded as a tear slipped down her cheek.

"What did I say?" Grinnell looked at Orla.

"Astrid's emotions are a little out of control. Your compliment touched her." He got up and placed his hand on her shoulder in support. "The crying is new. It started when my mate realized that some of her favorite clothes no longer fit."

"I heard that all emotions can be heightened during pregnancy. It's not unusual for that to happen."

Astrid rolled her eyes at his comment.

"Did I say something wrong?" Wow, how many times was he going to say something that would get some sort of negative reaction?

"I'm sorry, Grinnell," Astrid replied. "Everyone seems to have some great wisdom they feel they must tell me. Another lovely thing that has been happening is that every woman with children wants to tell me their lovely little birthing horrors."

"Oh dear," said Grinnell. "That explains a lot."

"And please don't tell me that the joy of holding my child will wash away the pain that could happen with childbirth."

"I wouldn't dare." He looked at Orla. "Another wonderful story?"

She nodded. Astrid grimaced as she rubbed her head.

"Are you okay?" asked Orla.

She looked up at him and smiled.

Grinnell watched her rest her head against Orla's shoulder as her eyes rolled into the back of her head. He stood in fear, afraid if Orla moved, her head would drop and she would hurt herself. A few securs later, she blinked and was okay. Grinnell didn't know what to think. "How often does that happen?"

"What happened?" asked Astrid.

Orla looked at him.

"Oh, your eyes were the same color for an instant, but now you're back to the one white and one violet." He wasn't about to tell her she had passed out for a few securs.

"So there is hope," she sighed. "I'm sorry, Grinnell, but I'm feeling a little drained. I think I should go rest a little before Grenta asks me to work on my Barou training a little more."

"Of course." He bowed as she turned then waited as Orla escorted her out of the room.

Grenta entered as they left. She spoke softly to Astrid for a few securs before approaching Grinnell.

"I have contacted the Barou council, and they have let me know that our leader went on a walkabout." She gave him a slight bow to acknowledge him.

He bowed back. "What is that?"

"Basically, she has stepped away from her position as leader to reflect on what she wants to do next."

Several servants moved around them to clean the room for the next time Astrid and Orla entered it. Grinnell gestured for Grenta to step outside for a micron.

"Great, at least I don't have to face the council." He felt more comfortable away from all the extra ears. He was pretty sure Grenta felt the same way. "Any idea where she went?"

"They believe she went into the nomad zone." She watched for a reaction.

His eyes got big, and he took a step back.

"No, no, no, no, no. I'm not going there." He shook his head. "Are you kidding? That's where a lot of Varal's soldiers ran to when they learned he had been defeated."

"I know that." Grenta looked past his shoulder, making him turn around. "It is also where you lived while Varal was in charge. You know how to get in and out without detection."

"I had one of Varal's best ships then." He noticed Orla coming toward them. "I'm not piloting an attack ship now. My ship is more for exploring."

"That's why you're not taking your normal ship," said Orla as he rejoined them. "Those soldiers knew if they surrendered, they would have to face their crimes. From what I've heard, they just want to be left alone. You're going in one of my newer ships, but one of our best, just in case."

"And if they decide to take the ship because of that?"

Orla grinned. Grinnell had stolen one of General Varal's ships when he'd decided he had enough of Varal's dictatorship. He'd chosen one of his best because he didn't want to get caught. Now he feared someone would do the same to him. "I think you'll find this ship to be perfect."

Grinnell nodded, but he didn't believe him.

"Come. Let me show you your new ship." Orla led the way. He stepped into a land cruiser with the royal crest and waited for Grenta and Grinnell to join him. The micron they were seated he took off.

"You love this thing, don't you?" Grenta asked through gritted teeth.

"You still haven't gotten used to riding in vehicles?" asked Grinnell.

"Never cared for them." She had a white-knuckle grip on the chair she sat in.

"She also thinks I race everywhere." Orla turned to look at her and gave her a wink.

"Keep your eyes on where we're going." Grenta made a little circular motion so he would turn around.

Orla laughed as he focused on landing the craft inside the massive hanger Varal had built for his fleet. "Since we took this place over, we've created several elite vessels. The one you'll be using is my personal favorite. I created it for my family. It has two sleeping quarters, a small mess hall, and a hanger deck, but there is a lot of storage area that can be converted into more living space if needed. I figured as my family expanded, I could convert the extra space into whatever we need."

"What sort of weapons does it have?" asked Grinnell.

"Enough to protect the ship ten times over." He stopped in front of a sleek ship. "I think you're going to fall for this ship."

"And if I do?"

"Oh, I know you will. And if you bring back the leader of the Barou, I'll make you one of your own."

Grinnell waited for clearance from the hanger command and took off the secur he got it.

"Smooth," he said to himself. Once he was out of the main flight lanes, he took it through a few maneuvers.

"Damn, Orla might be right," he said to himself. "This is nice."

He spent the next few horas getting to know the ship. By the time he hit the border of the nomad zone, he knew the ship backwards and forwards.

"Gods, I hate this place." It reminded him of his time running. He was good at hiding, but he didn't want to do that anymore. The planet the leader was on was a few horas away, so he decided to go through the woman's file once more.

He found it fascinating that even though men could also be Barou masters, no man had ever held the position of leader. They didn't have the stamina to make it through the tests. The current leader, Lawaya, had been off planet for over six lunas, which was the longest any leader had ever been away. In the past, she had kept up her communication with the council in case she was needed, but they hadn't heard from her in three lunas.

If Grenta hadn't contacted them, no one would have known about her disappearance. Secrecy was their second name. All he knew was what Grenta had taught him. From the file he had, this Lawaya was going to be difficult. He hoped he could be as convincing as everyone expected him to be.

The planet came into view until it was the only thing filling his viewscreen. Using the data in the file, he scanned for Lawaya but found no trace of her. This place was riddled with caves; could she be in one that his scanners couldn't penetrate?

"Change the scan for heat signatures and filter out all metals but iron." He watched as the computer did as he asked, but that didn't work either. Grinnell drummed his fingers on the arm of his chair. "Any suggestions?"

"There is a rare compound in the body of a Barou that helps with their power," stated the computer. "Although each scan has included it we haven't tried scanning for just that compound, no matter how minute."

"Do it."

It took a few microns, but they got a hit.

"Set us down as close as you can. I don't plan on staying long."

Once the ship touched down, he powered everything off and stepped onto the ground. It smelled so fresh here. The mouth of the cave was a little further than he would like, but the ship was still visible when he got to it.

He checked the exterior, looking for footprints or waste, but there was no evidence of anyone living here. The dark cave looked abandoned, but as he walked around a weird vibration went up his legs. What caused that? "Okay, that wasn't normal. Computer, what does your scan show?"

"There is an electronic barrier there."

"One that is shorting out?"

"I don't think that is what's happening, but the material it is made from isn't top of the line, which is why you felt the surge."

"How strong is it?"

"It will keep you out and will last for duras."

That figured. He wanted to get in and out quickly, but if Lawaya was hiding behind that barrier, he wasn't going to get what he wanted. Astrid needed this woman, so he wouldn't leave without her, but he was tempted.

Grinnell walked up to the force field and pressed his hand against it. "If that doesn't get their attention, nothing will."

He saw the weapon first.

"You're not wanted here," said a female voice.

Was that Lawaya? Why was she hiding? And why did she pull a weapon? Was she in trouble? He didn't have time for this. "Nonetheless, I'm here, and I need to speak to Lawaya."

"Go away!"

"Not until I speak with Lawaya." The woman talking didn't admit she was Lawaya, but if she was, wouldn't she use her Barou powers to disguise herself? "You can ignore me all you want, but I'm not leaving until I speak to Lawaya."

A young female arm grabbed his hand and pulled him into the cave. "Can you hide your ship?"

He hit a button on the metal band on his wrist and the ship vanished from sight.

11

She nodded and scanned the horizon.

"There isn't a soul out there."

"Ha!" She glared at him. "That shows what you know."

Grinnell couldn't help it. He rolled his eyes as he tapped his wrist. "Computer, are you picking up anything?"

"Two males are moving in on the cave as we speak."

So he had been wrong. "Where did they come from?"

"There is a small town nearby. It's close enough that our arrival could have caught their attention."

"You showed them where we were," the young woman scolded.

"This is something I can easily fix." It would take nothing to send them back the way they came.

"How?" She looked like she wanted to hit him.

He frowned. Why would she be so angry over this? "Computer, how far away are they from you?"

"Several klicks. They are approaching the cave from the opposite direction of my location."

"Then we can pretend that I found nothing and leave." He gave the young woman a knowing smile. These men will think he had left and be on their way, then he could get what he came for and be on his way as well.

"Yes. I can move to a remote location until you need me."

"Perfect." He looked at the woman.

"You—you can't stay here." She pressed her hand against her throat as she took a step back.

Not the reaction he expected. Didn't she realize he meant her no harm? "It's not permanent. I came to speak to Lawaya. Once I do, I'll get out of your hair."

"Um, you can't." Fear radiated from her. Looking behind her, she continued, "She's not here."

"Then you know where she is." Good. He did find the right person to take him to Lawaya.

"No." She blinked her overly bright eyes as she shook her head.

Grinnell noticed when he tried to make eye contact with her, she started looking everywhere but at him. She was lying, but why?

He heard his ship take off and knew the edge of the cave she had dragged him into had a good vantage point to watch their intruders. How he was going to handle her lying he wasn't sure, but now he couldn't go anywhere, so he was going to have to figure it out.

They watched the two men as they saw Grinnell's ship take off.

"His ship left?" asked one.

"You think he took her with him?" asked the other.

"I don't think he was here long enough to accomplish that." The one speaking looked at the other. "Let's set up camp. Once we're done, I'll contact our leader and let them know what transpired here. The stranger could come back."

"See? Told you." The young woman was close enough to whisper in his ear.

"Who is it they want?" He turned and watched her as she stared out at the men setting up camp.

"Lawaya." She moved away from the mouth of the cave. "I overheard them say something about needing a Barou for some mission the last time they were here."

"So they believe she is here as well." At least he had confirmation that Lawaya was on the planet if she wasn't in the cave he stood in.

"I'd know if she was here, and I promise she's not."

She sure was adamant about it.

"Then where is she?" He wasn't going to leave until he found Lawaya. Perhaps if he kept at it, he'd get a straight answer.

The young woman's gaze dropped to the floor. "I don't know."

CHAPTER TWO

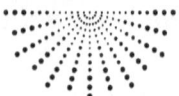

Mehanna had no clue who this man was, but he needed to go. It was bad enough that Lawaya had disappeared because of her. She couldn't take a chance that she'd make him disappear too.

It hurt to know she had caused harm to Lawaya. The woman had found her in this cave and had decided to take her under her wing and train her. Why? She had no answer. She wasn't Barou. She might have a little talent, but it caused more trouble than good. Lawaya didn't see it as a problem. She felt every talent needed discipline and training. So what if their abilities weren't the same? Training was training to her, and Lawaya had felt she could help her.

Boy, had she been wrong.

The problem was when she made a mistake like she had with Lawaya, there was no one to show her how to reverse it.

If only.

If Lawaya hadn't asked her what would happen if she did try to create something out of thin air, maybe none of this would have happened. The wonderful lady had shown her how she could change her image to a full-length mirror and had challenged Mehanna to create a mirror like the one she'd turned into. When Mehanna had tried to create the mirror, she'd ended up trapping Lawaya inside it. Thank the gods the mirror hadn't vanished, so when she went to the mirror she could see Lawaya, but she didn't know how to bring her back. She also couldn't talk to her. They couldn't hear each other, and Lawaya had nothing to write on to allow them to communicate that way.

But this man couldn't know that.

"What is your name, anyway?" He watched her.

"Mehanna."

"And how did you and Lawaya end up here?"

"I've lived here all of my life." She crossed her arms over her chest. Why was he watching her like that? "What's with the questions, anyway?"

"Small talk?" He shrugged. "Did you want me to call you 'hey you' all the time?"

"You won't be here long enough for that to be annoying." She tried to sound dismissive. Maybe he'd leave if she was.

"So you want me to walk out of here now?" He pointed to the mouth of the cave. "While those men are camping out there?"

Mehanna bit her lip. She had forgotten about them. "Of course not." She looked out to see if they had tents set up and a fire going already. "Hopefully, they won't stay too long."

"They look like they're ready to stay for a cycle." He looked around. "You stay here?"

"I have lived here all my life."

"Really? Here in this cave? You have no food, no weapons, no furniture."

Should she show him where she lived? She couldn't leave him at the mouth of the cave. He looked far too smart to not figure out she lived in another section. She hesitated for a micron longer, then said, "Follow me."

She checked a few times to be sure he followed as she weaved her way through several tunnels. When they arrived, Mehanna stopped and stepped to the side. "This is home."

He whistled as he looked around. "This is nice."

"Thank you, I think." She brushed a stray hair out of her face.

"What sort of security do you have?"

That made the hairs on the back of her neck stand up. "I'm sorry, but

I'm not going to tell you anything that you can use against me later. I have security. It works for me, and that is all that counts."

"Okay, let me rephrase that. You've lived in this cave all your life. A cave that is in a section of space that doesn't have access to the latest technology, yet you have a shield you shouldn't." He gestured to her wall of electronics. "And this looks far too advanced compared to anything else I've seen in this sector over the yepas."

"So you've spent time in this sector?"

He hesitated for a moment. "Yes, when Varal was in charge. I had stolen one of his ships and abandoned his army. This sector was the only place I could hide in the beginning."

"The beginning?"

"It's a long, sad story that is better left untold."

"As you pointed out earlier, those men are there for a while, so you can't leave. Your story can't be that long."

"It really isn't that interesting."

"Why don't you let me be the judge of that." She could tell he didn't want to talk about his past, but she didn't care. Mehanna sat in a chair and crossed her arms. She watched him as he hesitated and then stared at her as he decided what to do.

"My name is Grinnell. On Emori, I was the son of a farmer. My father wanted me to follow in his footsteps, but I found I had a knack with any equipment that moved. I repaired my father's old farm equipment. I could keep it running when my dad needed it, and when he bought new ones, he gave me the old ones to do whatever I wanted. I took parts from each and created a speedster and a hovercraft, just to name a couple of things.

"Varal got wind and gave my father an offer he couldn't refuse. If my father let him have me, he'd waive dad's taxes. As much as my dad didn't want to accept the man's offer, he knew it would help my family. I did too."

"You worked for that vile man?" She couldn't believe what she was hearing. She had followed the newsfeeds on Varal. His reach was far and demanding.

"Yes. I hated it, but I wanted to keep my family safe. I made sure I worked hard enough to keep out of trouble and tried not to do so much that I came under scrutiny. Then I heard my family was killed by Varal's men when he'd decided he needed my family's farm and my father had refused. I couldn't work for that man any longer. I took one of his fastest ships and ran. I came here for a while and just hid."

"I'm sorry for your loss." She didn't know what to say to him. She knew how evil Varal was and how many times he backstabbed someone to forward his plan. The pain Varal had caused Grinnell was very real, and a part of her wanted to wipe that pain away.

"My pain kept me alive. I found it was a good motivator. I started running contraband to planets. Planets that were out of Varal's reach at first, but then I found out about the resistance, and I worked with them. I still ran the odd job. Anything that kept me moving."

"That's how you met Queen Astrid."

He smiled. "You know who I am."

"Yes." She shouldn't have shown her hand, but she had to know if he was the Grinnell she had heard about. She knew about Astrid and how she searched for her betrothed. How Grinnell and his partner Leabo had helped Astrid defeat Varal. "I followed the newsfeeds. They never showed an image of you, which caught my attention. There's not a lot to do here so I did some searching and found one picture of you. You were in the background and not identified, but I knew it had to be you. It's one of the reasons why I was surprised to see you here, looking for Lawaya. The man I had guessed to be Grinnell was standing in front of me. The newsfeeds said you were supposed to be out there exploring."

"I was, but Orla called me back when Astrid became pregnant."

"Why?" She couldn't help her curiosity.

"Don't know, he never really explained. The one good thing was I was handy when he asked me to come for Lawaya. Astrid needs her."

"Astrid?" She looked at the ground again. "Oh, dear."

"You going to explain what's going on now?"

So he had figured out she was lying to him.

"I'm not lying when I say I don't know where Lawaya is. She found me in this cave and decided to train me." She paused for a moment. "I don't know who my parents are. I've been on my own for as long as I can remember. I've been in this cave for as long as I can remember. I can't

17

remember how I got here or how I knew there was a small village nearby where I could get food and items I might need."

"You had something to barter with?" He looked at the electronics again.

"Not in the beginning." She felt her cheeks heat up. "I went through their trash. You'd be amazed what people will throw away. As time went on, I created little gadgets that I could use to barter with to get better items."

"Are you telling me you created this security grid from spare parts you got from other people's trash and items you bought?" He looked at her creation. Just as she was ready to defend herself, he continued. "This is amazing. I know experts who can't pull this off."

That surprised her. "Thank you."

"I wonder what you could do with state-of-the-art equipment." He gestured to her security grid. "May I?"

She nodded.

"So you knew when I landed." He moved the camera around. "And you knew they were coming because they saw my ship land. That explains why you were so angry with me earlier, but I didn't know. My computer didn't show them as hostiles."

"Anyone this far away from any city is always hostile."

"I'm a little confused. If you traded with them, they have to know where you live." Grinnell looked at her. "Why are you hiding?"

"I never told them where I lived and tried to make it look like I was from another village. I knew if they knew I was here by myself they'd think they could take what they wanted, and I'd have nothing to barter." She placed her hands on her lap. "That's why I created this security system."

"Then I need to apologize. I never saw them as a threat. They were herding animals, so I took them as farmers. The computer agreed."

"Yet they don't have any animals now, do they?" She didn't mean to whine at him, but she couldn't keep it out of her voice.

"No." He turned the camera on the men outside. They had a nice fire going and looked very comfortable. "But they do seem to have plenty of food."

"I've seen them sit out there for duras." She stood and moved closer to Grinnell so she could see the men better.

"What are they after?" He looked at her.

"No idea. They started showing up here a couple of lunas ago, but I always stayed hidden in here, and after a few duras they normally just go away. From snippets I've recorded of the last few visits, they wanted Lawaya for some sort of mission. They needed something from her. I just never figured out what."

"Then they don't know a lot about the Barou race."

"Why do you say that?"

"Because I've seen Astrid's ability, and she could stand right in front of us and we wouldn't know it." He looked at her. "Where is Lawaya?"

"Um, I don't know. Like I told you, I don't know who my family is. I don't know if I'm from this planet or some other one. All I know is that I have a knack with computer parts, and I can create things." She held out her palm and rolled her wrist so that her hand did a circle. When she held her palm out again, there was a sweet fruit in her hand. "Now, before you ask me, I don't know. I just have always known that I could do that. It helped at first because if I was ever hungry, I could create this fruit to eat."

"Then you have magic."

She shrugged. "One dura a woman came to my cave. She was running from those men and hid against the cave wall. When those men camped outside, like they're doing now, she tried to come in but found my forcefield as you did. I knew she couldn't hold that form forever, so I pulled the forcefield deeper into the cave so she could slip in the mouth of it and hide in the shadows."

"Okay, so that explains how she and you became friends."

"She found out about my little talent and took it upon herself to teach me. When I tried to explain that I wasn't a Barou, she said a talent was a talent, and the best way to grow it was with discipline and training. That she was sure she could teach me."

He nodded and waited for her to continue.

She paced for a moment or two before walking to a corner that had a cloth-draped mirror. "Lawaya wanted me to create something from nothing and kept pushing until I caved. She created the illusion of a mirror and wanted me to make the same thing."

"It didn't go well, did it?" He moved closer to the corner she had moved to.

"No. I mean I did create the mirror but..." She pulled the cover off to reveal her creation.

Grinnell stared at the woman in the mirror. "Oh, my gods, is that Lawaya?"

"I didn't mean to do it." She waited for him to get mad.

"And you can't reverse what you did?"

She shook her head, too afraid any words would lead to tears.

He came up to the mirror. "What about breaking the mirror to release her?"

"And risk being wrong? I can't do that to her."

"What have you tried?"

"I tried reversing it, tried recreating it." She shrugged. "I don't know what else to do."

"How about approaching this scientifically?" Grinnell moved around the front of the mirror. He studied her creation.

"It wasn't created by science." How could he fix this when she had tried and couldn't?

"True, but science might reveal how to reverse this. At least let me try."

Grinnell felt better now that he had something to do. Mehanna had these eyes that made him feel things he never thought he'd feel again. He tried to convince himself that he was only feeling sorry for her. He couldn't imagine how he would have handled it if he had been abandoned at such a young age.

He found Mehanna quite pretty. Her hair was jet black and her eyes a crystal blue. Her skin had a slight blue hue to it as well. She was a little bit shorter than he was and thin. But being attracted to her wasn't why he was here. He needed to find a way to free Lawaya out of her prison so he could bring her to Astrid.

He knew the first thing he needed to do was measure the mirror and find out if there was any sort of frequency coming off of it. If there was, maybe he could use that to free her. The measurements were easy.

"Can I borrow some of your equipment to make what I need?" he asked Mehanna.

She nodded.

It took him a few horas to gather everything he needed. Once he had it done, he pressed his little contraption against the side of the mirror. He tapped the side of it and two small wires extended out and rested their tips against the surface of the mirror.

Grinnell watched the readings as they loaded to the band on his wrist.

"What is that?" Mehanna pointed to his wristband.

"A communicator mostly, but it also keeps me in touch with the ship's computer, so it can analyze any data I upload and give me the results."

"And what is it telling you?"

"That this mirror is real. Pure gold, even the reflective surface." He tapped on the device attached to the mirror again. "Whatever your race is, they create pure items."

"What do you mean?"

"There are a few races that can fabricate something the way you did, but it doesn't normally last. The quality isn't that good. Sometimes, with a lot of practice, they can perfect it to a point, but not like this. I've never seen anything like it." He watched the readings a little longer. "Hmm, I wonder."

"You wonder what?"

He ignored her as he tapped a few more times. "Lawaya, can you hear me?"

"Yes, yes." She placed her hands on the sides of the mirror. "Please get me out of this."

"Lawaya, I'm so sorry." Mehanna was amazed he was able to allow them to talk to her so quickly. Maybe he could free Lawaya from the mirror.

"Child, this isn't your fault. I should have taken the right precautions in case something like this happened, and I didn't."

"What do you see?"

21

"Here? Nothing. Not until you opened the portal. How much time has passed?"

Grinnell looked at Mehanna. He had wondered the same thing.

"Um, almost two lunas." She was looking at the floor again.

"What?" Lawaya's eyes widened. "Oh no, the council must be beside themselves."

"If we hadn't contacted the council, no one would have known," commented Grinnell. "They had kept your absence to themselves."

"Who are you?"

"I am Grinnell." He gave her a proper bow. "I work for Queen Astrid."

"Ah, I've heard she is very powerful."

"I've only known two Barou, so I'm not a good judge of that. I do know the two I know saved our lives a few times while we were battling Varal." He looked at Mehanna for a moment then turned his attention to the woman trapped in the mirror. "You are the reason I am here. I know this isn't the right time, but time is of the essence. You know Queen Astrid is pregnant, and there is something odd going on with her pregnancy. Grenta thinks it might have something to do with Astrid's Barou power and said you would know what to do."

"Me? Why?"

"The child seems to be draining her powers. I've been told that you would know how to help her."

"Then you were sent to release me."

"No one knows you're trapped in there, and the only one who can release you doesn't know how." He pointedly looked at the woman standing near him.

Mehanna continued looking at the floor of the cave.

—————

Grinnell looked out the mouth of the cave. The men were still camped right out front. He needed those men to leave but wasn't sure how to get them to move. His ship didn't have transport capabilities, which meant he'd be trapped until they did.

"We have a small problem."

"Besides Lawaya being caught in the mirror?" Mehanna tapped her chin as she thought. "No wait, that is a *huge* problem, so you can't be talking about that."

Her sarcasm made him crack a smile. "You know I can't leave until they do."

"I warned you about that."

"Okay." He frowned. "Um, I don't want to be crass, but how much food do you have? Enough to feed us both for a while?"

She flipped her wrist and offered him the fruit she could create.

"What about facilities?"

She tilted her head at that.

"Where do you go to relieve yourself?"

"Oh." A beautiful, soft blush filled her cheeks. "There is a small alcove for that."

"And where shall I sleep? I'm going to need a place."

"Come with me." She stood up and gestured for him to follow her. She walked down a short corridor and pointed to a small indention into the cave wall. "There is a spring that runs through this cave and that alcove exposes part of it. It should work for you. It works for me."

She walked a little further. "This is where I sleep."

He looked around at the spacious cave. A soft moss grew on little ledges throughout it where they could sleep. He noticed two areas were already in use. One must be hers, while the other belonged to Lawaya. It didn't take him long to find a spot for himself.

Grinnell tapped his wristband. "Did you learn anything new?" he asked the ship computer.

"They know you're here," it said.

"Did they detect you?"

"No, but once you stepped on the soil here, they knew there was an alien. I'm still researching how. They don't have the technology to detect you."

"Is that why they're sitting outside this cave?" He turned away from Mehanna. "Waiting to see what I do?"

"From the dialogue I've been picking up, they are after one of the two women with you."

"Lawaya, at least that's what my hostess believes." He glanced over at her for a moment. "Keep monitoring them and let me know if you pick up anything. If they plan on attacking, I need to prepare. As soon as they leave, we need to get out of here."

"I can't leave," said Mehanna.

"You can't stay here. They will keep coming back until they get what they want."

"And where am I to go?" She crossed her arms and shifted her weight to one hip.

"Anywhere you want." He wanted to smile. Her anger was real, but she had no clue how cute she looked trying to show it. "First, though, we need to find someone to reverse your spell."

"I've been trying!" She stomped her foot and clinched her hands at her sides.

He knew he'd hit a nerve. Maybe he should change tactics. "Don't you want to know where you come from? Who your parents are?"

"Why?" She crossed her arms again and glared at him. "They left me here all alone."

"That's not exactly true," said the computer.

"What do you mean?" they asked in unison.

"I'm picking up another DNA sequence like Mehanna's in that small town nearby."

"Someone from her race?" asked Grinnell.

"Someone from her family." The computer was quiet for a moment. "It is a sister. A twin, based on her age."

This woman had a sister on the same planet? What kind of game was she playing then?

"No." Mehanna shook her head as she backed away from him. "I have no family here. I've been by myself for as long as I can remember."

"Then it might not be Lawaya they are after." He tapped on his wrist pad for a secur. The computer showed her heart rate had increased, but her blood pressure, temperature, eye dilation, they all showed she wasn't lying. She sure was acting like she didn't know about the sister. Could that be true? "What have you learned about the town?" he asked the computer. "Is she a prisoner or a member of their society?"

"She is isolated, but not a prisoner. I'll monitor to see why she is separated from the rest of the people."

"I can't have a relative on this planet." Mehanna didn't look at him while she spoke. It was like she was talking to herself. "No one has ever come to look for me. Those people didn't even show up until Lawaya came into my life."

"And you started doing magic?" he asked.

"I've been doing magic the whole time. Remember the fruit?"

"That was something simple. You started practicing your art when Lawaya made you. Maybe something you did caught their attention."

"I don't know how. We were always in this cave." She gestured around.

"You do go and trade from time to time. Maybe they noticed you then but didn't know where you were until Lawaya came."

"Do you have a picture of this woman?" she asked, changing the subject.

An image popped up from the wristband that Grinnell wore.

Mehanna stared at the image like she saw a ghost. "My stars, she looks just like me."

"She has to be your twin. Computer, you did say they were the same age, right?"

"Yes. From my initial scans, I would say she is a twin but cannot verify that until I get a sample of her DNA."

"Okay, so I know the first thing we need to do once those men move," said Grinnell.

"And what is that?" Mehanna continued to look at the image of her sister.

"Get you and your sister to meet each other."

Grinnell asked to explore her cave, and she was happy to get him away from her for a micron. She needed to think. A sister? Her twin? How?

She had gone from being alone and invisible to having strangers showing up uninvited. What was she going to do?

Grinnell wanted her to leave the comfort of the life she built and go searching for people who didn't care enough to keep her. Not what she wanted. He also wanted her to go meet a sister she hadn't known she had.

There was something about the man, though. He had eyes that seemed to see into her soul. They were a beautiful slate color. He was much taller than the men on this planet. They were short and stocky, but Grinnell would tower over them. She had to look up to make eye contact with him. His body made her heart flutter. His shoulders were broad, but his waist was lean.

Mehanna sighed. Where was he, anyway? The cave wasn't that big, and he was intelligent enough to work his way through the place pretty quickly unless he'd found something that sparked his interest. That got her moving. He had better not be messing with her security system. It took her a long time to get everything to work, and one wrong move would shut the whole thing down and leave them defenseless.

She headed toward her grid, but a sound to her right made her stop. Someone was in her bathing area. What she found made her jaw drop. Grinnell stood under the small waterfall, naked and leaving nothing to her imagination. He looked like a god standing there with the water sluicing over his body.

He took good care of himself. The muscles of his back flexed as he rinsed his hair. He had found her soaps as well.

She moved away from the opening and pressed her back against the cave wall as she tried to slow her racing heart. Although she had never been with a man, she knew what happened. She had learned from newsfeeds and watching the local population. Mehanna wondered what it would be like to be with Grinnell. Then, just as quickly as the thought entered her mind, she squashed it.

What she wanted was him gone so she could work on freeing Lawaya. She'd created the mess and wanted to be the one to fix it.

Grinnell felt better after bathing. It always helped him find focus and help calm him. He had a goal, and he would achieve it. He had never failed Orla before, and some slip of a woman and her wayward abilities wasn't going to make this the first time he did. He knew several races that had the mage ability, but the slight blue tint of Mehanna's skin narrowed down the races to one he had heard of but very few people had ever seen them. Rumors said they hailed from a section of space not too far from where they were currently, but they weren't known for wanting to be found, so it wasn't going to be easy to find them. That rumor could be something they started so people wouldn't be able to find them.

He wondered about the sister. Both girls were left on this planet for a reason. Had their family put them both in the cave and one wandered off, or had they been with the townspeople and Mehanna the one that wandered off? Or had they placed each girl in their locations for reason? The big question was why. Why leave your twin daughters with people who didn't understand their abilities?

He tapped his wristband. "What have you learned about Mehanna's twin?"

"She is coddled and pampered by these people. She has magic as well, and they are afraid of her power. They do whatever she wants in return for her not using that power."

"Then she knows how to control it." Maybe she could free Lawaya.

"Not from what I've heard. They don't want her to use her powers because they are afraid of what might happen. She has had several problems in the past when her powers got out of control."

"Is she aware of her sister?"

"Yes. The communiques show she is the one who got these men to come out here. There must have been a magical pulse she picked up when her sister started using her magic with Lawaya."

"Then Mehanna's twin thinks she knows how to control her power and is hoping her sister will help her learn to control it."

"Yes. There is nothing to support her theory, but she believes if they are reunited, they will be able to help each other."

"Does the sister know how they got here?"

"Unknown."

"She hasn't said anything about their parents?" asked Grinnell.

"No. She hasn't spoken."

"At all?"

"Nothing since I started monitoring. She's been using tablets and hand gestures to talk."

"Interesting." Grinnell wanted to know why the sister wasn't talking. "And our guests?"

"Still out there. They have received communiques but nothing that has called them back to their home. Most of the missives were asking for updates."

"Which they don't have." He needed to talk to Mehanna. "I wonder how long they normally stay out there."

"According to the data on Mehanna's system, they are normally out there for a cycle or more."

"What makes them give up?"

"The weather. This area is well known for its torrential downpours and strong winds. It's not safe to be out when this type of weather hits."

"Just how bad is it?"

"The rain falls so hard that flash floods are common," said the ship's computer. "That's why most of these towns are built on hills. The rain falls so hard, it can crush anyone caught out when the rain starts."

"They don't have the technology to keep people safe?"

"That is where most of their advanced technology is. Their homes might not look like much, but they are built of the strongest material created."

"How did they survive if this happens a lot?" asked Grinnell.

"Like most storms, it doesn't cover more than a few clicks. It might attack two or three villages close together, but one a half a duras travel would be spared. They learned quickly, signaling all towns and villages when a storm was spotted. They realized it was safer on higher ground, which trees weren't destroyed by the storms, what sort of material withstood heavy downpours. It didn't take them long to adapt."

"They still look like nomads."

"That is part of their heritage. They have always traveled the planet. First to escape from the storms, then as technology took over they traveled to learn, trade, build their empires."

"Do you see a storm on the horizon?"

"No. but the conditions are perfect for one to develop."

Duro fell and still no storm. Grinnell wasn't sure if spending the duro in the cave with Mehanna was a good idea. He found her attractive. A little too attractive to sleep in the same room and not have a rough duro.

"I can keep watch toduro." He needed something to distract himself.

"There is no need." Mehanna gathered some items together. "They can't get past my security grid."

That wasn't what he wanted to hear. He needed a distraction. What else could he do?

"I need to bathe," Mehanna stated.

"Is that a warning to stay away from the bathing chamber?"

"Um, yes." She blinked at his comment. "I know you used it earlier and want to be sure you won't walk in on me."

Now that had his imagination going in the wrong direction. "No. I'll go rest, since I don't need to watch our visitors." He knew she didn't like him encroaching on her space, but he couldn't help it right now. There was only one way out of the cave, and those men were blocking it.

He gave her a slight nod and headed to the sleeping area. He picked a ledge that looked nice and soft and didn't show any use. Now what? Grinnell knew he couldn't disrobe. That might cause more trouble than he wanted. Stretching out, he laced his fingers behind his head and closed his eyes.

She came into the area quietly. He could smell the soft scent of the soaps she used as she entered. Grinnell kept his eyes closed as she approached her sleeping spot. He felt her hesitate, then he heard her voice.

"Are you going to be comfortable in your uniform?"

He opened his eyes at that. Sitting up, he felt his heartbeat pick up when he saw what she had on to sleep in. "I find this outfit very comfortable."

"Yes, but you've been wearing that the whole time you've been here. I can replicate something for you to wear while you sleep."

"You don't need to." What he wanted her to do was jump into her bed and cover up. The top she wore covered her body but hugged her so well it left nothing to the imagination. The bottoms were like small shorts, again skintight and making him want to see her without anything on.

"That outfit won't do well on the moss that covers these rocks. I'll be right back." She took off before he could stop her. In a micron or two, she was back with a bundle for him. "Um, I made a pillow and a blanket for you as well. The moss can wreak havoc with your hair and the air can get quite cool as it gets later."

"Many thanks." Grinnell took the small bundle from her.

"Okay, well, I'll see you in the dura." She turned and climbed into her bed.

Grinnell slipped into the outfit she made for him and folded his suit up and sat it on a nearby sill. He then climbed back up on his ledge and made himself comfortable. Sleep wouldn't be easy, but at least he had a pillow and blanket now.

CHAPTER THREE

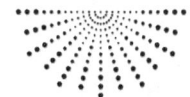

G rinnell was surprised that he slept through the duro. The moment he opened his eyes, his wristband started talking to him.

"There is a storm heading this way. It is a massive one, and several villages are in danger. That includes the one those men are from. They have already packed up and are moving out as we speak."

"How about this cave?" asked Grinnell. He sat up and grabbed his clothing. "Will we have an issue?"

"The mouth of the cave faces away from the direction of the storm, so you should be safe."

"How soon can you land?" Pulling off the clothes Mehanna gave him to sleep in, Grinnell climbed into his own and then stood.

"It will have to be after the storm passes. I will not have enough time to land and then take back off, and the storm could damage me beyond repair. Even though you might not see the storm for several horas, it is too close for me to land."

"Understood." Grinnell straightened his collar. "I'll try to have Mehanna and Lawaya ready when you can."

"You believe she will travel with you."

"I won't give her a choice." He picked up the clothes she gave him and folded them so he could give them back. Hopefully, they would leave within the dura and he wouldn't need them anymore.

"I will make preparations for two more to join us."

"I'm not going with you."

Grinnell turned at the sound of her voice. He didn't expect her to hear him talking to the computer. "You can't stay here, not now that I've made them aware that you do live here. It's not safe anymore."

She stomped her foot. "This is my home!"

"Mehanna, your sister will continue to send those men here until she gets you. Until I prove she doesn't mean you harm, I can't leave you behind. I wouldn't forgive myself if something happened to you and I had a chance to protect you." He liked the way she stood up to him. Mehanna wasn't afraid to speak her mind.

"And if she only wants to be my sister?"

"Then I will leave you here." He couldn't force her if her sister only wanted to spend time with Mehanna, but he still had to get Lawaya free.

"Let's go see her."

"We can't. There is a storm coming and we're going to have to wait it out."

"A storm?" Her beautiful blue eyes filled with worry. "How big?"

"The ship said it's a good size. That's why the men left." He frowned when she took off. He caught up with her in the security area. "The ship said we should be fine; the storm is coming from the opposite side of the mouth of the cave."

"Your ship hasn't been through one. I need to prepare. How much time?"

"You have six horas at the speed it's moving," said Grinnell's wrist.

"Good. We should have plenty of time to get everything done." She worked on the shield she had blocking the mouth of the cave. "Don't just stand there, help me reinforce the shield."

"Of course." He came to her side and worked on her shield. "I thought I would break something if I touched this system."

"I have to trust you not to break something. There's a lot to do." She worked on making sure her power source was secure and protected. "With your help, we'll be ready long before it gets here. Once we're done with this, we need to work on my garden."

"I didn't see a garden."

"That's because there is an opening in the cave itself where I could plant. That's the part of the shield I need you to work on next." She brought up an image of the garden.

"I see what you're talking about. What do you want me to do?"

"I'd like to allow a mist to come through so the plants can benefit from the rain, but most of the water needs to be rerouted to my reservoir." She showed him where the file was for the water cistern was, then moved back to what she was working on.

He was amazed at what Mehanna had accomplished. Everything she had worked together gave her what she needed to survive.

"This is quite ingenious." No wonder why she didn't want to leave. She had created her own perfect little world here.

"Thank you. I had a lot of time on my hands, so I read any book someone threw out in the beginning and tinkered when I found something I could work with."

He set up everything as she asked. "What's next?"

They spent the next few horas working side by side as, with Mehanna's guidance, they readied the cave for the storm.

Grinnell stood by the mouth of the cave as the clouds started to build. Mehanna came up to him and handed him a small pad. "I've had grids fail during storms so this should help us keep ahead of any failure."

"Never used a fail-safe program?"

"No. Never figured out how to make one."

"Ah." He turned and headed to the security center. "Now, understand I'm not a computer genius. That would be Orla, but I'm pretty good with them. I can create something quickly and it should hold during the storm."

"Will we need the pads?"

"They would be smart to keep handy as a backup, but if I do this right, we shouldn't have to do anything more than watch the rainfall."

Grinnell watched in awe as lightning filled the sky. Bolts hit the ground in succession. Sometimes so many hit the ground at the same time it was a whiteout.

"Pretty amazing, huh?" Mehanna said from behind him.

"Very. I find it beautiful." He turned to look at her. "Deadly, but beautiful."

"Wait till the rain starts. Lightning will strike it and water will evaporate. You'll see plumes of water vapor floating in the air."

"How did you survive this?"

"I don't know." She shrugged. "The first time I remember it raining like this I was asleep. I had gone to sleep thinking it would pass in the duro, but I woke up because I felt wet. The water had come in that deep. I knew I needed to protect myself from that type of rain. The good thing is that it doesn't happen that often. I saw the way the farmers could keep their animals on their land using technology so when they started throwing away their old tech, I took it and learned to repurpose it."

"How did you learn to do this?"

"Didn't you tell me that you had a knack for working with machines? I guess I did too. Any book they threw away I took and learned from it."

"So you knew how to read before you got here."

She nodded. "Just like how I knew to create the fruit to keep me alive while I learned how to grow my own food."

"That is amazing. What do you call the fruit?" asked Grinnell. "I don't recognize it."

"I don't know its name, and since I've been by myself, I never thought to give it one."

"Don't you think you should come up with one?"

"Fruit isn't good enough?" asked Mehanna.

Grinnell shook his head. "If that is what you want to call it."

"I do. It wasn't something I thought was as important as building my shield."

"How did you figure out how to make the force field?" It was a feat only the best could do.

"I found a book, actually a manual, which explained how force fields work." She watched him work on his failsafe program. "It covered the basics and the more advanced. I used it to teach me how to make them. I also found a training book on how to create computers. The rest just sort of came to me."

"I'd love to see what you could do with state-of-the-art equipment." He wondered what she could create if she had access to the computer on the ship. "I thought I was good until I met Orla, but I think you're better than any of us."

She blushed at that. "I did what I needed to do to survive."

"Exactly." Water started to flow past the entrance. "Where does the water go?"

"The lowest point is very close to here. It pools there, then seeps underground." She stepped up to the forcefield and watched as several bolts of lightning hit the ground. "This looks like it's going to be quite the show."

The rain started to fall, slow at first, then it picked up speed until it fell so hard he couldn't see anything more than a meter away. Lightning brightened the area, but it didn't help him see any further. A warm hand on his shoulder made him jump.

Mehanna laughed. "You okay?"

"Sorry." He gave her an embarrassed smile. "Guess I was staring so hard I didn't expect you to touch me."

"You're not going to see much right now. The rain will continue to fall hard for a few more horas. Once it starts to slow down, we can come back to see what the rain did." She gestured for him to walk in front of her so they could head back into her living area.

"What it did?"

"You remember the small copse of trees near the mouth of the cave?" She picked up two mugs she had sitting on a ledge, then handed one to him.

"Yeah, thought it was an odd place for trees to grow." He took the mug and gestured with it to show his thanks.

"You're right. They weren't there in the beginning. A rainstorm transplanted them there."

The rain had started to dissipate, and Grinnell found himself in front of the forcefield once again. He could now see more than halfway across the flat area. Water continued to rise, covering about one-fourth of the forcefield.

He was grateful the forcefield was strong. He'd hate to see what would happen if the rain broke through. Mehanna stood beside him, watching the storm. Water swirled against the forcefield, then it was pulled in a different direction. The ground showed once again.

A loud rumble filled the air. "What is that?"

Before Mehanna could answer the rumble turned into a roar as a wall of water headed straight toward the cave opening. Grinnell didn't think, he just scooped Mehanna up and bounded up several ledges until he thought they were high enough to be safe.

"My goodness, you're agile."

The water pounded against the forcefield, which held.

"Sorry. I just reacted." He released her legs so she could stand on her own, but still kept his arms around her until she could regain her feet. "I saw that water coming and knew we needed to get to safety."

There was something in the way she looked at him. It just seemed right when he lowered his face to hers and captured her lips with his. Her mouth fit his perfectly. Her hesitancy told him she had never kissed anyone before, but she wasn't frightened. Curiosity fueled her. He wondered how she would react if he deepened the kiss.

He brushed his tongue against the seam of her mouth, hoping she would open for him. A gasp escaped her, and he took advantage. His tongue searched for hers. She wasn't sure what to do, but as his brushed softly against hers she figured it out and swirled her tongue with his. His body felt a jolt, and he knew he needed to stop. Desire filled him sharp and swift, and he was pretty sure she wasn't ready for that.

He broke the kiss but couldn't step away from her.

"Why did you stop?"

"What?" He didn't quite understand her question.

"I was enjoying that." She tilted her head as she looked at him. "Why did you stop?"

He looked at her swollen lips and flushed skin. How should he explain this? "What do you know about relationships between people? Especially those that are couples?"

"Oh, you're talking about sex. Um, I know the mechanics." She studied his face. "Do you want to do that with me?"

He wanted to scream yes but didn't think that was the smartest thing to do.

CHAPTER FOUR

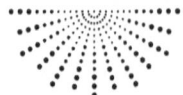

Did he want to have sex with her? Mehanna had always wondered about it. The things she read made it sound like a lot of fun. She had watched amusement stories that dealt with romance, but those people were also pretending. It didn't seem real when she heard couples from the village arguing. They didn't seem to be the perfect pairs she had seen in the feeds. She had to admit kissing Grinnell had felt really good. Her blood hummed, and she felt her body react to it in a very stimulating way.

"You don't seem to be the type of person to want to have their first time as a casual encounter."

"Oh, I never thought about it." She liked the way he held her. "I've been here alone all my life and thought I'd grow old and die this way."

"Until I invaded your little haven."

"True. But I knew those people from the village were coming, so I had to either leave you out there for them to find or allow you in."

"Thank you." He hesitated.

She knew he wanted to have sex with her. How did the feeds word it? He wanted her, but he didn't know if she wanted him. What had she seen in those entertainment feeds? Normally, one person took the hand of the other and brought them to their bedroom.

She took his hand and urged him to walk with her.

"What are you doing?"

"Am I doing this wrong?" She stopped and looked at him.

"No, but you don't have to do this. I feel like you've watched too many entertainment feeds. I find you very attractive, but this will be your first time. What if you do go home and find out your planet is one that demands the women to remain chaste until they find a life partner?"

"Why should I care?" She looked up at him. "They left me here. They didn't want me."

"There could have been a crash," he countered.

"No!" She shook her head. She got a little agitated when she spoke. "There was no evidence of a crash. I was left here."

He used their clasped hands to draw her close. The warmth of his embrace calmed her.

"They don't care about me, so I don't care about their rules. I want you. You plan on making me leave here, but sooner or later I plan on coming back. This might be my only chance to experience this, especially with someone I care for." She realized too late she said too much.

Grinnell smiled at her, then scooped her up in his arms and walked toward her sleeping area. "Does this fit into what you saw in the entertainment feeds?"

She wrapped her arms around his neck and smiled. "Oh, yes."

Once they reach her sleeping quarters, Grinnell looked around for a ledge that could hold the two of them.

"Um, my bed is over there."

"I know, but we need a little bit bigger space."

"Oh, there is a wider ledge toward the back of this room. I also have a few covers that we can use."

"Perfect." With her direction, he went to where the covers were. He refused to put her down, so she had to wiggle a little to reach them. Laughter escaped her when she tried to place the cover on the soft moss that covered the rocks.

"It doesn't have to be perfect. I promise you won't care later." He released her legs and let her slide down his body. Now he had to make sure she still wanted this. The moment had passed. She could change her mind. Her nerves could get the best of her.

She looked up at him, and he knew she feared the same thing.

He brushed his knuckles along her jaw. He dipped his head toward hers. He went slowly, giving her a chance to stop him if she did change her mind. If she pulled back, he would back off, offering to hold her for a little while.

Her arms wrapped back around his neck as she closed the gap and pressed her lips against his. He took control at that point. Grinnell eased her back onto their bed. He was as nervous as she was. His father had hired a teacher to educate him on how to please a woman, but he had never had to use his training on someone so naive before. He hoped he didn't botch it.

He placed soft kisses along her jawline and throat as he opened the closures on her top. Once she realized what he was doing, she did the same for him. Gentle touches followed bits of clothing until they were both naked.

Grinnell needed to arouse her. The moment had passed, and he could tell by the way she mimicked what he did, but there was no desire behind her movements. He pressed a kiss against her collar bone. His hands started caressing her. They glided over her soft skin, caressing and stroking all the right places. Her hands started to explore his body the same way he was exploring hers.

She was hesitant, but when she heard him moan when she brushed a hand against the inside of his thigh, she became bolder. He moved down her body enough so he could take the tip of her left breast into his mouth. The secur she felt the heat of his mouth surround her nipple, she moaned herself. Forgetting her exploration, she gripped his head with both hands and held him close.

If she liked that, how would she react to what he was going to do next? He continued to focus on the one breast as his hand worked its way down her body to her folds. His fingers slipped in and gently stroked her. He took his time, making sure he pushed her need higher. He felt her body shake, and he knew what he was doing was working.

Breaking her hold on his head, he moved down until he could replace his fingers with his mouth. He latched onto her, drawing small circles around her core with his tongue. He slipped a finger inside her and heard another moan. She was so tight she gripped his finger in a vise and as he slid his finger in and out, he heard her breath become shallower. Her body shook again as her muscles clamped down on his finger. Mehanna's legs started moving, showing she didn't know what would happen next. Grinnell knew she was reaching for something she didn't know how to find.

He moved again, this time back up her body, driving into her body deep and quick. Shock filled her face at the invasion. She felt pain, but it didn't overshadow the release she was close to having. Grinnell gave her a few moments to adjust to his size before he started to move. He did slow, short strokes at first, then he shifted to deeper ones once he felt she was ready for it.

She looked up at him in awe, and he knew he'd done the right thing. He rocked into her, setting a nice pace. One she could keep up with if her body responded the way he expected. It didn't take long before she moved with him. He picked up the tempo, and she kept up with him. Her legs moved against his. Creeping up with each move.

He slipped an arm under her left thigh, bringing the leg up higher and tilting her pelvis so he could fill her completely. He drove in deep and heard her breath stop. Her hands grasped at his back. She wanted more. He started moving faster, filling her again and again. Her body started to shake.

"Don't fight it. Let it flow over you. Let it take control."

She had no idea. All the feeds she had seen never prepared her for this. Mehanna had pleasured herself many times, but it had never felt like this. It was just out of her reach. Grinnell slipped his other arm under her other thigh and brought that up as well. Now he had total control, but oh stars it felt good. He pounded into her faster, harder, and each time he filled her, her body tightened just a little more.

It was close. Whatever she was about to experience was very close. She felt everything tighten and then felt a euphoria fill her. It started deep inside her and then, like the way a light filled a room, it filled every part of her. It bubbled in her stomach and then spread out to her fingers and her toes. Her heart hammered in her chest. It took her breath away.

It had been a glorious three duras. They had made love when they wanted to, ate when they needed to, and slept when they had to. Their little world held just the two of them, then a communique from Orla came and shattered their little cocoon.

"Grinnell. Have you found her?"

"Yes, but there is a complication." How was he going to explain that Lawaya was trapped in a mirror?

"What sort of complications?"

Grinnell paused, not sure how to answer the question. He looked at the mirror when Lawaya banged on it. "Um, Orla, can I have a moment?"

"Of course."

Grinnell halted the communiqué so Orla wouldn't hear or see what was going on.

"Is there another Barou with her?" asked Lawaya.

"Grenta." He frowned, not knowing what she was getting at.

"That will do." Lawaya crossed her arms over her chest. "I can use Grenta to help Astrid right now, then you can figure out how to release me from this prison."

"I thought Grenta was banned by the Barou."

"She was, but I have the power to restore her Barou status. That was why I needed time to think. She never should have been banned in the first place, and I needed to come up with a strong reason to reinstate her."

"You want me to bring you to Astrid while being trapped in the mirror?"

"I don't have a problem with it. Her health is most important. Mehanna will release me. I know she can do this."

"Orla?" Grinnell focused on his conversation once again. "I should be lifting off in a few horas. I need to take care of something first."

"Hurry, Grinnell. Astrid is getting worse."

"Yes, sir." He ended the call.

"What do you need to do?" asked Lawaya.

"I want to talk to Mehanna's sister. She must know something about what happened. She knew Mehanna was here."

"So you think she was the reason those men kept coming here?"

"No," Mehanna said. "They didn't come here until Lawaya came."

"I do." Grinnell looked at Mehanna. "They didn't start coming here until you started training. Your sister might have felt your power and realized it was like hers and wanted to know who had the same talent."

Mehanna remained silent. Grinnell could almost see the wheels turning. She had never looked at it that way.

"It shouldn't take me too long," he reassured her.

Grinnell decided that sneaking up wasn't the way to handle this. These people were still cleaning up from the storm and were moving about too much. They'd spot him easily. Instead, he walked to the center of their village. He heard them whispering as he passed. They knew he had come on a spaceship. They wanted to know if he was going to take "her" away. From the snippets he caught, it sounded like they *wanted* him to take her away.

They were afraid of Mehanna's sister.

No one approached him, but a few looked at him, then glanced at the building they wanted him to go into. He sure hoped they weren't leading him into a trap. He entered and saw the woman he was looking for. Mehanna, or her mirror image. They were identical.

"You're him, aren't you?" asked the young woman.

"Him who?" Might as well find out what she knew.

"The man who came from space. You're going to take her from me." She sighed. "I had hoped I could talk to her; maybe learn how she controls her magic."

He wanted to laugh at that. Mehanna had no control. "What can you do?"

"Me? Frighten the villagers. That's my magic power. That's why I'm here." She gestured to the room. "The walls absorb anything that gets out of hand, which is a lot." She looked at him. "Do you know how she controls it?"

"She's had a little training." He felt like he was talking to Mehanna.

There was no evil in this woman, just sadness that she couldn't control things the way she wished. "What is your name?"

"The people here call me Mayanna, but I don't know what my real name is. You can call me May." She moved about the room for a moment. "Can I go with you? Meet the woman with the same powers? Maybe learn a little from her?"

"Isn't this your home? These people raised you, correct?"

She nodded.

"Wouldn't they be upset if you were to leave?" He was surprised to find her talking after the computer told him she hadn't talked with any of the villagers. What did she do, save it up until Grinnell saw her? He didn't think she had stopped for a breath yet.

"These people have been very sweet to me, but they don't want me here. They're afraid I'll destroy their village. They don't even want me to talk to them. You're the first person I've spoken to in a long while." She walked around the room. "My power started to develop about three yepas ago, and I've caused more than enough trouble for them."

Grinnell frowned. Mehanna had been taught how to use magic to make the piece of fruit when she was a child. Wasn't this woman taught how to do the same thing?

At his frown, she asked, "What?"

He decided to be honest. "Your sister has been able to make a piece of fruit since she was a child."

"My sister? Really?" Hope filled her face. "I have a sister. Wait, you said she's had her magic since she was little?"

"Yes. Did you have a special talent? Something that could be considered magical or good luck?"

"Not really. The family I grew up with told me I was left in the center of town with a note saying someone would be back for me, something that has never happened."

"This isn't making a lot of sense. Why did you send men to Mehanna's cave?"

"I didn't." She looked shocked. "Oh! The people here must have done it. They have wanted to help me control my talents, and when I felt magic like mine in the air, they must have tried to find it."

"So they camped outside her cave because they thought she could help you?"

"I think. They didn't harm anyone, did they?"

"No." Grinnell thought about what she said. "But if they didn't have the magic, how did they know where to look?"

"Oh." May clasped her hands in front of her. "I told them where I felt magic. I could feel it coming from the south. They questioned me about it, but I never expected them to try to find it."

"So you told them where you thought it came from." He nodded. "That explains why they camped outside. They weren't sure if they had the right cave and hoped your sister would come out to find out why they were there. My next question is do you know who left you?"

"I don't remember much, but I was young. I was told I had been found curled up and sound asleep. They did keep my clothes and a blanket I was found with. Would you like to see them?"

"I could scan them and tell you where the materials came from. That might make it easier to figure out where these two came from," said the ship.

He agreed. He gave May his best smile. "That would be great."

―――――

Mehanna watched the entrance. Grinnell had left several horas ago, and she was getting worried. He had told her he could be awhile, but the thought of him being in trouble bothered her.

She went to her computer center and checked all her screens to see if they were picking up anything.

"Why am I behaving this way?" Mehanna never had anyone in her life before. Why would she worry about a man she didn't want to stay in the first place?

"Because you're attracted to him," said Lawaya. "He is the first person you've been around, and he is a kind heart."

That made her sound like she craved companionship, and she had done quite nicely without anyone all her life. "I barely know him."

"Yet you slept with him."

"What makes you say that?" The mirror wasn't in that section of the cave. How could she know that?

"I can see the signs," said Lawaya. Before Mehanna could ask her what she meant, Lawaya tried to explain why Grinnell wasn't back yet. "You need to look at this logically. He walked there, which would have taken him a hora, maybe a little more. Then he had to talk them into letting him see her. I wouldn't expect him back until closer to sundown. You need to be patient."

"I know, but those people have been after you, or me. I don't know." She looked at Lawaya. "I just don't trust them."

"And it's good to be a little skeptical. He'll be back. That ship of his will keep him safe."

She wasn't sure about that but didn't think arguing with Lawaya was smart, so she just continued to stare at the monitors. Finally, she saw someone heading to her cave. Mehanna raced to the entrance but waited when she realized two people were approaching. Who did Grinnell bring with him?

"Mehanna? I have someone I think you should meet."

She stared at an exact image of herself. She couldn't believe it. Mehanna stepped out of the mouth of the cave to get a better look.

"You look like me?" they asked in unison. The two women circled each other, looking for differences.

"Do you have a mole?" asked May.

"The one right here?" Mehanna pointed to her hip.

"Mine is on my stomach."

"Can you do this?" Mehanna flipped her wrist and produced a piece of fruit. The red skin held the soft meaty center intact. She liked the sweet and tart flavor. The seeds in the center and the stem made her wonder if it grew on trees.

"No." May's eyes widened as she picked up the fruit from her hand. "Oh, please do that again."

"Ladies, I know you two have lots of questions for each other, but I have a mission that I must complete, and to do that I need you two to come with me." Grinnell gestured toward the ship waiting nearby.

"You mean we can go into space?" May looked at him with childlike wonder.

"Yes. I promised Mehanna I would help her find her home. It's your home as well, so you should come with us."

Mehanna looked at her cave, then looked at his ship. She didn't say a word, but he know she didn't want to leave.

"I promise to bring you back, if that is what you want, once we find your home. Will that make it easier for you to leave? I know you want to help Lawaya get freed from the mirror and none of us know how to do that."

"Someone is trapped in a mirror?" May looked from Grinnell to Mehanna. "How did that happen?"

"It is a long story," said Grinnell. "One that should wait until we're on the ship."

Once the ship had broken through the atmosphere and he could turn over control to the computer, Grinnell went to speak with his guests.

"I'm going to need a few horas to prepare rooms for you. This is Orla's ship. Only one room had been created, and I never even used it since I tend to stay in the cockpit."

"We can share," said May.

"This ship is capable of having several rooms. I just have to set it up. You two can sit in the galley until I come to get you. Learn a few things about each other."

"I would like to learn how you make that fruit," May said.

"It's a natural reflex," May replied. "I'm not sure if I can teach you, but maybe you can figure it out if I repeat the motion enough."

Grinnell showed them where they could relax and headed to the cargo area.

"Alright, computer. I know we will be at Emori in a few horas, but I have promised to take these two to their home planet, and I don't know how long that will take."

"Orla promised to make you your own ship."

"You think he can get one ready for me in a few horas?"

"He might be working on one for you now and will have it ready when we arrive."

47

"Okay," said Grinnell. "Creating these rooms for them will show them that I'm telling the truth about helping them find their homeworld. Anything I do here can be transferred to another ship, right?"

"Yes."

"Good." The cargo hold was huge. He used a tablet to map out two bedrooms. Then he created a third room that was especially for Mehanna. She didn't want to leave her cave, and he hoped what he created for her would make her feel more comfortable.

Once he had the rooms set up, he went back to the ladies.

"Your rooms are ready if you're ready to see them."

They nodded as one. He found it eerie. Was that a twin thing? These two girls didn't grow up together. How could they be in sync so quickly?

He brought them to the first room.

"May, these are the colors you had in your room in the village. You can make changes as you see fit, but I thought this would be a good start."

"Thank you, Grinnell. Do you mind if I rest a little? I'm not used to so much activity."

"Of course. I'll show Mehanna her room. We should be landing in a few horas. I'll have the computer alert you."

"Thank you."

He ushered Mehanna down the hall but walked past the bedroom he had set up for her. He stopped in front of a large set of doors.

"I know you didn't want to come." He turned toward her. "And you were worried about leaving your equipment behind."

"You told me it would be safe."

"And I didn't lie to you." He pressed a button, and the doors opened.

She watched as they revealed her cave. Well, part of her cave, the section that held all her computers and surveillance equipment.

He had brought it all here.

"Thank you." She wrapped her arms around him and kissed him. It was quick but filled with such joy that it jolted him.

By the gods, he wanted another one.

Orla was standing outside the ship when they landed. The worry lines creasing his face made Grinnell feel guilty. He should have been back sooner.

"My friend." They clasped hands and bumped shoulders. "I see you have brought some friends."

Grinnell turned and found the two women peeking out the doorway. "Ah, yes. Mehanna was working with Lawaya and May is her twin."

"And where is Lawaya?"

"I'll bring her to you in a few microns. Why don't you bring your mate out to the garden? Lawaya said she needed sunlight and lots of space."

"Is there a problem?"

"Only a little complication. Where is Grenta? I need to speak to her before I bring Lawaya to you." Grinnell smiled, trying not to show how nervous he was. "Lawaya needs to speak to her before we start."

"Okay." By Orla's tone, he wasn't sure if he should force Grinnell to explain his odd behavior or let this play out and see what Grinnell was hiding from him. "I'll send her here to you."

"Thank you." He headed back into the ship before Orla could ask him any questions. A sigh escaped him. One problem dealt with. Now he had to deal with Grenta.

She stood at the bottom of the gangplank yelling for him.

"Grenta, come on up." He came to the door and gestured for her to come up.

"You know I don't like the close confines." She stood at the bottom with her arms crossed over her chest.

"I do and normally I wouldn't ask you to do this, but it's important." He had to convince her to come onto the ship.

"Is Lawaya on the ship?"

"Um, yes." Why did she ask that?

"Then I can't come aboard." Grenta smiled as she spoke. "I'm not allowed to be in the same room she is in. In fact, I'm not allowed to be on the same planet."

"That won't be a problem." He smiled back. If she fought too much he would go down and bodily carry her on to the ship.

"What do you mean?" She frowned at him. "What have you done to her?"

Grinnell watched in amazement as she stomped up the gangplank and barged past him.

"If you have harmed her." She stopped when she reached the main part of the ship.

"I am not harmed, Grenta."

Grenta turned toward her voice. Her jaw dropped when she saw the mirror. She spun on her heel and glared at Grinnell. "What did you do?"

"Grinnell had nothing to do with this. It was an accident, pure and simple. It was Grinnell who gave me the ability to communicate with everyone."

"We need your help," said Grinnell. "She can still help Astrid, but she needs to use your hands."

"No." She shook her head. "I can't. I'm no longer part of the Barou. I made promises that I must keep."

"You never should have been banned," said Lawaya. "We all knew that boy had an evil streak. He never should have been allowed into the academy. My predecessor took him in because he came from an affluent family. She hoped if we could train him, it would allow us to get a strong backing. She didn't look at his soul when she accepted him."

"I killed him." Grenta looked down.

"You protected us." Lawaya's words made her look back up.

"I should have handled it differently." Grenta wrapped her arms around herself. "I should have been more careful."

"All these yepas you have been mourning him. You have been punished enough. I decree that you are no longer banned and are a full member of the Barou once again, Grinnell, are you a witness?"

"Yes, ma'am."

"Good." She then spoke to Mehanna. "Mehanna, are you a witness?"

"Yes, Lawaya."

"And May, are you a witness?" She shifted inside the mirror so she could see May.

"I am." May nodded.

"Computer, send a record of this to the Barou homeworld."

The computer took a few microns before responding. "Done."

"Now, let's go help Astrid."

Four people entered the garden.

Grinnell hoped they did a good job hiding what happened to Lawaya. He and Grenta were up front and Mehanna and her sister were behind them, carrying the mirror.

Orla had Astrid moved to the garden. He'd also had a beautiful lean-to erected to keep her out of the sun.

Seeing his friend unconscious and looking so pale made him feel worse. Orla had kept just how bad she had gotten from him. "I'm sorry it took so long to get back."

"Time to explain everything," said Orla.

"I agree," said Grinnell. "But first let me introduce my new friends and give you a little history. This is Mehanna and May. They are from one of the races that have the ability to do magic, but she and her sister were never trained. They were left on the planet you sent me to when they were children. Lawaya met Mehanna and learned her story. She felt a talent was a talent and wanted to help her learn to use her powers."

"Okay." Orla looked at the way he and Grenta were keeping the two sisters behind them. "What happened?"

CHAPTER FIVE

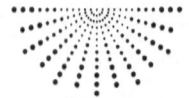

He and Grenta stepped aside and revealed the mirror.

Orla stared at the woman trapped inside.

Grinnell bet he didn't expect this.

"Grinnell, why did you hide this from me?" asked Orla.

"What would you have said if I had gone and said, 'Oh, by the way, Lawaya is trapped in a mirror?'"

"I would have asked if you had been drinking."

"And I had hoped we would free her first." Grinnell released a small sigh. "Lawaya told me she can still figure out what is going on with Astrid and should be able to help her."

"Your man has worked as hard as he could to get us here quickly," said Lawaya. "Grenta, tell me what has been going on so far."

"Astrid has been working on her Barou talent while she was pregnant. We were working together when I saw the power drain out of her. She told me she was fine, but I knew she needed a break. That was when I noticed she had two different color eyes. I knew what that meant."

"So the child she carries is a strong Barou."

"And Miran."

"Miran?" She looked at Orla. "That blood runs in your family?"

"Yes, ma'am."

"That does complicate things a little. I will have to separate the Barou power from the Miran first. How long has she been unconscious?"

"Almost a cycle."

"Grenta. Check her vitals. How strong is she?"

Grenta took a few moments to gather that information. "Heart, lungs, pulse are all strong. She is a strong Barou as well. I have seen her talent in action, and she is one of the best."

"Part of her problem is the mixture of the Barou and Miran blood." She rested her hand against the mirror. "We need to create a cap to keep the child from trying to take over."

"I'm not sure that is what's happening. The spikes happen at odd times. Could the baby be trying to control its power from within Astrid's body?"

"You think the child is that strong?" asked Lawaya.

"Astrid is a lot stronger than her mother." Grenta guided May and Mehanna so they could bring the mirror to Astrid's side. "I was wondering if adding the Miran shapeshifting blood to the Barou mage blood might be causing the spikes. This is the first time the two bloods have mixed, so we don't know what could happen."

"Tell me about Astrid's training."

Once May and Mehanna placed the mirror where Grenta wanted it, they stepped back.

"She is half Barou, as you know, and her mother passed when she was young. Her father was killed by General Varal, and she escaped to find a champion to help her take her planet back. That champion was Orla. I think the extenuating circumstances that brought her powers out made her much stronger than she would have been if her life had been a simple one." Grenta touched the unconscious woman's hand. "Each time I teach her something, she works at it until she masters it. If she doesn't grasp it right away, she gets angry. Her emotions fuel her power."

"So the anger allows her to figure out how to do things quicker."

"It's not always anger. One time she was so tired I refused to teach her anymore, and she got so silly we ended up laughing so hard tears fell from our eyes. She tried once more and mastered it."

"Alright. Orla, I know a bit of the history of the Miran blood. Normally the firstborn."

"Normally? I was told always."

"There have been a few families where more than one child inherits. Especially if the firstborn dies at a very young age," Lawaya said. "Tell me a little about your family."

"My mother had the bloodline. I was the first of twins. I don't know much else because when our parents betrothed us—" Orla gestured between himself and Astrid. "—I came to live with Astrid as her pet. The only way for a Miran to bond and mate properly is for them to grow up with their mate."

"Really?" Lawaya was quiet for a moment. "So you spent all of your life on this planet? Did you ever go home?"

"Once I was old enough I did."

"And Varal was in control by that point." She watched Orla brush a few strands of Astrid's hair. "Was Varal from this planet?"

"No. Astrid's father needed a general to help keep his space safe. There had been a few incidents with people trying to mine the moon. The general came along at the right time, and at first, he seemed perfect. It wasn't until much later that we realized that Varal was the one behind mining the moons. He had tried to get to the ore and got caught, so used it to his advantage to take over the planet and have the access he wanted."

"I heard the newsfeeds on your exploits in thwarting him, but I'd love to hear the real story."

"There wasn't much to tell," Orla said. "When her father passed, we used the royal time of mourning to escape the planet. Then we worked our way to my homeworld. Astrid's father told her to go find her betrothed to get her off the planet."

"Then she didn't know you were her destined mate."

Orla shook his head. "No. She believed my twin was who she was betrothed to. That's how we met Grinnell and Grenta. We needed a pilot and Grinnell is the best. He kept us safe throughout our mission. I consider him my best friend. Grenta was living on my planet when we met her. She knew she could be in deep trouble with your people, but she also knew that Astrid needed to learn to control her power. She is more than a teacher. She is family."

"What sort of things did she do with her power?" Lawaya asked. "Things that surprised you."

"Oh, well, she created a Miran tail, which was impressive since she hadn't had any training then." Orla paused as he thought. "Then, with Grenta's help, she was able to hide our landing party from the guards searching for us."

"I only helped her focus," added Grenta. "She did the rest all by herself."

"And then there were the doors."

"Doors?" Lawaya looked confused.

"We infiltrated one of Varal's strongholds and were caught. We had to escape, and somehow she manipulated the security doors so they wouldn't slide down. I have asked her to tell me how she did that, but she said it was a Barou secret."

"She learned to manipulate inanimate objects?" Lawaya looked a Grenta. "Only a master has that ability."

"The situation was dire, and she had to return safely." Grenta looked at her hands. "What she did was against Barou rules, but I had to make sure she had the right ammunition to do that."

"How much did you teach her?"

"I only had microns, so I gave her the basics." Grenta looked at Lawaya. "I was no longer part of the Barou, and I knew Astrid had been able to master a lot of the more advanced techniques faster than anyone I had trained before her. I felt what I did was right, and I still stand behind it."

"I'm not upset with you teaching her how to do this technique, but she never should have been able to do what she did." She looked at Orla. "It takes masters yepas of intense training to be able to accomplish what Astrid did after a few microns of training. She could be the strongest Barou out there."

"Astrid could well be," said Grenta. "Once she's tested, she might even believe it."

"Amazing." Lawaya smiled. "Grenta, have you been training her while she's been pregnant?"

"Of course. She still has a lot to master."

"I think you had more than one student. Here's what you need to do. Place your hands on either side of her womb and speak softly to the infant. Let her know that she is very strong, and you promise to train her when she is born, but for now, she needs to let her mother be in control so her mom can make sure she comes into this world strong."

Grenta nodded and did as Lawaya asked. She rubbed her hands against Astrid's stomach, relaxing the child and the hold she had on her mother. After spending a few microns telling the child how smart and loved she was, she whispered how excited everyone was to meet her and wanted her healthy. Asked her to let her mom have control, and she promised to train her when she was old enough. She hoped she made it through to the child when she stepped back.

Orla watched his mate as he spoke to Grenta and Lawaya. "I don't know what I was expecting, but it wasn't that."

"Sometimes it is best to keep it simple."

Astrid's eyes fluttered open.

———

"Astrid." Orla was at her side quickly. "How are you feeling?"

"I'm not sure." She felt a little lightheaded. "How did I get here?"

"You fell unconscious, and I couldn't wake you. Grinnell brought the leader of the Barou to help wake you up."

"What?" She sat up. "What about Grenta? She's not supposed to be anywhere near the leader."

"It is alright, child." Grenta sat on the bed beside her. "Lawaya has reinstated me. You no longer have to take the test to prove you're Barou."

"That doesn't matter to me as long as you're safe." Astrid took her friend's hands in hers. "You told me they could put you to death if they wanted to."

"I would never do that to Grenta."

Astrid looked to where the new voice came from and saw nothing but a mirror. She looked back at Grenta. "Where is she?"

"In the mirror."

"What happened?" She tried to stand, which brought Orla to her side to help her keep her balance.

"It was my fault," said another new voice.

Astrid turned to where Grinnell stood. "And who is your friend?"

"This is Mehanna and her sister May."

The two women bowed to the queen of Emori.

"And why do you think this is your fault?" she asked.

"Because my abilities got away from me, and I trapped her in there."

"Are you Barou?"

Mehanna shook her head.

"But you have some sort of ability to manipulate matter."

She shrugged.

"Very good," said Lawaya. "That is what I thought too. I felt the training could be the same."

"It makes sense," said Astrid. "That is what we do, but our manipulations of matter or energy don't last."

"What is a Barou?" asked May.

"We have the ability to create illusions that a non-Barou will see as real."

"Can we see?"

Astrid waved her hand and a bouquet of flowers appeared. She handed it to May. Dewdrops glistened on the petals.

"This is amazing. How can you say it's not real?"

"This is how," said Grenta as she passed her hand through it. It broke up into a thousand glittering fragments.

May tried to grasp at the glitter as it started to disappear. "Oh, you must do that again. I've never seen anything like that before."

"All in good time, May," said Lawaya. "I still plan on working with your sister once I get out of this mirror."

"I can work with May," said Grenta, "while you and Mehanna try to free you from the mirror."

Astrid was grateful that Grenta was going to help the young woman. She knew her mate had worried about her, but she didn't know why. She took his hand and pulled him back to sit on the bed she had been on. "So how long was I out?"

"Too long."

"Orla."

"Almost a cycle."

"What?" She didn't feel like she had lost any time. "What happened?"

"I don't know." He took her hands in his. "You were working with Grenta and passed out. When we tried to wake you, we couldn't."

"How did you get Lawaya here?" She looked over to where the mirror rested.

"I sent Grinnell after Lawaya when your eyes changed color. Grenta told me that wasn't a good sign."

So her friend and her mate had kept this from her. "Why not?"

"It said our child might be stronger than you are."

"Really?" She rubbed her belly and spoke softly to her womb. "You are?"

"Lawaya said that when Grenta was teaching you, our daughter was trying to master the same technique." Orla placed his hands on her womb as well.

"We don't know the sex of our child." Astrid turned so she could lean against him.

"I know, but that didn't stop Lawaya from saying our child was a girl."

"How would she know?" asked Astrid.

"I don't know, but she is very convincing." He linked fingers with her.

"Boy or girl, our child will be loved."

"That is very true." Orla hugged her. "And they will be spoiled."

"May, you have the ability your sister has." Grenta watched her. "Were you taught anything?"

"No. My sister can create food that you can eat, but I was never taught anything."

"Have you tried to use your talent?"

"With disastrous results."

"What happened?" Grenta pointed to a chair for May to sit in.

"I don't know." May sat down. "I tried to make a new outfit. I had been wearing the same thing for too long and no one would make me a new one, so I thought I'd try to do it myself."

"What went wrong?"

"I wish I knew. Instead of making clothing, I set my home on fire."

"Oh, my." Grenta stood. "Show me."

"Okay," May stood as well. "I wish for new clothing. What I have is old. The cloth is simple. The design beautiful. Cover me in elegance and style."

"Hmm." Grenta walked around her. "You have everything worded, but where is the emotion?"

"That was what set my place on fire."

"Your power, controlled or not, is based on your emotions." Grenta stopped in front of her. "Most of us awaken our power with strong emotion. For Astrid, it was the death of her father."

"I haven't had something so devastating as that."

"You were separated from your twin sister and taken from your family at a young age. I would think that would have triggered your power."

"Yes, but I didn't know that until recently." May looked at Grenta. "The people I lived with treated me well. Now that I have powers that I can't control they're afraid of me, but they raised me like one of their own."

"How about you show me what you can do?"

"That's it. Everything I've tried doesn't work."

"Okay. Let's start with your focus."

Grinnell walked with Mehanna. "Orla would like us to stay for a few duras. He has been working on making a ship for me, but it's not quite ready."

"I thought the ship we came in was yours."

"That is Orla's ship. He loaned it to me because finding Lawaya was of the essence."

"And now?"

"He wants to make sure our mission to find your homeworld is successful. This new ship will have a larger engine and can go into deep space. The other ship doesn't have that capability. It will also have a better cloaking device and a powerful defense system."

"Why?"

"Because I think your home planet is in a sector of space that has a lot of pirates. I want to be able to protect us if need be."

"Then you asked for this new ship."

"Orla told me if I liked his, he would build me one. He must have started on it lunas ago. All he needs to do is a few modifications and we can leave."

"You know you don't have to help me. You have what you wanted."

Grinnell stopped walking and turned her toward him. "I promised you that I would help you. I never go back on my word."

The secur May saw her sister she started talking. "Oh, my stars, these people are great. If you want to learn more about our powers. They seem to know it all. Grenta showed me how to make a flower. Now it's only one, but it's a start." She continued chattering away while she created a single flower. "Nesdura she's going to work with me some more so I can learn to control my powers."

"That's wonderful, May." Mehanna placed her hands on May's arms. "Maybe you need to take a breath?"

"Sorry." She laughed. "I'm just so happy to have someone willing to teach me, to teach us. Will you learn with me? Grenta said you'd be here a few duras while they get Grinnell's ship ready."

Mehanna searched her sister's face. "You're coming with us, aren't you?"

"I want to learn, Mehanna. I've always wanted to learn. I don't care about where we came from. They didn't care enough to come after us."

"I want to know why they left us." Mehanna stepped back and clenched her hands. "Make them explain themselves."

"I will go home somedura, but I want to control my powers first. You don't seem to have the problem I do where they just flare up. In a small space like a ship, I need to not be afraid that I'll destroy something accidentally by snapping my fingers or by laughing too hard."

"It can't be that bad. I'll help you."

"How? You can't control your powers. Let me do this." She placed a hand on Mehanna's shoulder. "You're my sister and now that I found you, I don't want to lose you again. But if I can't control my powers, it will make both our lives miserable."

"If you are sure." Mehanna wasn't happy about the idea, but she knew how frustrating it was to not have control. She wanted to go home so she could free Lawaya and learn to control her powers so she wouldn't make the same mistake. They had the same goal. They just wanted to achieve it differently.

Orla rested a hand against the hull of the ship. "I love this ship."

"I thought you loved your ship."

"Oh, I do." Orla grinned. "But when we had to make changes to this so you could have heavy armaments, larger engines that would allow you to go longer without needing fuel and change the paint job so you can camouflage the ship better. I fell in love all over again."

"I thought I was your only love," said Astrid, who now stood behind them.

"You know you're my best love."

"Good answer." She walked to his side and wrapped an arm around his waist. "At least your other love is an inanimate object."

"She is designed the same as the one you took to find Lawaya."

"She?" questioned Astrid.

"Most vehicles are dubbed female unless they do something that is totally male," said Grinnell.

"And that makes absolutely no sense."

"The interior is the same," Orla said. "I didn't format anything, but the command area, and you can make changes to make the ship more comfortable for you."

"What about the items I asked you to install?" Grinnell asked.

"Cargo three."

"Thanks."

Grenta approached with May and Mehanna. The two women were carrying Lawaya in the mirror once again and followed her to the ship.

Grinnell shifted his weight when the ladies caught up to them. Orla noticed that Mehanna went to his side. His lovely mate had pointed out that the young woman had kept to Grinnell's side since they arrived. She thought there was a budding relationship between them. He teased her and asked if she was playing matchmaker. She reminded him that all she did was observe.

He felt his mate's hand tighten on his waist when Mehanna edged her way to Grinnell's side.

"You ready?" asked Grinnell.

Mehanna nodded.

"Lawaya, I know you'd rather be around us, so I had the computer create a small niche for your mirror to rest in. It will keep you safe and allow you to watch the screens as we travel."

"Thank you, Grinnell." She looked at Astrid. "I will make sure you receive your confirmation from the Barou homeworld as soon as I can. Once I'm released from this prison, I want to test you, but I'm going to mark you as a fledgling master until I can do that. The things I saw you create were much better than most of our full-time students."

"Thanks, Lawaya. I look forward to finding just how good I am." She placed her hand on her stomach. "But perhaps we should wait until the baby is born."

"That might be a good idea."

May went to her sister and hugged her.

"You sure you don't want to come with us?" asked Mehanna.

"You sure you don't want to stay with me?" countered May.

"I'm going to miss you."

"And I you." May hugged her again. "Come back quickly."

"I will try."

May moved to Grinnell and as she hugged him, she whispered. "I've had duromares of home. Please protect her and bring her back safe."

"You remember your home?" he asked softly.

"Yes." She pressed a small chip into his hand. "Everything I have dreamed is on this. It's a copy of my diary. I've been having the duromares for yepas, but they didn't make sense until I met my sister."

"Why not give this to her?"

"She is still child-like in many ways." May looked at her sister for a moment. "She wants to know why they left us and hopes the answer will give her peace. My dreams won't show her what she wants to see. I fear she would ignore it, but you have been out there; you know evil."

He nodded and stepped back.

"My friend, I wish you could spend a little more time with us," said Orla.

"We'll be back before you know it, with Lawaya freed from the mirror," said Grinnell. They grasped elbows.

Orla pulled him close. "My mate thinks there is something between you two," he whispered, indicating Mehanna. "Is that true?"

There was no way he was going to answer a question like that. He didn't know what was happening between them. "I'm happy we were able to help Astrid," he said instead, as he smiled as he stepped back from Orla.

"My hero." Astrid wrapped her arms around Grinnell's neck. "Thank you."

"My queen."

She pressed a kiss against his cheek. "She's sweet. Treat her well."

"Yes, ma'am. I promise."

Once the goodbyes were done, Grinnell climbed the gangplank and entered the ship. Mehanna and her sister entered next, carrying Lawaya's mirror.

"Put her right here." Grinnell pointed to a small niche against the wall. He helped them settle the mirror. Once they were done May exited the ship.

"Lawaya, this spot was created to keep you stable but still allow you to see everything."

"Thank you, Grinnell. I was worried you'd make a room for me. Something I don't need."

"This has a forcefield to keep you safe, and it can be made opaque if you want some privacy."

"And how am I to activate it?"

"The easiest way is to use a thumbs up. The computer had been programmed to watch you for any motion to let it know what you want. We can work on other movements, but I thought that would be the first one we could start with. I have also programmed the computer to interact with you. All you have to do is mimic talking with your hands." He parroted the movement with his hand.

"Yes, Captain. You wish to speak?"

"I want to be sure you can register her movements."

"Of course."

"Go ahead, Lawaya."

She shrugged and opened and closed her hand like she was imitating talking.

"What would you like to talk about, Lawaya? I have been programmed in many subjects."

"Good," Grinnell said. "Computer, this is a test to see if her movements register. From this point on, when she makes that movement, you should have a subject ready in case she isn't sure what she would like to speak about. Lawaya, try having the computer activate your privacy shield. I'll reverse the order as soon as I'm sure it works."

"You realize that the moment the shield goes up my mirror will go dark."

"I've programmed something that I hope will help keep your mirror active. If it doesn't work, then we'll try something else."

"Alright."

Grinnell sealed her in and activated the screen inside the shield. He hoped he gave it enough time.

The first thing he noticed was the shocked look on her face when the shield dissipated. "Was there something wrong?"

"What was that?" She pressed her hands against the glass of the mirror. "It was so white."

"Good, it worked. That was from the mountains of Emori. It's frozen rain. Quite beautiful." He pressed a few keys on a tablet he held. "I can program just about anything you might want."

"I would love to have a nice forest scene. One I can pretend to walk through."

"Done."

"What's next?" asked Mehanna.

"Well, I have to do my preflight checklist, but I thought you might want to settle into your room if you like."

"Um, sure."

"Come with me." He led her down to the cargo area.

"This doesn't look like the sleeping quarters."

"It's not. I thought you'd be more comfortable here." He opened the door to reveal her computer system. "I had everything brought here, but I know you'll want to tweak it. I thought this would be more fun than watching me while I go through my boring checklist. Once we break the atmosphere, I'll come back and get you."

"Oh, thank you, Grinnell." She pressed a quick kiss against his cheek and then practically danced into the room.

He knew she loved what he did for her. That thrilled him to the bone.

Everything went off without a hitch, something that didn't always happen. Grinnell watched as the atmosphere gave way to space. He set the autopilot and went to cargo bay three.

He walked in to find Mehanna on her hands and knees, crawling around one of her terminals.

"You are not going to get the best of me." She crawled in between two units so the only thing Grinnell could see was her derriere wiggling at him.

"Is there a problem?" he asked, trying to keep his voice from cracking. She had no idea how the view aroused him.

Bang!

"Ow!" Mehanna sat on her butt and rubbed her head. "No. Just trying to get something plugged in. Had the same problem when I first put it together."

"You know you could program the computer to give you a longer cord so you wouldn't have to fight with it like this." He offered her his hand and helped her to her feet.

"That would take all the fun out of it." She dusted the seat of her pants off. "Are you done with your work?"

"I am. I thought you'd like to see where your room is."

"Okay." She didn't sound excited. Maybe there was something wrong.

He took her hand and led her down the hall. She pressed her hand against the panel to unlock the room. The doors slid open, and they stepped in.

"Oh, you recreated my sleeping area." She wandered into the room. "Thank you."

"You don't sound very excited. I thought this would make you feel more comfortable."

"Oh, it does." She clasped her hands behind her and gave him her best smile.

"Then what is wrong?"

"Nothing." She brushed her fingers against the moss that covered the slab. "You have gone out of your way to recreate what I had in my cave."

He took her face in his hands and lifted it so he could look into her eyes. Unshed tears glistened there. "Hey. Talk to me."

"You haven't wanted to touch me since we left my home. I had thought maybe you would want to again now that we're alone, but I see that I'm wrong."

"What? That's not—look, I think I need to explain a few things." He took her hand and led her to the bed. "I wasn't ignoring you or avoiding you. Physical relationships can get a little complicated, and I didn't handle it right. I wasn't sure if you wanted anyone to know about what we shared, and I never got a chance to ask you so decided to let you make the first move. Between Orla needing my help with a few things and the instant bond between you and your sister, I didn't see how I could get you alone."

"But we did take a few walks. You could have said something then."

"I know, but you seemed a little overwhelmed, and I knew the moment Astrid found out she would try to play matchmaker, and I didn't think you'd want that kind of attention." He took her hands in his. "But I promise to make it up to you starting right now."

She gave him a smile that took his breath away.

CHAPTER SIX

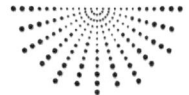

Mehanna felt a little thrill race through her. Her sister made her question what had happened between her and Grinnell when she'd told her about them. He hadn't shown any desire for her, but now she knew that he was trying to be a gentleman like she had seen in the entertainment feeds. Now what? She looked up at him. "So how do I make the first move?"

"You could whisper in my ear that you need me."

"I do." She leaned into him. "I need you."

"And I need you." He wrapped his arms around her as his lips claimed hers. He urged her back onto the bed. His hands moved about her body, touching, caressing, as well as removing her clothing.

She felt the cool moss against her back. The heat of his chest against her breasts. How she had missed this. His mouth moved from her lips to her throat, traveling down to a breast. A sigh escaped her when he latched on. She felt each tug to her toes.

Her breath hitched when she felt his fingers slip into her folds. She held her breath when his mouth released her breast and started to work down her body. Grinnell planted a kiss against her ribcage, then her belly button. He paused there for a moment, swirling his tongue around it before he continued down her body.

She arched her back when she felt his mouth at her core. Each time his tongue touched her, heat filled her. Soon she was on fire and wanted more. She wanted, no, needed to feel him deep inside her. Her legs started to move. It must have given him some sort of signal because he moved back up her body and took her lips with his as he drove into her.

They started moving together. Grinnell released her mouth and turned to her throat instead. Each time he drove into her she felt everything tighten a little before relaxing, only to do it again when he drove into her once more. Like a coil, her body tightened a little more each time. Her body started to vibrate. She met him thrust for thrust, wanting that release she could only find in his arms.

Her blood zinged through her veins. The release she wanted was getting closer. She could almost feel it. Mentally begged it to take over. To take her to that place where joy was in control.

Grinnell changed the tempo, driving into her faster.

It made her blood pump quicker. Then it started, bubbling up and filing her until she lost contact with everything but her release. She floated along in euphoria. Joy. She sighed her happiness.

"Wow." Grinnell shifted and brought her into his arms. That was more explosive than any other time. Maybe keeping themselves apart wasn't a bad thing. He didn't want to move. Didn't want to break the spell they weaved with their lovemaking.

"I know." Mehanna's voice was soft. "Does it get better every time?"

"It does with you." He pressed a kiss against her temple. "I think our time apart was good for us."

"And you don't have to fly this ship? You did on our way to Emori." She rested her head against his chest.

"That was because the planet was a lot closer. It's easier to manually fly when it's a short trip." He brushed his fingers against the arm she rested on his chest. "We're going to have to search a little. Your homeworld is cloaked in mystery. All anyone knows is the legends we have heard. Astrid stocked our library with all the stories and books that have any reference to your planet. All we need to do is have the computer organize it by content. Then we'll start reading. We're going to have plenty of time."

"How do you feel about doing some fun reading?" Grinnell asked Lawaya. He handed Mehanna the two tablets they would be reading from.

"How do you plan on having me do that? I can't turn pages or scroll."

"No, but you can tell the computer to do that."

"I don't have a problem, but if all of you are reading, won't me talking to the computer every time I want to turn a page stand out?"

"It will be fine, Lawaya. Let the computer know what word or motion you want to use so it will know to advance what you're reading. Our goal is to find the references we've heard about Mehanna's planet."

"There is something in my books at home that gave a lot of information."

Mehanna gripped Grinnell's arm when she heard Lawaya say that.

"Can you use the computer to access those books?" asked Grinnell. That information could save them lunas of searching.

"I can ask the council to transmit them to the ship, but they'll have to see me in order to approve my request." She looked around where she was trapped. "I'm not sure how they would take this."

"We could record you at a close distance. If they can't see the mirror, they might not question anything."

She smiled. "You don't know the Barou masters. We're trained to see through other Barou's images. They will see through this. I just need to come up with a reason that they will understand."

Grinnell contacted the council and found they were excited to speak to their leader. He focused the view screen toward the niche where she rested.

"My sisters."

"Lawaya, we've been working hard on keeping everything running as you asked."

"And you've feared my silence."

"We hoped you were well, but just couldn't communicate with us."

69

"That much is true." Lawaya smiled at her Barou family. "I met a young woman. Although she isn't Barou, I felt her abilities were close enough that I could train her."

"Is that why we haven't heard from you?"

"Part of it. It is also why I'm contacting you. She is magical, and I remember reading about a planet that had magical people. Grinnell and I want to take her home."

"Grinnell?"

"Yes." She signaled for him to step forward.

"Hi." He wasn't quite sure what to do. "Don't know if you remember me, but I was the one who contacted you a few cycles ago, looking for Lawaya."

"Yes," responded the woman. "You needed her for someone?"

"Astrid, Queen of Emori." Grinnell smiled. They did remember him.

"And how is she?"

"Much better." Grinnell caught a hand motion from Lawaya out of the corner of his eye and nodded. "And I understand that Grenta has been reinstated?"

The woman nodded. "We received the missive from Lawaya."

"Good," replied Lawaya. "Grenta helped me with Astrid, and I never believed she should have been banned."

"Why do you look different?" asked the woman she was speaking to.

"Because I'm trapped in a mirror."

"What?" The woman turned to look at a few of the women behind her.

"I wondered when you'd say something." Lawaya laughed. "I told you I was working with a young woman who had magical powers. She's very powerful but was untrained. There was a small snafu, and I'm now trapped in a mirror. It's one of the reasons I need the book where I read about her planet. We're hoping that someone from her planet will be able to release me."

Mehanna gave her a sad look. "I'm so sorry, Lawaya."

"Child, all of us have had our power go haywire," Lawaya replied. "I believe Astrid told you about her tail."

"She did."

"Come and speak to the council." Lawaya gestured for Mehanna to step beside the mirror. "I'm sure they fear I'm doing this under duress, and I want them to meet you so they understand that is was a very powerful, sweet woman who didn't know how to control her abilities."

"You think I'm powerful?" Mehanna stepped to her side so the camera could pick her up. "Um, I wish I could reverse what I did, but I don't know how. We're hoping someone from my homeworld could either release her or teach me how to do it."

"How did you end up out here?" the woman asked. "Your people don't normally leave the planet."

"I don't know. Do you know where my homeworld is?" She couldn't keep the hope in her voice out.

"No, but our library has the most comprehensive information on all known races. Lawaya was right in contacting us even under the current conditions. If there is any info on where you're from, we should have it." The woman talking looked down for a moment. "I'm sending twelve books to you. They should have the info you're looking for."

"Thank you." Lawaya looked at Grinnell and Mehanna. "Sorry, but this is for my eyes only. You have to be a Barou master to read any of our literature."

"We have plenty to read," said Grinnell. "I'm just glad that we have access to special information that could help us."

"Thank you for helping us," Lawaya said to her fellow Barou. "Hopefully the next time you see me I will be free of this mirror."

"Are you okay?" asked the woman who had been doing all the talking.

"I am. Grinnell set up a way for me to speak." She smiled again as she looked at him. "I didn't know how much time had passed until I was able to speak to them. I am sorry that you didn't know where I was or what happened to me. I am safe and will be home soon."

"As long as you are safe."

"I promise these people have my best interests at heart." She looked over at Grinnell again, who nodded, letting her know that the books had arrived. "We've just started our journey, so it could take some time."

"Hurry home."

"I will try."

Grinnell ended the communique.

"I loaded the information they sent for you to read." He pulled up the screen so she could see the information. "The computer is waiting for your instructions."

"I'm a little worried that I won't be able to read. We don't know what the mirror world has done to my senses."

"True, but you can talk and understand us, so I think the only thing we might have to do is adjust for any distortion."

She nodded.

"Ready?" asked Grinnell.

"Yes."

The cover of the first book came up.

"It's a little fuzzy." Lawaya frowned. "Can you sharpen the image?"

The computer made a few adjustments.

"Well, that's good for the cover." She swiped her finger like she was turning the page, but nothing happened. "Grinnell, nothing is happening."

"That's because you haven't given the command to the computer. If you want to use a movement to give the computer a command, you have to tell the computer out loud what it means. From that point on it will follow that command while you are looking at the screen."

"I forget that the system has limitations."

"I'll leave you with the computer." Grinnell took Mehanna by the hand and led her away.

"Grinnell is very thoughtful," Lawaya said. "Computer, I do want to use hand signals. I don't want to disturb our lovebirds with a voice command when they need to be alone. I want to have both."

"Of course. How do you wish to proceed?"

"Motions first. As far as the books go, I'll probably just do this." She motioned her finger like she was turning a page. "If I want to turn more than one page, I'll count on my hand how many I want to go. When I start a book, I always want to start with the table of contents. I know what I'm looking for, so I don't need to read the whole thing."

"Understood."

"When our couple gets a little amorous, I'll make a motion like this." She pulled her hands up and then pushed them down. "That will mean I want the shield."

"If it makes it easier, you can use either gesture as well to signal the shield."

"That would be easier."

"I can pick up nuances, but I need to know your personality first. As time goes on, I will be able to anticipate what you want or need. The mirror might be a problem for you, but it doesn't keep me from seeing your facial expressions and reading your personality."

"Do you understand the concepts of love and hate?"

"Emotions are not something I feel, but I can recognize them by the data I have."

"So what do you see happening between Grinnell and Mehanna?"

"They are sexually active. Grinnell is very attentive to Mehanna. She, on the other hand, doesn't seem to be sure about what to do."

"That's what I see as well. I want to give them the space they need for Mehanna to realize she's in love with Grinnell. She has never been around people, so this is very new for her."

"Do you think she will embrace this or run from it?" asked the computer.

"That is something I've been wondering. She's never had her heart broken by someone, yet she was abandoned. It could cause the same reaction. As innocent as she is, I think as long as she feels Grinnell's affection, she'll embrace it."

"It will be interesting to see how this plays out."

Lawaya agreed. She wondered if she'd end up with the shield up all the time. "If the shield is up, how was I able to see the images Grinnell loaded?"

"Good question," said the computer. "The cloth Mehanna used on the mirror sealed you in. The only time you were aware of anything was when the cloth was removed. Clear or opaque, the shield doesn't touch your mirror. It surrounds it. It's surrounding it right now, but you can still function."

"Then I should be able to read the books while the shield is opaque?"

"Of course."

"Great. I don't sleep while in here, so it will give me something to do."

"You can also speak to me whenever you wish to talk," said the computer. "I'm programmed in many subjects."

"You don't think Grinnell or Mehanna will be paying any attention to either of us?"

"They do seem to be preoccupied with each other."

Grinnell led Mehanna to where he normally controlled the ship. "This is where I'll be if you need me. I created a spot for you near Lawaya. I wasn't sure what you'd prefer, but here you can get comfortable as you read. If you doze off, which I think everyone has done when reading the way we're going to, the space will convert into a bed for you."

"Okay."

"Did you want it to be more like the cave?" asked Grinnell. "I can create something like that for you if you'd like."

"This is fine." She looked around for a moment. "Um, I'd like to be with you."

"Oh, you want to distract me." He wrapped his arms around her.

"Well, no, but I would be more comfortable if I could, I don't know, ask questions if I need to. If I'm over here and have to come over to where you are to ask questions, I'd feel like I'm intruding."

"You'd never be intruding." Grinnell gave her a quick hug. "Computer. Can you expand my area to allow Mehanna to join me? I'll need another screen for her."

"Done."

He brought her to where he had set up his pilot seat. "Normally, when I'm captaining a ship, I don't have a room. I stay here instead."

"You sleep here?"

"Unless I have a co-pilot. I never know if something is going to happen. If I have an emergency to contend with and I'm in my quarters, I'll lose precious securs trying to get to the bridge. This way, I'm right here and can react immediately."

"That's smart." She looked around and spotted a pillow-covered bed, for lack of a better word, for her to lounge on. It looked comfortable, but she didn't feel very comfortable.

Grinnell took her hand and led her to it.

"You can make changes to this if you want. The screen can be mounted, suspended, or you can hold it in your hand." He took one of the two screens he had handed her earlier. "I loaded about ten titles for you to work through. I recommend you not read the whole book. Most of the books have a table of contents that will help you with your search. The computer also marked the sections that might have the info we're looking for."

"Why don't you just ask the computer to search the files?"

"The computer sees everything in black and white, right or wrong. It would give us information quickly, but it might miss something small because it wouldn't get an inference."

"So you used it for some of the books."

"It scanned all the books and was the one who gave me the list. I gave it key words to look for."

"And what am I supposed to look for?"

"Well, anything we know about a race that has magic is legend." He sat and pulled her down beside him then pulled up one of the books to show her how to quickly find what they were looking for. "We have lots of races, like the Barou, or Miran that have abilities, but they're limited, like you saw with Astrid's talent. She can create almost anything, but it doesn't last. Orla is a shapeshifter. He can go from humanoid to a Miran, but that is all. I've met people who can turn into anything. But I've never met anyone who can do what you and your sister can do." He pointed to the table of contents showing extinct races. "I'm betting your people came out into the galaxy and found that people wanted what they could do and decided that keeping to themselves was the smartest thing to do."

"What we can do isn't all that." She tapped on the link. It opened to the section that spoke of races that are gone but whose remains were found in digs. She closed that and went to the section that spoke of the legendary races.

"Maybe not to you, but even your sister found the fruit you could create amazing. Imagine if you had been trained since you were a child. What you would take as something natural would be magic to someone else. Some would accept you, but others would be afraid of what you could do. Then you have those that would covet what you could do. They

75

would be thinking of all the things they could make you do if they could control you."

"Never thought of that." She sat back from the book and dropped her gaze.

"And now you're wondering if I want to control you."

She looked up at him.

"Now you want to know if I'm reading your mind." He took her hand in his.

"It did cross my mind." She played with his fingers.

"General Varal did that to me." He brushed his knuckles against the back of her hand. "He controlled me by hanging my family over my head. Telling me they would be safe as long as I did what he wanted. He lied to me. He killed my family anyway. Having it done to me made me swear to never do that to anyone. It tore me up inside, and even though it forced me to flee and I'm better for that, no one should go through what I went through."

"I didn't mean to make you relive what Varal put you through." She took his hand. "I've been by myself all this time. I never thought about how others would see my abilities. Especially since I think my powers are a hindrance, and I'd like nothing more than to have them go away."

"Really? Are you afraid of your powers?"

"No." She sighed. "Yes, maybe a little. Not being able to control it upsets me. Look what I did to Lawaya. What if it happens again, but the next time it's worse? I don't think I can live with myself if someone died because what I can do goes haywire."

"I get that, but you have a beautiful gift. I watched Astrid try to control her talent, and in the beginning, it embarrassed her to no end. Now, I understand that her power isn't the same, but there were moments when it could have caused harm. She could have had her powers fail her or she could have tried to show off and have it go berserk."

"But it didn't happen to her, did it?"

"You're right. It didn't happen to her, but she felt the same fear because it could have." He smiled. "That's what you're doing. You're not thinking about what you can achieve, but what might go wrong."

She remained quiet.

"I gave you something to think about, haven't I?"

"Yes."

"Then why don't you get comfortable? I have a few system checks that I need to do and will be back. I promise not to bring this up until you do."

She smiled.

Grinnell stood over his control panel, checking the readings and making sure everything was within acceptable norms. Happy with the readings, he checked on Lawaya once more before going back to where Mehanna sat. He found her on her stomach, knees bent, feet waving in the air. The image made his heart skip a beat.

He slipped into his seat and pulled up his screen. May's diary had also been loaded. How would Mehanna feel if she knew he had her sister's diary and was reading it? Would she be upset that May had given it to him instead of her? Grinnell decided to read that when she was sleeping or otherwise occupied.

"This is interesting," said Mehanna.

"What did you find?" He went to sit down beside her.

"This book speaks of people who controlled magic. They could turn the dura into duro. Make it rain."

"That sounds like the people we're looking for. Does it tell you anything about where they came from?"

"Not yet. The people who wrote this saw them as gods. It sounds like they came to the planet as explorers."

"What was the name of the planet?"

"Um, it's called Teraforna. I think." She handed him her screen. "How would you pronounce that?"

"Teraforna is right." He looked at the information. "This planet is in a section of space that I wanted to avoid."

"Why?"

"It's not safe."

"You had said something about the space around my planet not being safe, didn't you?"

"Yes. The planet I found you on is just inside a section called nomad land."

"Why is that area so bad?"

"When we defeated Varal, a lot of his loyal soldiers ran to that section of space. It hasn't been explored a lot, so it's easy to find a place to hide."

"And the section we're going to?"

"It's a little further out and a little more developed, but this is where Varal's reach ended. Anyone running from him went there."

"So you ran there as well."

"I went to the fringes of Varal's reach but not into that territory. The area we're talking about still isn't governed. If I had flown the ship that I had stolen from Varal into that area, I would have been attacked. They wouldn't have cared that I stole it. They would have taken it from me to either sell for parts, ransom it back to Varal, or keep it for themselves to try to control a small section of the quadrant."

"And you're afraid that it could happen now."

He nodded. "This ship is top of the line. One that any pirate worth his salt would want to have. It's not a could but a when. I need to figure out how we go into territory we don't belong in and get back out without trouble. I need to keep everyone safe."

"Can I help?"

"Yes. Continue reading. Maybe we'll find some information that will keep us away from that sector."

"But you don't think that will happen, do you?"

"I live by the rule that what can go wrong will go wrong. It makes it easier to prepare for everything."

A large planet loomed on the screen.

"Why are we going to this planet?" asked Lawaya.

"I want to be sure we have all our supplies," said Grinnell. "We need enough fuel, food, and equipment to make it to the planet we decided on and back without having to stop."

"You want to be as self-sufficient as possible, even if we get attacked."

"No one is boarding this ship while I'm the captain." He set the controls to start their descent. "I'm known here as a pilot. Nothing more. I doubt the information of me working for the queen of Emori has spread this far. It's not something I would deny, but it's not something I'll announce either."

"Lawaya, you're going to be in charge of the ship while we're on the planet. The computer will monitor the area around the ship and keep me posted, but I'm relying on you to let me know if something doesn't feel right."

"I will do my best."

He powered down the ship and pulled up the shields. "I've hidden the royal seal but the ship itself has to be visible while we're in port. It was the only way we could land here where we can refuel and restock."

"You think there will be a problem?"

"No, but we are on the fringes of regulated space, and there are spies for those in the next quadrant."

Mehanna clung to his side. The noises, the people, it was too much for her.

"You okay?"

"I should have stayed on the ship."

He laughed as he slipped an arm around her waist. "Tell the computer to minimize the background noise so you can focus on my vocal direction."

She spoke softly into her mouthpiece and sighed when the sound around her lowered to a volume she could tolerate. "Can we make the crowd thin?"

"We're almost out of the port. Open space isn't too far away."

"I hope you're right."

"Grinnell!"

He knew that voice anywhere. They had protected each other while running from Varal. He turned and smiled. "Leabo!"

They grasped arms as they pulled each other close and pounded each other on the back.

"How have you been, my friend?"

"Good," Grinnell responded. "And you?"

"Happy." He smiled as he turned with them to head for the massive opening that led outdoors. "Who is your pretty friend?"

"This is Mehanna. I'm helping her find her homeworld."

"I see." Leabo paused for a moment. "Is it one of those things where time is of the essence? I've been trying to get in touch with you. I need your help."

"With what?" Grinnell gave Mehanna's waist a quick squeeze. "Is it something I can do once I help Mehanna?"

"My request is something that is time-sensitive but shouldn't take too long. How about you two come to the evening meal and I'll explain everything?" He looked at Grinnell. "Have you booked a room yet?"

"No. We were going to stay on the ship if we needed to stay overduro."

"Then why don't you stay with me? We can catch up, and it will give you a break from the ship." Leabo noticed Mehanna tighten her hold. "I do only have one extra room at my place. Is that okay for you two?"

"That will be fine, my friend." Grinnell smiled as he looked down at Mehanna who loosened her hold a little. "Mehanna has led a sheltered life, so I thought staying in town would be a bit much for her."

"I totally understand if staying with me is a little too much. Just thought it would give you a little relief from the confines of the ship."

"How about we meet you for dinner and then decide if we want to stay? That way, if Mehanna wants I can take her back to the ship." He patted his friend on the back. "Right now, I want to take her out to the tents and give her a chance to see the wares the people here have. She never experienced anything like this."

"That will give me the time I need to get everything ready. I'll meet you just outside the main doors of the port in three horas."

"Sounds good."

"Who was that?" asked Mehanna once Leabo had walked away.

"Oh, sorry. That was Leabo." He took her hand and led her outside. "He was my co-pilot when we helped Astrid and Orla. We met several lunas after I had escaped with Varal's ship. When Orla offered me the position to head up his space fleet, Leabo could have been my assistant, but he opted to work privately. Whenever he has needed my help, he has contacted me. I've helped when I could. I bet Orla told him about our quest and that we were going to be here this dura."

He took her down a wide path. They rounded a corner, and the noise got loud again. Riots of color filled the sky.

"What is this?"

"Welcome to the Bazaar."

CHAPTER SEVEN

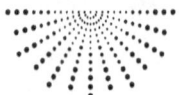

T he colors, sounds, and oh stars, the smells surrounded her. Mehanna still clung to Grinnell as she looked around in awe. "I've never seen anything like this."

"Not even in your newsfeeds?" he asked.

"It didn't hold a candle to this." She gestured around her. "What should we do first?"

"How about a treat?" He led her to a booth that had all kinds of sweets. He picked one of his favorites and paid for it. They walked away from the booth as Grinnell handed the pastry to her. "This might look small, but it packs a lot of flavor."

She popped it in her mouth. The sweetness filled her mouth, followed by an explosion of flavor. Joy filled her. "I could eat a dozen of these."

"That's why I love these things. You'll notice the flavor lingers for several horas." He smiled. "And I picked up a few more for later."

"Does everyone have the chip you have to pay for things?"

"This planet uses a barter system. Most of the off-worlders normally only have the chips to pay with, but you'll see people trade animals, labor, items they have made, food, and plants."

"If I want to buy something, would they be willing to buy the fruit I make?"

"Yes, but you would have to make them ahead of time. If you make them in front of any of these merchants, you run the risk of one of them wanting you for your talent."

"Hadn't thought about that. I don't want you to pay for everything."

"I get that. You're helping me go through all those files so we can find your planet. Consider it payment for your help."

"You're helping me, Grinnell. Not the other way around."

"Still, other people wouldn't be willing to go through all those files. They'd make me do it by myself."

"That's not very fair."

He shrugged.

They walked around, stopping whenever something caught their eye. Grinnell stopped in front of one that had some beautifully patterned material. He nodded to the woman there.

"I have bolts if you wish to make garments."

"Have any ready-made garments?" asked Grinnell. When the woman frowned, he added. "For the lady."

"Oh, of course." She looked at Mehanna. "I have several outfits about your size that I can adjust to fit you perfectly."

"What's wrong with my clothes?"

"Nothing," said Grinnell. "But I thought you might want to try the clothing of this planet. I normally wear what is popular on the planet I'm visiting."

"Are you now?"

He nodded. "Do you see anything you like?"

"Um." She touched several cloths. "This one feels nice."

"Does a color jump out at you?"

"This one." She touched a dark blue pattern with shots of pink throughout it.

"Very pretty," the merchant said. "That will look good on you." She took a few measurements and went back into her tent, then came out with a small bundle. "Would you like to try it on? I can wrap your clothes up to carry with you."

She looked at Grinnell.

"Go. I can't wait to see you in it."

She smiled at him, then followed the woman into the tent.

Grinnell knew this could take a few microns, and if he stood there waiting he'd be a mark for one of the many thieves looking to find someone easy to manipulate. He decided to check out a few of the neighboring booths. Nothing caught his attention at the first two. Great, he was going to find himself right back at the tent Mehanna was in, staring like a fool.

The third booth had wines from a local vineyard, and he picked up several for dinner later. The fourth one had crystals of every size and color. One was the exact color of Mehanna's eyes. It was several carats in size.

"Ah, you have a good eye."

"Are these created or mined?"

"Mined, of course."

"Uh-huh, that's why they look perfect. Just like created ones do." He picked up the one he was eyeing. "How much?"

"Sixty credits."

Grinnell started laughing and handed the stone back.

"For you, I'll give a twenty-five percent discount."

"Not enough." He moved toward the next booth. The price wasn't a problem. He just knew how and where they were made, and if he wanted to, he could get one for a fourth of the price. This one, though, was beautiful and right in front of him.

"What do you want to pay for it?"

"Fifteen credits."

"I would make no money off that."

"I know what they're worth."

"You also know that you might never find this exact color."

Grinnell shrugged. "I know."

"Fifty-five credits."

"Twenty."

"Fifty."

"Twenty-five."

They looked at each other.

"Forty," offered the merchant.

"Forty if you throw in this small crystal as well." Grinnell pointed to one of the small crystals the man had displayed on a black silk cloth.

The merchant looked at the piece in question and smiled. "Done." He slipped the stones into a small cloth bag. "I have mounts you can choose from as well."

"Thanks, but no. I don't have the time."

The flap of the tent Mehanna was in opened and she stepped out. She was a vision. The woman even had her hair swept up and a piece of the cloth was braided into it. She came to his side, her expression showing her curiosity. "Are you buying something?"

"I found some wine for our dinner with Leabo."

The merchant came out and called Mehanna over to get her old clothing. Grinnell took that moment to purchase the stones and slip the bag into a pocket.

"She is very pretty, and I know why you went to that stone. Good luck, my friend."

"Thank you." He slipped his chip back into a front pocket as he turned his attention back to Mehanna. "You look beautiful."

She clasped her hands behind her back. A slight blush filled her cheeks.

"This feels so different." She looked around, then stepped close. "I feel free, like—like I'm naked." The blush deepened.

He slipped an arm around her. "There is no need to be embarrassed."

"I'm not embarrassed." She put her arm around his waist. "It's just very strange."

"You never thought to make yourself a dress in your cave?"

"It wasn't practical. I'd see them on the feeds and knew I'd tear one up too fast."

"And now?"

"I'm still worried about that, but I'm not doing the same things that I would do at home."

"Would you prefer pants? We could get you some new ones and a few tunics if you'd like."

Mehanna remained quiet.

"You can still keep the dress."

She brushed her hands down the material. "I do like the dress."

"And we can get a few more dresses."

"I don't want you to spend all your credits on me."

"Don't worry about how much it costs. Clothing is something we need. We need it to fit in. I always have an allowance for that."

"I will pay you back."

"If that will make you feel better." He looked down at her. "So, which is it? Dresses or pants?"

"Dresses." She said it softly.

"Let's go pick out a few more."

That evening they met Leabo at the main doors of the port. He smiled when he saw them.

"Mehanna, you look lovely."

"Thank you." She brushed her hand against the material of her new dress.

"Did you have fun at the bazaar?" Leabo asked her as he led them back out of the port doors.

"Oh, yes." She smiled and nodded. "I've never seen anything like that before. It was a lot of fun."

"Glad you had fun." He led them past the bazaar. "My home is also my business. I live above where I work."

"Do you regret not accepting Orla's offer?" asked Mehanna.

"Honestly?" He pointed to a road to the right of the main road. "No. I enjoy what I do. I get to travel to some exotic places and meet a lot of different people. Don't get me wrong: There is a lot of boring paperwork and research on many cases. Every once in a while, though, I get that gem that makes it all worthwhile."

"Like the one you want me to help you with?" They followed the road until they came to a two-story building.

"Yes—well, sort of." He led them up the stairs to his quarters. "It's an intriguing story that I hope you like."

Wonderful aromas wafted past them when the door opened.

"When did you learn to cook?" asked Grinnell.

MAGICAL QUEST

"Oh, I didn't. I hired my secretary to cook for us. If you want something I cooked, I have some bread and jelled fruit to serve you."

"That's not cooking." Grinnell laughed. "And I bet you bought both items."

"Of course, I did." Leabo laughed as well. "You know I can't cook, so I had two choices. Either order from a local restaurant or blackmail someone I knew could cook to make a meal for us. I did promise her that she could join us."

"Someone you're sweet on?"

"Maybe? I don't know. It's my secretary. She helps me with the business. Has a good head for finances. We get along great."

"Pretty?"

"Every time I look at her, my heart stops."

Grinnell laughed again.

There was a quick knock and the door opened.

"Am I late?" A pretty young woman came in with a large basket. Behind her came three other women carrying more food.

"Are we feeding an army?" asked Leabo.

"I'd rather have too much instead of too little." She directed the other women to set up everything, then she thanked them and allowed them to go home. "Besides, you're not the cook, and I always end up bringing you my leftovers. This time, you'll have enough for a few duras."

"She knows you well, Leabo," said Grinnell.

"A little too well at times."

"You couldn't do without me, and you know it." She moved a large bowl to a side table and then lifted the lid.

"I see how toduro is going to go." Leabo shook his head. "If you two are going to be against me, you should at least know each other's names."

"Oh, I know this has to be Grinnell. You've been talking about him all dura." She gave him a bow. "My name is Sarha. I am the one who keeps Leabo's business afloat."

"Hey! I work just as hard as you do." Leabo's tone showed he felt he needed to defend himself.

"I'm sure you do," replied Grinnell. He bowed as well. "This is my companion Mehanna."

"It's a pleasure, Mehanna." Sarha bowed to her.

87

Mehanna bowed back. "Nice to meet you."

"I'll have everything ready quickly." Sarha pulled out plates from the cabinets, then she grabbed the silverware. She crossed to a small pile of linens and finished dressing the table. Each plate was filled, then she gestured for everyone to take a seat.

"Oh, wait." Grinnell swung the bag he had slung over his shoulder around. "I bought some wine for us to enjoy."

"Thank you for that." She took the containers and went to get wine glasses. As she poured the wine, she smiled. "You got some of our best wine."

"Leabo told me he wanted my help, so I needed something good to choke on when he tells me what he wants."

That made everyone laugh.

The meal went well, with Leabo and Grinnell telling stories about each other and themselves. Mehanna hadn't said much, but she did seem to enjoy the stories.

"And you, Mehanna?" asked Sarha. "How did you meet Grinnell?"

"Um, he came to my cave."

"Cave?"

"Mehanna lived a solitary life before I showed up." Grinnell placed an arm over Mehanna's shoulders. "She did live in a cave. That was home for her."

"I come from a large family," said Sarha. "I don't think I could handle a lot of time on my own. I'm too used to having someone interrupting me at every turn."

"And she proves it every dura," Leabo said. "If you think she is loud, you should see her with her family. They start talking all at once, but her voice can cut through the din."

"It must be lovely to come from a large loving family," murmured Mehanna.

"What do you need my help with?" asked Grinnell, wanting to steer the conversation away from talk of family.

"Oh, right," Leabo said. "We received a missive from a woman on a planet just inside the forsaken zone. She is looking for two sisters. Twins, really. They were left on a planet, and she wants to find them quickly."

"Any reason why?" He felt Mehanna's hand slip around his waist and give him a squeeze.

"She said the girls were in trouble." He gave him an odd look. "Why?"

He looked at Mehanna who nodded her head. "Because I think you're talking about Mehanna and her sister."

"What do you mean?"

"Mehanna and her twin sister were left on a small out-of-the-way planet just inside nomad's land."

"You think they could be the sisters?" Leabo sat forward.

"They do fit the bill."

"She said they had a mark." He pulled out one of the missives.

"Mark?" asked Mehanna.

"Yeah. That's how I'll know I have the right girls." He gestured for Sarha to turn her back. He lifted her hair and pointed to the nape of her neck. "There is supposed to be a mark that looks like a crescent moon there."

Grinnell lifted Mehanna's hair. There on the nape of her neck was a crescent moon.

"And this woman?" asked Grinnell. "Did you ever meet her in person?"

"No. She did everything the old way. Her missives are on paper like this. She had it hand-delivered to me. That's what caught my attention. She knew to contact me. It was addressed to me personally. When I suggested we meet in person, she refused. She is afraid of something or someone. All she has promised is that no harm will come to the girls and that time is of the essence."

"I'll need all the information you have."

"I have it right here." He handed over a small pile of paper.

"Did you tell her that you were going to ask for my help?"

"Had to. She's a bit paranoid and demanded pictures of all involved. I sent yours just in case you said yes."

"Good thing you did."

Grinnell was happy to get clearance to leave the planet. He read every bit of correspondence between Leabo and the woman who hired them. She only signed with a single initial.

"I have no idea how to find this woman," he said. "She never mentioned what world she lives on. The only thing we know is she lives in the forsaken zone." He handed the notes he had been going through to Mehanna. "This could take lunas, if not yepas. If you don't want to waste time chasing this down, we could do it after we find your planet."

"True, but she might know where I come from." She took the notes. "If she is just inside this forsaken zone, then we could find her in duras. She could save us lunas in our search."

"That is true, but what if this is just a ruse, and she wants you for your power? We do have to think of that."

"Wow, you sure are a pessimist." She set the papers down.

"I am pragmatic and look at the stark reality." Grinnell checked a few readings. "I know better than to trust people and always try to figure out what they really want."

"And if she is exactly as she seems?" She touched his back so he would turn to look at her. "All she wants to do is to protect me and my sister?"

"Then I'll be very happy for you." He placed his hands on her shoulders.

"And will still question everything won't you?"

"Of course." He smiled as he pulled her close.

Grinnell activated the cloaking device the moment they entered the forsaken zone. He constantly checked the monitors for anything out of the ordinary. He was amazed at how quickly Mehanna found little clues in the missives Leabo received. They now knew where they were going. The planet they were headed to would be the first one just inside.

They had coordinates to find the woman who sent the missives without having to land at the public port. He had turned off their transponders so no one should detect their presence. He landed their ship in a clear area of the woods that supposedly surrounded the woman's house.

Grinnell shut down the computer and turned to look at Lawaya. "I hate leaving you here alone again."

"I'll be fine," she responded. "You want me to look for oddities once again?"

He nodded.

"I hope this woman has the information you two are looking for."

"I hope we find her before anyone knows we're here. I'll be in touch with you from time to time to make sure everything is okay." He picked up a satchel he had packed earlier and took Mehanna's hand. "You ready?"

"Not sure, but that won't stop me."

"Then let's go."

They stepped off the ship and Mehanna watched as it disappeared. "I find that amazing."

"Technology is great at times like this." He looked at the map his computer put together. Not wanting anyone to know they were there, he left anything that could be detected inside the ship. He did bring a weapon, but he made sure it was nothing in it that could be tracked. The heavy firearm was in the satchel he carried.

The map led them through the wooded area to a small stream.

"According to this, we should follow the stream north. It should lead us to her home." He put the map back in his bag. "We can still turn around and go home if you don't feel comfortable."

"No." Mehanna shook her head. "We've come this far. I need to know why she's been looking for me and my sister."

"I sent a transmission to Orla and let him know what was going on. I wanted someone to know where we are just in case and to see if your sister wanted to join us. She deserves to hear what this woman has to say as well."

"I wish she had come with us. Thank you for letting her know what is going on."

"She needed to stay and learn. You would have fought with her if you thought staying was wrong."

"I know. I would have stayed too if I didn't need to release Lawaya from the mirror."

"Your guilt is something you need to shake off. What happened wasn't your fault. It was a fluke. You should look at this as a good thing. Your ability must be strong to trap anyone in a mirror."

"A good thing?" she shook her head. "I made a mistake."

"I don't see it that way, and I don't think Lawaya sees it that way either. You are powerful, just untrained."

"You are very powerful," said a new voice.

Grinnell spun toward it, wishing he had his weapon strapped to his side. A tall thin woman, whose build looked a lot like Mehanna's, stood in front of them. The slight blue tint of her skin proved she was of the same race that Mehanna came from.

"I know you don't like not being in control, Grinnell, but I must be sure we're safe," the woman said.

"You know my name."

"Of course. Your friend Leabo sent your picture as well as your bio. I did a little research on top of that." She smiled. "And this is Mehanna all grown up. You turned into quite a beauty, my dear."

"Then you know me."

"I do." The woman studied her. "But you don't know who I am, do you?"

Mehanna shook her head.

"I wondered what he did to you before he put you on that planet."

"He?" She looked at Grinnell. "He who?"

"I guess I should start at the beginning. You and your sister lost your parents in a freak accident, and with no other relative, our leaders appointed you two a guardian."

"You still haven't answered the question."

"I know. This is difficult for me. On our planet, we're free to do as we wish, but off planet we don't speak anyone's name. Unless, of course, they are off-world as well. I can't even tell you where the planet is."

"Why not?" asked Grinnell.

"To protect our people. Too many people are looking for our planet and our power. But I'm talking in riddles, and my goal is to help you remember so you will know what you're up against." She turned and headed upstream. "Come. Let me ply you with food and drink and I will do my best to explain without breaking any of our laws."

Mehanna followed, then turned to check to see if Grinnell was coming.

He couldn't believe they were going to trust this woman. They didn't even know her name, and after her explanation, he bet she wouldn't tell them what it was. Grinnell picked up his gait to keep up with the two women. There was no way he would leave Mehanna's side. Her safety was paramount to him. Not knowing what to expect had him fearing everything.

No one spoke as they followed their leader. A lovely little house came into view with an assortment of animals, some he didn't recognize. One, feline in design, twined between their host's legs.

She scooped it up and petted it as she welcomed them to her home.

"It's not a mansion, but I've been very happy here." She put the animal down. "Now. I want to know what you can do, Mehanna."

"That's easy." She flipped her hand and brought forth the bright red piece of fruit.

"Ah, a fandel. It has several vitamins that you need to stay healthy. And you were taught that before you left our home planet."

Grinnell had wondered what it was called. He hadn't recognized it when she first created it.

"There was no one to teach me anything else."

The woman looked confused. "But you should have figured out other things along the way."

"Like what?"

"It doesn't matter if you don't know anything else." She paused for a moment. "Did you know you had a special ability?"

"No. I lived by myself. What I could do was so natural, I never thought of it as odd until I met…"

"Who? Grinnell?"

Mehanna shrugged.

"Someone else." She looked at Grinnell. He looked back, not adding anything. She turned her attention back to Mehanna. "And you're embarrassed by it."

Mehanna remained silent.

"Alright." She crossed her arms over her chest. "If you want my help, you need to tell me what is going on."

She couldn't believe that Mehanna hadn't unlocked her mind yet. That was the first thing she had to teach her. What had Moorac done to her?

"It doesn't matter," Mehanna said.

"It does. Whatever it was has taken any confidence you might have had." She paused for a moment. "If you can't be honest with me, then I can't help you."

Mehanna sighed. She looked to Grinnell, which she did a lot, then she spoke. "I met a Barou master. She decided to try to train me."

"And that didn't go well," prompted the woman. "What happened?"

"I—I…"

"She's trapped in a mirror on my ship," Grinnell answered for her.

"Trapped?" The woman's brow furrowed. "The Barou can create like we can, but their images are nothing more than illusions, right?"

"Yeah," responded Grinnell. "They dissipate after the Barou stops concentrating on it."

"How did she get trapped?"

"She created a mirror and she wanted me to do the same thing," said Mehanna. "I was having trouble. She kept pushing me to try. It took me horas to make the mirror anywhere near as nice as the one Lawaya made." A quiver entered her voice. "She was so proud of what I did though. She got up close to check it out but when she touched it, the damn thing sucked her in. It happened so fast, and no matter what I try I can't get her out."

"Have you offered her your hand?"

"Of course." She quieted for a moment. "I tried grabbing her hand before she went into the mirror. I banged my hand against the mirror when I couldn't get her out. There were times when I pressed my hand against the mirror, and she pressed her hand against mine from the other side. Nothing ever happened."

"But you never tried to put your hand into the mirror."

"I don't know," Mehanna said. "I've been so busy trying to get her out I can't remember if I even thought to offer my hand that way."

"Grinnell, you said you have the mirror on the ship?"

He nodded.

"Will you go get it and bring it here?"

"Of course. You'll have to give me a couple of horas though. It's a full-length mirror."

"Here." She waved her hand and handed him a small circular disc. "This is an antigrav disc. This should help move it."

"I have these on my ship. It's making sure I can get her through the woods without a problem."

"Ah." She thought for a moment then flipped her hand. A small silver box appeared. "This will allow you to shrink it down to a smaller size. Just place it on the base of the mirror and set the adjustments to the size you need."

"And this won't cause harm to Lawaya?"

"No," the woman said. "She won't realize any change in size. It only affects the mirror."

"I'll be back as soon as I can."

Grinnell wasn't sure if bringing Lawaya to this woman's house was a smart move, but he hadn't been happy about any of the decisions so far. Mehanna did trust the woman, and he was following her lead. At least until he felt their lives were in jeopardy.

He had explained everything to Lawaya before he brought the mirror to the small home. He wasn't sure how he felt about the recent turn of events. If Lawaya was freed, he no longer had a reason to help Mehanna. He was helping her so she could free Lawaya. If she freed her this early, she might not need him anymore, and he wasn't sure if he could walk away.

He wasn't quite sure why, but he would do whatever she wanted him to do.

The house came into view. Grinnell straightened his shoulders. Pulling the mirror out of his backpack, he sat it on the ground and pressed the button so it would go back to normal size. He had brought the equipment he had added so they could talk to her. It sat in his bag just in case they needed to use it.

Mehanna and their host came out when they saw him. He wished he knew the woman's name.

"Good." The woman came up to the mirror to check it out. "Mehanna, this is very good. The detail is amazing."

Mehanna hung back while their host checked out the mirror. Grinnell moved to her side.

"You okay?" he asked quietly.

"Yes. This is just the worst. She knows so much, and I know so little."

He put an arm around her shoulders in support. "But she's willing to teach you."

"So was Lawaya."

"True, but this woman has the same power as you. She's been through the training you're going to get. I'm sure any mistake you make, she has made too."

"Although I might not have made the same mistakes as Mehanna, I have made my share, Grinnell," the woman interrupted. "It should be enough to be able to correct anything that could go wrong." She gestured for Mehanna to come to her. "Now very simply offer your hand, palm out."

Mehanna did as she asked. As she held out her hand their host grabbed her hand by the wrist and pushed it into the mirror.

CHAPTER EIGHT

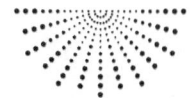

"Lawaya, if you can see her hand, take it." She made gestures so Lawaya knew what she wanted her to do.

Grinnell watched in amazement as Lawaya took her hand and Mehanna pulled her out.

"Lawaya!"

"Oh, my stars, Grinnell." She pressed her hands on different parts of her body to prove she was really out then turned to look at her prison. "Oh, thank you so much, Mehanna."

Mehanna stared at the mirror, too. "I can't believe that worked."

"Remember, sometimes the simplest thing to do is the right thing."

Lawaya went to their host and bowed. "I am Lawaya, Barou master and leader of my people. I am indebted to your training."

"I am Tosci. At least that is my nickname, but anyone who knows me calls me by that name."

"You are afraid someone will find you," Lawaya stated. "Is Mehanna in danger?"

"She's the center of it."

Now, why couldn't *he* have gotten that answer? He hadn't asked the direct question Lawaya did because he didn't want to upset Mehanna. Perhaps he should have. "What sort of danger?"

"This is going to be a long conversation, and I don't know if it is something I should say in front of Mehanna."

"Why not?" asked Mehanna.

"Because your mind is blocked. It was done on purpose. I would rather free your mind with your talent than scar you with information that will rip those memories open."

"How long do you think that will take?" asked Mehanna.

"I don't know. It depends on how strong the block is, and how strong you are."

"Can we start now?"

"Of course." She directed Mehanna to stand under the shade of a tree. "Now, this is going to be a little silly to you, but I want you to make your fruit. The one thing you retained. Make it over and over, as fast as you can."

"You're kidding."

Tosci shook her head. "This should be mindless for you."

Mehanna gave her an odd look but did as she asked.

Tosci led Grinnell and Lawaya away from Mehanna and spoke to them in soft tones. "Mehanna needs to remember on her own. That way, she can control the power that will surge through her once she breaks the block."

"The block is stopping her memory and her power?" asked Lawaya.

"Yes. For most of us, our power is tied to our emotions. Mehanna is the same way. She never had anything to push her to breakthrough."

"I don't agree." Grinnell thought about May's journal. What he had learned so far was their minds had been wiped, so they'd had to figure out how to survive on their own. Their power was there, but neither one had tapped into it the way the person in her duromares had expected. "She had to learn to survive on her own. She is highly intelligent and created her own forcefield to keep herself safe from her environment. This power you're talking about doesn't hold a candle to her mind."

"You care for her a lot, don't you?" asked Tosci.

Grinnell didn't answer. He hadn't examined his feelings for Mehanna yet, and he didn't want to do it in front of this woman.

"We both do," said Lawaya. "I saw her security system as well and without any sort of training, she was able to create something very advanced."

"That doesn't surprise me. She is brilliant. When she knew how to use her talent, she could do things that one else could have at her age. Without that knowledge, she had to put her ability somewhere."

"She did a good job," commented Grinnell. What he was learning made him think. "The person who did this to her. Why? Did they hate her and her sister that much?"

"Oh, no. Quite the opposite. Both sisters have more power in one finger than most of us have in our entire body. He wants that power, but he couldn't tell which one would be stronger. So he thought if he sent them away, the one with the most strength would be the one who came back home. His goal is to bond with the one who is the strongest and have a child. That child would be what he will control."

"Then she can't go home."

"Grinnell, how do you plan on stopping her?" asked Lawaya. "You know how headstrong she is."

"But now that she's freed you from the mirror, she doesn't need to go back to her planet."

"She still wants to know why they sent her away."

"Can't we tell her?"

"Excuse me," said Tosci. She walked over to where Mehanna was working. The pile of fruit was getting big. "Now make the pile vanish."

"What?"

"You heard me. And don't try to eat them all. You'll never get it done, and it will make you quite ill." She watched Mehanna think for a moment then stoop and pick up a handful. "Oh, you can't throw them out of sight either."

"What exactly do you want me to do? Just wave my hand and say begone?" Her jaw dropped when the fruits she had created vanished from sight. "Oh, my stars!"

"I told you that the simplest thing is sometimes the right thing to do."

Mehanna nodded. She stared at the cleared ground. Waving her hand, she commanded the fandel to reappear. It took her a few microns, but she got the wording right, and all of it came back.

"Now continue to work with them, give them commands to sort, stack, whatever your imagination will come up with." Tosci moved back to where Grinnell and Lawaya watched. "Where were we?"

"You were going to explain why we can't tell her why that man sent them away?"

She nodded. "You might tell Mehanna, but I know she's not going to believe you. If she does, she'll want to confront him. Her pride is on the line. You are going to be in danger as well, Grinnell. He wanted her to remain chaste. When he finds out you two have been together, he will kill you to keep her at his side."

"What about May? Is she in danger as well?" asked Lawaya.

"It all depends on who has the most power. As children, Mehanna was the most powerful, but May showed signs of equaling her. He wants the most powerful of the two, but if they turn out to be close in strength, he could marry one, then keep the other as a backup. If their power level is that close, it might not matter to him which one bears him a child as long as he gets that child to control."

"I can't see them bowing to anyone like that," said Grinnell.

"He is very powerful. He knows some of the ancient arts of mind control. He could lock them inside their own minds, so they won't fight him." Tosci watched as Lawaya went to help Mehanna.

"Then it's even more imperative to stop her from going to your homeworld." Grinnell would restrain her if it would keep her safe. She might be really mad at him, but he didn't care. Her safety was what was important.

"I know, but I don't think stopping her will stop the inevitable. He will look for her when he finds out she has left the planet he put her on."

"How dangerous is this man?"

Tosci looked at him. She waved her hand and watched as his eyes bulged. "You can't breathe because I took that ability away from you. I can also cause you so much pain that it will make you curl into a small ball and cry out for relief. The man I'm talking about is ten times stronger than me. He can make you hear and see things that aren't there, that no one else can see. He could trap you in your mind for the rest of your life." She released him.

Grinnell fell to his knees the moment she released him, sucking sweet air into his lungs. He wanted to hurt her, but at the secur, he couldn't do anything. Once he regained control of his breathing, he looked around. Didn't Mehanna or Lawaya see his plight?

"Oh, I also blocked the others from seeing what I did to you. You needed to know what you'd be up against. He doesn't care about your wants or needs. He doesn't care about anything but what he wants. He'll destroy you to get that."

"So, you're trying to scare me." He stood up. "I don't scare easily."

"I didn't think so, but how do you plan on battling someone who has abilities like ours?" She clasped her hands behind her back so he would know she wasn't going to use her powers against him again.

"I don't know, but I do know that people have been successful. You wouldn't be hiding your planet if you didn't fear anyone off-world. He might be mean and powerful, but he has to have some sort of weakness. I just need to find out what it is."

"I will help you."

"How?"

"Because I know him. He's my brother."

CHAPTER NINE

Mehanna swore that Grinnell and Tosci just vanished. It broke her concentration. She looked over at Lawaya, who was cheering her on. Mehanna had been stacking the fruits in various piles. When one hit her in the head, she looked up and wished she hadn't. They were floating above her, but now starting to drop due to her lack of focus. With the movement of her hand, she froze them in space so she could walk out of range before allowing them to drop to the ground.

"That was quite pretty."

"What was?" Mehanna looked at Lawaya, who had been standing with Tosci and Grinnell until a few microns ago. Seeing her free of the mirror made her feel so good.

"The fruit." She pointed to a few pieces that were still floating above their heads. "You had it dancing around your head in a rhythm."

"Really? I didn't even know I had lifted them above my head."

Lawaya watched as the fruit bounced against the ground. She studied Mehanna for a few microns. "You're worried about Grinnell."

"He and Tosci just disappeared. I feel like I should be able to see them, but I can't."

"You started playing with the fruit without thinking about it. I think that is what you need to do."

"Not think about it?" Mehanna didn't understand.

"Don't try to figure out how they disappeared, just assume you should see them. Open your mind to the possibilities of what you are capable of."

It made sense. She *had* been told that sometimes the simplest things were the right ones. She should be able to see them. She closed her eyes, focused her mind, then opened her eyes. The area to the right of Tosci's house wavered before her eyes. Why was it wavering?

"Show me," she said it softly, hoping the area wavering would clear up. Instead, images filled her head. She heard and smelled things that weren't anywhere near her. Laughter surrounded her. Two little girls ran down a hall.

That's Me and May.

How she knew that she wasn't sure, but it felt right.

The two girls were playing.

"Shh," said May.

"I'm sorry. We don't get to play very often." Mehanna smiled but curbed her laughter. "Should we build our shield so he can't hear us? He probably won't look for us if he thinks we're quiet. He expects us to study all the time."

"He told us to get ready for dinner." May brushed her hands down the formal outfit she wore. "He'll be mad if we muss up our clothes."

"Who do you think he has brought to dinner this time?"

"Probably another man to talk into marrying one of us," said May. "That's all he's done lately."

"I don't want to leave you."

"I feel the same way." May reached out her hand to her sister.

"Girls, it's time."

Mehanna recognized the woman talking to her younger self. It was Tosci. She was there too?

"Yes, ma'am." The girls chorused. They followed her down a hall before the memory disappeared.

More memories floated to the surface. Always with the two of them.

She felt her power surge through her. She remembered how to wield it. Simple things came to her as well as the more complex.

She looked at the area where she thought Grinnell and Tosci went and saw it clearly. Grinnell was rubbing his throat. If she harmed him. Mehanna wrapped her ability around Tosci, restricting her movements. "You're not allowed to harm him."

Tosci looked over at her and smiled.

Mehanna walked to where they stood. "What did you do?"

"I'm fine, Mehanna." He rubbed his throat. "Tosci was showing me how difficult a time I'm going to have if I try to take on this maniac that is after you without being prepared."

"Moorac will kill you."

"You remember," said Tosci.

She nodded.

"We need her to help us." Grinnell pointed to Tosci.

"You know that is his sister." She didn't understand why, but she wanted Grinnell away from Tosci. The thought of her harming him made her skin crawl.

"Yes, she told me." He took Mehanna's hand in his. "She also hates him for what he did to you girls."

She hadn't realized she was holding her hand up to attack until he took it. "Then why didn't she stop him?" Mehanna also realized she still held Tosci in the hold she put around the woman when she first saw through the magical shield Tosci had created.

"I think you need to ask her."

She looked at the woman who had been there for her and her sister until they needed her. Releasing the magical hold she put on Tosci, she chose her words carefully. "Why should I trust you? You left with no explanation."

"I didn't leave. I was banned."

"Banned?"

"I tried to talk my brother out of sending you two away. He became angry. So angry he banned me magically. I couldn't enter the house as myself." She focused inward and Mehanna found her childhood pet in front of her.

"Sara?" She picked up the small feline and hugged it close. "I thought some wild animal got you."

"What's going on, Mehanna?" asked Grinnell.

"When Tosci disappeared, I found this sweet feline. It started to come around at duro. I'd stand in my room looking out the window into the duro sky and hear its cries. I would sneak out to feed her, and she learned to climb up to my window at duro." She sat the animal down and watched as it shifted back into Tosci. "You were still with us."

"I couldn't leave you. If my brother hadn't decided to pilot that damn ship himself, I would have gone with you to that planet. He could detect my power in a small environment. It takes a lot of energy to maintain a shift like that. It's not the same as it is for a shapeshifter. He would have realized that the cat wasn't real." She inhaled then let her breath out slowly, wanting to maintain her composure. "I think my brother knew, or at least suspected, I was still trying to help you girls. That's why he brought you to that planet himself."

"Why didn't you follow?"

"Ships are very rare on our planet. It took me lunas to get off our planet just to get away from him. By that time, I had no idea where he brought you, and I searched his house to find anything to hint where he could have taken you. So I came here and started searching."

"He stuck them on a small planet that didn't have space travel," said Grinnell. "You could have been on the next planet in that solar system and never would have found them."

"The man is very smart. Did you ever see him on the planet, Mehanna?"

"No. I had been left out in the middle of nowhere and stayed there." She clasped her hands in front of her. "I don't know why, but I feared the indigenous people, so I never allowed them to know where I lived. I went through their trash and grabbed anything I thought I could use, but I did it when they were sleeping. I hoped they thought I came from a nearby village and thought it worked until recently."

"He probably wanted to keep you and your sister apart, so he put that fear in you."

"Did he put the ability to build computers and force fields in me too?"

"No," said Tosci. "That was all you. You were very good at anything you wanted to learn about. But you should remember that, since you broke through the block he put on you."

"My memories are still coming back to me. Little snippets of the life I lived before. Were we nothing more than an experiment to him?"

"I didn't think my brother was capable of such cruelty. His desire to be the most powerful wizard on the planet drove him to do things I never expected."

"Do you consider yourselves wizards?" asked Grinnell.

"Some do. We do have the ability of what some call magic. The old stories and legends called those people wizards. Others called them witches and warlocks. We never saw it as a special power because we all have it. That's why we have kept to ourselves."

"Some of your kind did leave your planet because we have heard of you," Grinnell said. "The stories call it Mystic."

"The name means 'ground' in our language," said Tosci. "Ironic, isn't it?"

"If Moorac is that powerful, how am I supposed to free myself from him?"

"I'm not sure if this will make sense. When we were young, my brother was a good student. He learned everything he was taught and pushed to get high grades, but I never thought he was obsessed with it. He was always praised because he did well. Then he met a young boy from another section of our world who was very gifted. He was also a bit of a brat. He challenged my brother and bested him. My brother never got over that. Before, when we were in school if I happened to do better, he would congratulate me, but after that his anger was a force to be reckoned with. It scared me. I never tried to best him in school again. I did push myself to be the best, I just never showed him what I could do." She looked at Mehanna. "I had hoped this dura would come where you wanted to defeat him. You can do things naturally that we had to train hard to accomplish. But my brother is very good. And he will use whatever he can to try to force you to do what he wants."

"You believe he will use Grinnell to get to me." She tightened her hold on Grinnell's hand.

"You care for him. I can see that." She looked from Mehanna to

Grinnell. "My brother will see it too and that will anger him because he wanted you for himself."

"If he wanted that, he shouldn't have sent me away." Mehanna took a deep breath. "You said you will train me?"

"Yes." She looked at Grinnell. "Your ship can scan for others?"

"All I need is his ID code and I can track him anywhere."

"Even if he can hide it?"

"Why would he hide it?" said Grinnell. "He has no idea who we are or what we're up to."

"My brother seems to know things that he shouldn't. I wouldn't be surprised if he did know everything already." She brushed her hands on her outfit. "But I am probably just being a little paranoid."

"If he is as good as you say, why hasn't he found you? You seem to be very comfortable here. You don't strike me as a woman afraid for her life."

"I have safety measures in place." Tosci waved her hand to reveal a dome-like structure over them. "If he comes near here, I'll know."

"Then how will my ship's security system be of any help?"

"Because I can enhance certain technology to search for magic as well. It will give us an extra layer of protection."

"I'll take you to my ship."

"Thank you." She looked at Mehanna. "I'd like to start your training right now. Lawaya can work with you as well."

She showed Mehanna what she wanted her to work on and explained to Lawaya what it should look like if she mastered it. She also told her what to do to get Mehanna to practice the next level. Once she was sure Mehanna knew what she wanted to do, she gestured for Grinnell to lead the way.

"I know you wanted to talk to me alone," said Grinnell.

"I know Mehanna, and I know she will believe that she can fix my brother."

"And you know better."

"He is obsessed. I don't know what happened with that boy that could have caused my brother to snap the way he did, but I think my brother doesn't want to be fixed. He wants to get even."

"I had wondered." He led the way down the stream until they got to the clearing where he had left the ship.

"I am sorry about what I did to you earlier, but you needed to see what my brother is capable of."

"I've been through the cruelty of General Varal." He pressed a button on his wristband to bring the ship into view. "I don't think he can do anything I haven't already been through."

"How can you say that? He'll kill you and make Mehanna watch."

"Varal made promises to me then killed my family. Mehanna knows this." He gestured for her to follow him up the gangplank. "If she knows how cruel this Moorac could be she would know how he would handle our relationship, and I haven't seen her regret anything that happened between us."

"That is a wonderful sentiment, but how are you going to react in the moment?" she asked.

"You don't have to worry about me." Why was she pushing so hard?

"Prove it to me."

"How?" he led the way up into the ship.

"I could read your file."

"Sure. Computer? She needs proof that I can handle someone like Moorac." He sat down at his station and pulled up his files as well as his security information. "Now understand that you only have access to what I have opened here."

"So what happens if I try to open something I shouldn't?"

He shrugged as he stood. She'd be frozen in place. He'd like to see her magic get her out of that one.

She took the seat he vacated and opened the file. It didn't take her long to load the data Grinnell requested so the ship would have the tracking info he needed to find and follow Moorac's ship. Next, she turned her attention to Grinnell's file.

"There isn't much there," he told her. "Varal wasn't one for keeping records, only a list of who he wanted killed."

"Did you keep a journal?"

"I'm not sure I feel comfortable with you reading my innermost thoughts."

"Okay. I get that." She looked up at him. "But my brother can be cruel. I've seen him in action. I need to be sure you can stand up against him."

"Varal blackmailed me into working for him by promising my family would be safe, then he killed them."

"My brother can lock you inside your mind, facing your worst duromare over and over again."

"You don't think I did that with the slaughter of my family? I had heard the rumors and slipped away from Varal to find out if they were true. If Varal had caught me, he would have killed me."

"That isn't the same as he making you watch as he kills your family over and over again."

"My imagination did that for me." Grinnell clenched his hands. "You don't know what it was like for me to lose everyone I loved and then find myself being hunted. I had to think on my feet. I hid the best I could until I found a way off my home planet. I didn't know if I would ever come back to it. I had to learn the social customs of a dozen planets on my own by trial and error, and quickly. If I got it wrong, I was punished. I've been jailed, beaten, drowned, electrocuted. What else is there?"

"I get it, but I want you to be prepared. I can teach you a few tricks to use that might break his concentration for a secur, but the secur he realizes you don't have any power yourself he'll either ignore you or use you as an example."

"He still bleeds, doesn't he?"

"Of course, but you have to be able to touch him first, and that would be the problem."

"Others have gotten the best of your people, and they didn't have your powers."

"That is true, but we were innocent in the beginning. We trusted the wrong people. Believed they had our best interest at heart. My people learned the hard way that if we weren't careful, we could be used."

"With your abilities? I don't see how anyone could get the best of anyone from your planet."

"Yet you didn't suspect anything when you met Mehanna."

"Of course I did. The fact that she could create her fruit from thin air made me aware of the possibility of where she came from. I just don't know where the planet is."

"So you're here to find my world."

"No." He frowned. "I needed to find Lawaya. When Mehanna

showed me she was trapped in a mirror, I promised to help her get Lawaya released. We brought Lawaya and her mirror to Emori so Lawaya could help Astrid. Then we followed a trail that led us to you."

"And I showed her how to release Lawaya. You know you have fulfilled your promise."

He blinked. He had been released from his obligation and hadn't even thought about leaving. How did he feel about Mehanna? Why hadn't he made plans to leave?

"Mehanna, you don't seem to be focused," Lawaya chided.

"Sorry." She straightened her shoulders. "I keep getting these memories, and I'm not sure if I should trust Tosci. I know that her brother is the true villain, but she went along with a lot of what he wanted to do."

"Do you think she is working for him?" said Lawaya.

"I don't know what to think. I'm not sure if I like the fact that Grinnell is with her by himself."

"You're jealous."

"What?" she shook her head. "No."

"Yes. You two haven't talked about how you feel about each other, and you know he has fulfilled his promise to you. He could climb on his ship and leave."

"He wouldn't leave us here with no way off this planet," Mehanna defended.

"He could send another ship for us."

She shook her head. "Grinnell wouldn't do that."

"You sure?"

"Yes." Mehanna had to back up her words. "He could have left at any point, you know that. Once you helped Astrid, he could have sent me on my way, but he didn't. He wanted to help me face the people who sent me away."

"He promised to help you free me."

Mehanna stared at her as her words sunk in. She was right. He no longer had to help her. What would he do?

Grinnell walked back to Tosci's house in silence. What would Mehanna want now that he had fulfilled his obligation? He realized he didn't want to leave her. The question was, how did she feel about it?

"You are deep in thought," commented Tosci.

He looked at her.

"You're afraid she'll send you away, aren't you?" She smiled. "You love her."

"I don't think you should be commenting on something you know nothing about." Grinnell didn't want to think about the feelings bubbling up inside him. He hadn't had time to examine them yet.

"We'll see."

The house came into view and Grinnell straightened his spine.

Lawaya turned and spotted him and gave him a knowing smile. Okay, why did she smile at him like that?

Mehanna looked at him a little oddly. Then she wouldn't look back at him. She looked at her hands, the sky above, even the ground, but not at him. Just by the way she was acting, he knew they'd had the same conversation he and Tosci had. He wished he knew what they had said to each other. It would give him a better idea of how to speak to her. First, though, he had to get her away from everyone.

He felt like the odd man out while the three women talked about what Mehanna could and couldn't do. He wanted to grab her by the hand and drag her away but wasn't sure if that would be smart.

Tosci announced she was going to fix dinner and Lawaya volunteered to help, and just like that, they were alone.

Now he had to figure out how to broach the subject.

"So, are you going to leave now?" asked Mehanna.

Well, that was to the point. Might as well be just as to the point.

"Do you want me to?"

She blinked at his question. The look in her eyes told him she didn't.

"Say something."

"I would miss you."

"Okay. If you want to play this game, fine. You never answered my question. Do you want me to leave? If you do, I'll jump on my ship and never look back." Grinnell pointed away from them. "But you want me to stay, I'm in all the way. I'm not going to let you use me, then send me away later."

"Even if all I'm trying to do is protect you?" She looked at him with those beautiful eyes that revealed what she really felt.

"Even then." He placed his hands on her shoulders. He wanted to wrap his arms around her, protect her from anything that could cause her harm. "How can I be there for you if you push me away?"

"He can be quite cruel." Her gaze didn't flinch. Like a mirror to her soul, he could see she didn't want to send him away in the depths of her eyes, but she feared what Tosci's brother could do to him.

"I've been shown."

"Tosci." Her voice had a bitter tone to it.

"She wanted to be sure I understood what Moorac can do." He brushed his hands up and down her arms. "I know I don't have the ability that you do, but he still bleeds. I asked."

She laughed at that. Mehanna grasped his hands with hers. "I don't want anything to happen to you."

"And I feel the same way."

"There is a way you can tap into my power." She started swinging their joined hands.

"What? How?"

"If we bonded." She didn't look at him. Probably because she didn't want to see how he would react to this information. "You would be able to use my power."

"Really?" The implications were enormous. "No wonder why he wants you. If he could access your power, he would be hard to beat."

"It's also why we decided to hide." She broke the hold she had on his hands. "There were people who pretended to care, pretended to care only to get us to bond with them so they could access the power we have naturally."

"You realize this bonding is for life." He slid his fingers under her chin and lifted her face so she had to look at him. "Can you see me in your life forever? We don't know that much about each other. You don't know that much about you. Those memories are still coming, aren't they?"

"I do know my heart."

"And what does it say?"

"That we have something special."

Her simple statement shook him to the core. "Are you sure? I'm the only man you've been with. What if you meet someone else you find attractive? If we bond, you would be stuck with me."

"I know that the entertainment feeds were fake, but it showed me what made women happy. You make me happy," she said simply.

He smiled at that. "Mehanna, I don't want you to make this decision because of what we have to face. You need to make this decision because you want to spend the rest of your life with me."

"Grinnell. I wouldn't have given you my body if I didn't feel something for you." She touched his face. "There is magic between us. I know you felt it too."

"That isn't the reason for us to bond. Not for life."

"What do I have to do to prove to you that I do want this? Moorac has nothing to do with my feelings for you." She smiled. "My question is, do you feel the same way I feel? Or was our time together just superficial to you?"

CHAPTER TEN

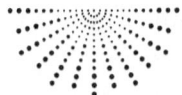

"What are they talking about?" asked Tosci. She looked out the window to see the couple standing close to each other.

"I'm assuming they are talking about the same thing I told Mehanna. That his obligation was over with." Lawaya looked out the window with her. "They are now trying to figure out what the next step is."

"Next step?"

"Whether to part ways or continue their relationship." Lawaya picked up the tray they had filled with food and drink. "I think they make a cute couple."

"Cute won't keep them alive."

"They are stronger together. Don't forget that."

"You sound so sure." She opened the door.

Lawaya nodded her thanks before heading outside. "You have kept yourself isolated out here. I have had the joy of joining couples together. I watched them grow together. Some have that special spark. The same spark that those two have. I just don't think they realize it yet."

They carried their meals outside to the large wooden table Tosci had out there.

"How did you make this mammoth thing anyway?" asked Lawaya.

Tosci just smiled and wiggled her fingers.

Grinnell stepped up and offered his help. With it, they had their food on the table in no time. He and Mehanna sat side by side as they ate.

"You two are quiet," commented Lawaya.

"I offered to bond with Grinnell, but he thinks I need to think through it a little more."

Tosci started coughing. Lawaya patted her on the back.

"I think he's right." Tosci's voice came out rough. "You barely know him."

"I do know him. He had many times where he could have taken advantage of me but didn't." She looked at Lawaya. "He could have grabbed your mirror and left me behind. Instead, he promised to help me free you and now, even though he has fulfilled his promise he still wants to help me. That says a lot about him."

"Are you in love with him?" asked Lawaya.

"Love?" She looked at him, considering. "That is a good question. What does love feel like?"

"Does he make your heart flutter when he stands close to you?"

"I don't know." She looked at her hands. "Maybe?"

"Perhaps this is a conversation that me and Mehanna should have privately? Asking these questions is putting her on the spot, and not fair for you to ask while I'm sitting next to her." Grinnell put a supportive arm around her. "Are you going to ask me the same things? You know I am honest, and I will tell you that it is none of your business."

"You're right." Tosci placed a hand on Lawaya's arm. "I can open my home to everyone. Mehanna can sleep with me, Lawaya can have the extra bed, and we could prepare a pallet for Grinnell."

"Or we could stay on the ship and not crowd your small home," responded Grinnell.

"Why don't you two stay on the ship?" offered Lawaya. "I can stay with Tosci toduro."

Tosci frowned.

"You don't trust me," said Grinnell. He heard Mehanna suck in her breath. "It's okay. I don't trust you either."

"You make it hard for me not to like you." Tosci laughed. "I would have said the same thing."

They ate their meal in happy companionship, using small talk to keep from discussing the pros and cons of Grinnell and Mehanna bonding.

Once they finished eating, Grinnell ushered Mehanna back to the ship.

"So when can we talk about it?" asked Mehanna after they were out of earshot of Tosci's home.

"Once we get back to the ship." He had a hold of her hand and was leading her past the creek. "If you are serious, there are things we need to discuss."

"Like what?" she asked.

"Once we get back to the ship," he repeated. It came into view quickly, and he hurried them into the hull. "We don't know if this Moorac has found this place or not, and I don't want to take any chances."

"He hasn't been here."

"How do you know?"

"I'd sense his magic."

"Okay. That's good to know." He sealed the door behind them. "I'm ready to talk."

She looked at him. "I'm not making this decision on a whim."

"Yes, but have you thought it all the way through? Like where will we live?"

"I don't care. In the beginning, I wanted to go back to the safety of my cave, but I didn't know where I came from then and that was all I knew. Besides, you built me my cave in the cargo hold, so I have all I need here."

"And once all this is done? Once life goes back to normal?"

She shrugged. "I don't know. I have so much to learn about other worlds. Will you teach me?"

"Of course, but we don't need to bond for me to do that."

"Let me ask you this. If there was no Moorac, would you have left the moment Lawaya had been released from the mirror?"

"I—" He blinked. Would he have left? "I don't know. I am attracted to you, Mehanna. And if there was no Moorac, I probably would have found an excuse to stick around. It doesn't matter. I won't allow anyone to force us into a situation we're not ready for."

"Grinnell." She took his hand. "Why are you fighting this?"

"Mehanna, I've never thought I'd find someone I could love. My life is good, but after all I had been through, I can't burden anyone with that. It's not fair."

"You love me?"

"I—" He hadn't planned on blurting that out. "I do."

"I love you too." She wrapped her arms around him and sighed. "And you fighting this makes no sense now."

"I have seen the worst side of people, and you haven't. As much as I want to, I can't protect you from everything. How are you going to feel when you see that side? When you see me interact with that side because I need their help?"

She leaned back to look at him. "You're afraid that I will think less of you?"

"You're so innocent, and the galaxy isn't." He brushed a few stray hairs off her face. "I don't want that for you."

"You want to take me back to my cave and leave me there?"

"Leave you?" He shook his head. "I was thinking that could be our little haven. The one place where we could escape the rest of the galaxy."

"You still haven't given me a good reason for us not to bond."

He pulled her close. "I'm afraid I'll hurt you."

"How? Because of what you did when you were running from Varal?" Her forehead creased. "I don't care about that. I know you had to do things to stay alive. Things you regret. But it's not like you continue to do these things. You work for Orla and his mate. You're well respected now."

"And it would only take one person to come back into my life to ruin all of that."

"Do you think so little of your friends to believe they would condemn you because of something you did in your past? Didn't Orla and Astrid meet you while you were hiding from the general?"

"Yes."

"Then you're worrying about nothing." She brushed her fingers through his hair. "General Varal really hurt you if you think no one would respect you because of how you kept yourself alive while that madman was in control."

He looked at her like he wanted to say something, but he remained silent.

"I see." Mehanna backed up and started working on the seals of her clothes.

"What are you doing?"

"Me?" At his nod, she smiled. "I'm going to seduce you."

Her comment brought a smile to his face. "Why?"

"Because I need to show you that I don't care what you did in your past. I only care about the future, our future. I do want to spend the rest of my life with you, and I want to start toduro." She opened the seal on her top, and let it slide from her body. Then she opened her pants so they too would fall to the floor.

"You aren't playing fair." Grinnell stepped close. "I sort of like it when you don't play fair."

"You are so funny." She worked on the seals of his clothing as well.

"Now what are you doing?"

"Making everything even." She opened his shirt. "I shouldn't be the only one naked."

"I agree." He started pulling his clothes off as fast as he could. "So now we're the same."

"We are." She took his hand. "And I'm tired of standing, so why don't we continue our conversation somewhere comfortable?"

"You are asking for it."

"Not yet." She clasped her hands behind her back and smiled at him.

"Oh!" He scooped her up in his arms. Holding her close, he whispered in her ear, "I'm going to make you beg for it."

She wrapped her arms around his neck. "Not if I get you to beg for it first."

"I have created a monster, didn't I?"

"When it comes to making love? Oh yes." She pressed her lips against his jaw. "You awakened a beast."

"Then I think we need to feed that beast." He brought her to his captain's chair. Since he'd had it altered, it would hold them quite nicely.

"She is very hungry."

He sat her feet on the ground, allowing her body to slide down against his. His whole body reacted, making him hard in securs. Grinnell captured her lips with his while his hands moved about her body, touching all the places he knew aroused her.

She broke the kiss and leaned back. "Wait. I promised to make you beg for it."

"And I did the same." He pulled her close again and nibbled at her throat. "And I plan on winning."

Mehanna wrapped her warm fingers around his erection. That made him stop what he was doing and look at her.

"I see I have your undivided attention." She gave him a sultry smile. "So how were you going to make me beg?"

"My first idea was to get you comfortable, then I was going to kiss you all over. Then I was going to use my mouth to focus on those areas that love my attention." His hands caressed her as they moved about her body. "And I didn't mention what my hands can do."

"True, and I do love how they make me feel." She sifted her grip on his erection and slid her hand up and down his length.

He rested his forehead against hers. "You aren't fighting fair. I can't focus on anything but what you are doing to me. I need to feel your body take me in before I explode."

"So are you begging me?" She brushed her finger against the tip and watched in satisfaction as he shuddered and nodded.

"Please." He urged her to move backward. "You know I'll make it up to you."

She felt the soft cushion of the seat brush the back of her legs, and Grinnell worked his magic. She wasn't sure how he got her to lie on the soft cushions, but she felt his weight as he drove into her.

Mehanna sucked in her breath as she arched against him. She wanted this as much as he did. He set them on a good strong rhythm, and she met him thrust for thrust. Her legs wrapped around him, giving him better access and giving her the friction she wanted.

Her body hummed. She felt her muscles tighten as he drove into her again and again. Great gods, this wasn't going to take long. She could already feel the beginnings of her orgasm. Grinnell's lips claimed hers.

He picked up the pace. Mehanna knew he felt the beginnings of his release. She could tell by the way his breath hitched and his body shook. They moved together, racing toward their goals. Mehanna felt her body clench as her climax flowed over her. She felt him tense as he reached his as well. Grinnell pressed soft kisses all over her hairline.

He gathered her in his arms and sighed. "So tell me more about this bonding you want to do."

She settled her head against his chest. "It's pretty simple. It's normally a long ceremony with half the planet in attendance."

"What?"

The stricken look on his face made her laugh. "What did you think? It *is* simple. The ceremony is for show. We could bond, just the two of us, then go on our merry way. We could bond then have a ceremony for friends and family. We could have the ceremony first. But the bonding is always just between the couple."

"You know, that wasn't very nice." He brushed his fingers across her back. "You scared the crap out of me."

"Yeah, well, you've been fighting it so much I thought I'd lighten the mood."

"I've been fighting it for your protection. You wouldn't think to bond with me if you weren't afraid of what that man could do to you."

"That's where you're wrong." She levered herself up so she could look him in the face. "I didn't know about the bonding until recently, but I didn't want you to leave me once we got Lawaya out of the mirror. I know you're the first man I have been with, but it has been wonderful every time. I have watched enough of those streams to know what to look for in a successful relationship, and I think we have that."

"I do too," Grinnell agreed.

"Then let's bond."

"I don't know if that is wise."

She sighed and rested her head back on his chest. "You don't think you're worthy, do you?"

"I have done a lot of not so nice things in my life."

"As I said, you had to do things while you were running from Varal, and no one would blame you."

"I blame me. There were people who asked for my help, and I told them no. They couldn't pay."

"You mean you didn't want to take what little money they had." She lifted her head to look at him again. "If you felt they had a good reason, did you help people? Let them ride for free if they couldn't afford to pay you? Like Astrid and Orla? I bet they didn't have any credits to pay you."

"No, but—"

She pressed two fingers against his lips. "No buts. I'm betting you told people no because you felt they were safer where they were, and you're beating yourself up because every once in a while you were wrong."

"They lost their lives because I told them no." He moved so he could sit up. "I had a chance to make a difference for them but didn't."

She sat up with him. "How many died?"

"I don't know." He wasn't looking at her.

"I don't believe you. I believe you know the name of every person you feel died because of you." She touched the side of his face. "And I bet you also know the names of everyone you helped. So tell me, how many died?"

"Six. Six families. A total of sixteen people."

"And how many did you save?"

"I don't know."

"Yes, you do." She shifted her weight so she was up on her knees. "Tell me."

He finally looked at her. "Why is this so important to you?"

"I learned that a good leader, in fact, a great leader, which is what you are, understands that he isn't perfect and realizes there are risks. He also doesn't let those risks paralyze him with fear."

"I'm not paralyzed with fear." He wrapped his arms around her, shifting so they were lying down again. "You keep trying to find something that isn't there."

"You are letting it keep us from bonding, so there is something there."

"This is for life, Mehanna. What happens if we get past this and you decide you don't want this? Or worse, you meet someone you want to be with more?"

"I know you think I haven't lived yet, but I promise that I want this. I have watched those feeds all my life. I know I haven't lived the lives I saw on those screens, and you'll use that as an excuse to tell me no when you want to say yes." She touched his face. "I can see it in your eyes. But I saw the good and bad in people and relationships. People killing their loved ones. Marrying for money or power. You are a good man, and I love that about you."

"Are you trying to flatter me?"

"I'm just telling the truth." She pressed a soft kiss on his mouth that brought a smile to his face. "You have this wonderfully lopsided smile that takes my breath away."

"And you have these beautifully bright eyes that show me your soul."

"Really?" She blinked. "And what do my eyes tell you?"

"That you're not going to stop until you get your way." He brushed a few stray hairs out of her face. "I sure hope you know what you're doing."

"You are going to bond with me?" She planted a quick kiss on his lips. "Oh, my stars, you make me so happy."

He couldn't help but laugh. He pulled her down for a kiss, one filled with promise and love. "So how do we do this?"

"It's pretty simple." She got up on her knees and gestured for him to do the same. "Now put your hand on my heart."

He pressed his hand on her heart, just like she did.

"Now you can say something with it, but all you really have to say I bond with you."

"That's it?"

"Like I said, it's pretty simple." She adjusted her hand. "I'll go first."

"Good."

"Grinnell, you bring great joy to my life, and I can't wait to spend the rest of my duras with you. I bond with you." A slight glow came from her hand.

"I get it." He made sure he had his hand on her heart properly. "Mehanna, you have brightened my life in ways I never thought possible. I want to spend the rest of my duras with you. I bond with you."

A glow came from his hand as well. It spread up their arms and encompassed their bodies.

"I think we're glowing."

She smiled. "We are. That's how you know the bonding took place. The glow will fade in a secur or two. And the bond will seal once we make love again."

"I should be able to help with that." He wrapped his arms around her.

"I sure hope so. I'm kind of counting on you to work your magic."

"Magic, huh? We are magic together." He lowered them to the cushions. "So I have to ask. Those couples who do the ceremony first. Do they glow the whole time?"

"No." She laughed. "The glow does dissipate, but it does flare at times."

"Really? Like when?"

"Oh, sure. You'd ask that now."

He interrupted her with another kiss. When he broke it, she spoke again.

"Some women who become pregnant will glow from time to time."

"Okay, good to know." He brushed his fingers through her hair.

"Can we stop talking now?"

"Do you have something else you want to do?"

"Oh stars, yes." She pulled him down for a kiss.

"You know Tosci is going to figure out everything, don't you?" asked Grinnell as he led her back to the woman in question's house.

"I do." She wrapped an arm around him. "But I don't care. She will just have to deal with it."

He wrapped an arm around her as well. "And what about your sister? Will she have to deal with it too?"

"May wanted us together."

She said it so matter-of-factly that it surprised him.

"Okay, but what about Moorac?" He walked next to the creek so Mehanna could walk on the drier section of the path. "The moment he figures out you have bonded with me, he will go after your sister."

"I know. I've thought about that too. We need to protect her, I'm just not real sure how yet."

"And your overly protective guardian?" he asked. "You know she was against this in the first place."

"She was just trying to protect me." She leaned into him. "Now that it's done, she'll have to help us."

"I hope so."

The house came into view.

"Here we go." Grinnell took her hand, and they walked into the yard.

"It's about time you two showed up. We have a lot of work to do." Tosci gestured for Mehanna to follow her. Grinnell went to stand next to Lawaya.

"So did you mate?" Lawaya asked softly.

"Now you know I'm not going to answer that." He didn't look at her but watched Mehanna instead.

"How long do you think you can keep us in the dark?" She pointed to Tosci. "That woman is a bloodhound."

"You are focusing on the wrong thing. We need to think about how we're going to defeat that man without getting ourselves killed."

"He uses magic." Lawaya wasn't deterred. "I can disguise myself, and they can use magic against him. But you, my friend, need to stay as far away from him as you can."

"Can he tell the difference between magic and the Barou power?" Grinnell asked, still trying to steer the conversation away from their bonding.

"You mean if I were to create something, would he know it's not really there?" Lawaya shifted her weight as she thought. "The way our powers work is that only a master can see through another Barou's imaging. So as long as he's not aware that we're Barou, our illusions should trick him."

He looked at her. "So you could trick him into thinking you have magic too?"

"I guess. At least for a little while."

"And if we had more help?"

She stepped back and shook her head. "I can't ask the Barou council to sanction this."

"I'm not thinking about the council." He touched her arm and smiled. "I'm thinking about our friends on Emori. We have two more Barou masters, another magic wielder, and a shapeshifter. The odds are better with them."

"And what if they don't want to help?"

"There is only one way to find out." Grinnell turned and headed back to his ship.

"Would you please focus?" asked Tosci.

"I *am* focusing," Mehanna answered as she watched Grinnell race away from the yard. Where was he going anyway? "I just find these basic moves just that. Basic. I remember, Tosci. Why can't we move on to something more challenging?"

"How long has it been since you've used your power regularly? And making fruit doesn't count."

"Okay, so it has been a while." She looked at Tosci. "But everything you have given me, I have mastered without an issue."

"I know." She placed her hand on Mehanna's shoulder. "But I have to push you. You have to best him."

Grinnell turned on his communication system. It took a few microns for Orla to appear on the screen.

"My friend." His smile looked strained. "How are you?"

"Good. How's Astrid? Any baby Mirans yet?"

"No." Orla laughed. "She's close, but we still have a little time."

"I have a favor to ask."

"Before you start, I have a few things to get you caught up on."

The look on Orla's face made Grinnell pause. "Of course."

"We've had a visitor."

"Really?" He didn't like the sound of that.

"Yeah, I'll send you over the details."

"Okay." He wasn't sure why Orla was sending him a file when they could just talk about it.

"Great. Check out the files and get back to me. I told him we'd do our best to find what he is looking for, and I know you're the best." Orla closed the commline before Grinnell could respond.

What was in those files? He opened them up and found every bit of data Orla could record on Moorac. He had been to Emori. In fact, he was still there. It hadn't taken Orla long to figure out who he was and why he was there. Orla didn't trust the man and feared that he would manipulate him to say what he wanted, but Moorac couldn't manipulate technology. Hence the file. Orla figured Moorac couldn't control the specialized technology he had to communicate with his ships, mate, and anyone else with the same inserts. So he'd set the file up to send the moment Grinnell contacted them.

That was good to know. Maybe Grinnell could manipulate his device to make their situation better. As he worked through the files, he found out Orla had thought the same thing. He sent him everything he needed to make changes to their inserts.

This was going to take time.

———

Mehanna worked hard on everything Tosci threw at her. She wanted to prove that she was up for the task. A soft beep filled the air.

"What was that?" asked Tosci.

"What?" Mehanna thought she could ignore it for a few moments, but Tosci's curiosity wouldn't let her.

"That beeping I keep hearing."

"It's this device." She pulled a small metal disc out of a pocket. "Grinnell gave it to me so we could communicate."

"Why would he want to communicate with that when he's always around?"

"We've never used this, but he gave me one when we left the planet I grew up on, just in case we got separated." She stared at it. Pressing the button, she held it to her ear.

Laughter came out of the disc.

"You don't hold it to your ear, you hold it out in front of you. Like a tiny screen." Grinnell smiled at her. "I just wanted to let you know that Moorac has been on Emori."

"Oh no." She almost dropped the device. "What about May?"

"She's safe. Orla said she and Grenta are traveling the planet while she's being trained, so she's safe. May is aware he's there and knows not to return to the palace."

"We have to go get her." She was ready to drop everything to go save her sister.

"I agree, but I have a few things to take care of here at the ship, and you need to get in as much training as you can before we face this man." He paused for a moment. "I'll escort you back to the ship before it gets dark."

"Okay." She wished she could talk to him more. She wanted to know everything he'd learned about her sister. He was right though. She needed to focus.

"You are smitten with him," Tosci commented.

"Can we not talk about Grinnell right now?"

"Why?"

Mehanna knew she had to tread carefully, or Tosci would figure out they had bonded. She wasn't sure if she was ready to face this woman's wrath.

"My sister could be in trouble. I need to get back to her."

"Alright."

Mehanna wasn't sure if Tosci believed her, but as long as she didn't ask any more questions, she could relax a little.

They worked for horas. She fought her fatigue as time passed, but she mastered everything she was taught.

"Lightning is one of the hardest things to master." Tosci held out her hand and created a lightning ball. "It took me five yepas to learn this. Another three to be able to throw it."

"That long?" She rubbed her forehead. "How good is Moorac's? I don't remember him using lightning."

"I don't know. That's why I want you to master this. It is extremely difficult. If he hasn't mastered this, it will give you the advantage."

"And if he has?"

"Hopefully it will level the playing field."

CHAPTER ELEVEN

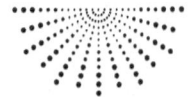

Grinnell made some great strides in his new creations. He wanted to test them out but had promised to walk Mehanna back to the ship. He didn't feel any different, yet he found he wondered what she was doing. He also wondered what he could do to put a smile on her face, even more than usual. Her smile made his heart flutter. His focus was fractured where he normally could focus on the task at hand.

He came to the house to see Mehanna creating a bright blue ball, only to watch it disappear as quickly as she made it.

Lawaya came out of the house when she saw him approaching. She met him near the line of trees.

"How is she doing?"

"I think she's doing great. I know she knew a lot of this when she was a child, but she is very impressive at how quickly she is moving through them. She doesn't hesitate, even if she hadn't done it in a few yepas." Lawaya handed him a cloth bag. "I prepared an evening meal for you two."

"You didn't have to do that. You know we can get something on the ship."

"Yeah, something prefabricated. This is homemade and fresh." She held out the bag.

He took it and slung it over his shoulder. "Thank you."

Grinnell watched as Tosci held up her hand and commanded Mehanna, who stopped working with the blue ball and create a fireball instead. He wasn't sure how to interrupt, or if he could interrupt. He found he didn't have to.

"It looks like your escort is here," commented Tosci.

"Are we done?" asked Mehanna.

"Do you want to be done?" asked Tosci as she looked over at Grinnell.

"I want to kick your brother's ass, so if you want me to work more I will."

"Good answer." She gestured to Mehanna to go to Grinnell. "Keep working on the lightning. You will master it if you keep at it. Just be careful where you practice."

"Safety first."

Tosci smiled. "Go, enjoy. I will see you nesdura."

"Thank you." She dashed to Grinnell's side. Taking his hand, she led them away from the house.

"Are we in a hurry?"

"I just don't want her to change her mind, and the longer we linger, the bigger chance we have of her suddenly remembering something she wants to show me." She took his hand and led him away from the house. "We could be here for horas if I don't take advantage of her releasing me."

"I don't think she would push you that hard unless you asked her. She wants us to succeed." Grinnell helped her around a few overgrown roots. "I know she's pushing you because she cares."

"And when she realizes we bonded, she'll be pushing you as well."

"I can handle that." He slipped an arm around her waist. "As long as I'm with you, I can handle anything."

Mehanna gave him a beautiful bright smile that made his heart skip a beat.

"How much practice do you need to do?"

"I'm not sure. I'd need a safe space to work in."

"I can set up a place on the ship for you." He adjusted the bag on his shoulder.

She pointed to it. "Lawaya?"

"Yeah, she didn't want us to starve."

"I think she was bored. She started going through Tosci's pantry and just decided to make a meal for us. She made too much. That's why you got the bag."

"Was it good?

"Delicious. I wouldn't mind having more."

The ship came into view.

"Then we'll eat first."

"Did you give them some of the food you made?" asked Tosci.

"I did," replied Lawaya. "I thought instead of eating the food the ship can create for them that a good fresh meal would be perfect."

"You didn't know what to do with yourself and thought you could contribute by cooking for us."

"True." Lawaya filled a plate and handed it to Tosci. "There's still plenty."

"Figured as much."

"You know they have bonded, right?" Lawaya picked up her plate.

Tosci nodded. "I could see it in her eyes."

"I expected you to get mad." Lawaya walked to the table and set the plate on it.

"It won't do any good. What is done is done."

"Are you going to say something?"

"I'm going to wait a dura or two. I want to see if she is going to tell me."

"And if she doesn't?"

"Then we'll both know she's not mature enough to face my brother."

They entered the ship and received a greeting from the computer.

"Good to have you back, Mehanna. Grinnell missed you."

"He did?" she turned to look at him.

Being caught, he shrugged.

"I hope he didn't pine for me all dura."

"I kept busy. Would you like to see what I've been working on?"

"Sure."

He took her hand and led her to one of the cargo holds. "Since everyone is worried about the fact that I'm not magical, I have created my own magic."

"Really?"

"Watch." He slipped something onto his hands and then tapped a few keys on a keyboard. "I haven't completed it to a point where I can take it off the ship yet, but I think you'll get the idea."

A target appeared in front of him. Grinnell pointed at it. Mehanna sucked in her breath when she saw fire shoot out of his fingers.

"How did you do that?"

"I created a glove that I can wear that will work as a weapon."

"If he suspects you have a weapon on, he could use it against you."

He nodded. "I know. That's why I'm not ready to show anyone else yet. I need to make it seem like it's coming from me. I plan on using technology to make Moorac think it's magic."

Mehanna found his weapon ingenious. She could remind him that he could access her power, but since she didn't know how to teach him, she would wait for Tosci to do it. It also wouldn't hurt for them to have some sort of backup that could confuse Moorac. "I wish I could master my lightning as easy as you created that."

"Hey, that wasn't as easy as you think. How are you creating your lightning?"

"I try to create a ball of it." She worked on creating one while she spoke to him. "But I'm not doing something right."

"I think you're trying too hard. Just create a ball."

She did that easily.

"Now catch it on fire."

"Fire? But I want lightning."

"I know, just try this. If it doesn't work, you don't have to try again."

"Alright." She focused on the ball and caught it on fire.

"Now all you have to do is turn the fire to lightning."

She blinked. Could it be that easy? Using the technique Grinnell just showed her, she changed the fire from red and yellow to a blue color. That was what she thought lightning should look like. The fire turned blue, but it still looked like fire. She knew lightning arced. She had seen enough of that on the planet she grew up on. Maybe that was what she was doing wrong. That lightning frightened her, and she was letting that fear control her now. She had to get past that. She remembered how her hair stood on end when she was filled with static electricity. That was funny to see. Mehanna used that image to change the fire to strands of hair dancing around the ball. Then she widened them.

There in her hand was a perfectly round lightning ball.

"Blue, huh?"

"It's the color I know." She snuffed it out and made it reappear. "It's not perfect, but it is better than what I was creating. Thank you."

Her bright smile was all he needed.

"Should I change the fire to lightning?" He took his glove off. "Would that make my weapon look more like magic?"

"It might. It's something we'll have to talk to the others about." She snuffed out her second ball as well. "Tosci knows this kind of stuff the best."

"Do you trust her?"

"Shouldn't I?"

He shrugged. "I don't know. She is related to Moorac. He's still family to her, and that bothers me."

"She does still love him. I can see that in her eyes. But I think she believes she's lost him. Power does corrupt."

"Okay. I get that, but what if she thinks she can save him?" He picked up the satchel that held their meal and led her back to the galley. "Or if he convinces her that he has changed only to get her to drop her guard?"

"There are a lot of ifs that we can't predict." She sat at the table while he brought out the food. "But I understand that I shouldn't trust her completely."

"Good. I hope she is trustworthy, but we need to be smart about how we handle this. If he can control minds, we have to prepare for the fact that he could turn us against each other." He sat at the table next to her.

"I know." She took the clay bowl he handed her. "Lawaya went out of her way to make sure we had everything we need."

"I think she didn't care for the rations I served us."

"But she never had any. She was trapped in the mirror the whole time."

"Yeah, but she saw them. I'm thinking she couldn't get past the look of them. They don't look very good, but they are nutritious and filling."

"Maybe we should bring her a sample of your rations so she can see they're not that bad."

"That sounds like a good idea."

They arrived early the next dura, Grinnell carrying the satchel back. "I brought our morning meal."

Lawaya's face lost its smile. "I have prepared the morning meal."

"And we thank you for that, but I would be remiss if I didn't offer a sample of the foods stored on my ship. You never got a chance to taste it. We can save your meal for middura, right?"

"Of course," she replied. But she didn't look happy.

"I promise it tastes better than it looks. You didn't get a chance to try it."

"And she's not sure she wants to," laughed Mehanna.

"How about you, Tosci?" asked Grinnell. "Are you willing to try?"

"Someone else's food? Yes. You never know what you'll like unless you try it."

"Good." Grinnell laid the food out on the wooden table she had outside. "It's designed to give us everything we need, and it doesn't taste bad."

"But you are used to the taste, right?" asked Lawaya as she eyed the food dubiously.

"I don't find them too bad either," chimed in Mehanna.

The four of them stood around the table and Grinnell watched as the two women took a bite.

"Okay, so it's not that bad," admitted Lawaya. "But do you think this is better than what I cooked for you nodura?"

"Of course not, but I wanted you to know that we're not suffering through awful rations on the ship."

"I knew that."

"I've been working on a few things, too," added Grinnell, changing the subject as he ate.

"Oh?" asked Lawaya

"I'm the only one who doesn't have some sort of power so I'm making my own."

"How?"

"I'm creating a glove that will give me powers like yours."

"You're going to use technology to have magic?" Tosci looked between him and Mehanna.

"Why not? Most people would come in with guns blazing, but you said he couldn't detect the difference between technology and magic. If I give him something that looks like magic, he won't know it's technology."

"What have you come up with?"

He looked at Mehanna. "I think she should show you what she worked on first."

Mehanna stepped forward. "Grinnell helped me master the lightning ball."

"Show me," said Tosci.

She created a perfect lightning ball.

"Good. Can you make it move?"

Mehanna had it moving in a figure eight above their heads.

"And what do you have to show us?" asked Tosci, turning to Grinnell once she was happy with the control Mehanna had on the lightning.

Grinnell held his hands out, having one palm on top of the other. As he opened his hands, a small ball of fire danced in them. It grew as he opened his hands more. Even though he was using technology, he hoped it looked like magic.

Tosci came close to look at his hands. "How have you mastered this so quickly?" she asked.

"Mastered?" asked Mehanna. Then it dawned on her. "You knew."

"How could I ignore the way you two act around each other? I just waited for you to tell me."

"And I wanted to enjoy our bonding a little more before you could berate me for making such a decision."

"I would never berate you." Tosci gestured for Grinnell to create the fire again. "The decision to bond can't be taken lightly, and you were doing it to protect Grinnell. You didn't say you loved him, or you wanted to spend the rest of your life with him. I didn't want you to make a rash decision."

"I didn't." She walked to Grinnell's side and took his hand. "We didn't go into this for a temporary fix. I do love him, and he loves me. I do want to spend the rest of my life with him."

"I hope you two are ready for the fight of your life." Tosci looked from Mehanna to Grinnell.

"We are," said Grinnell.

"Then I will train you best I can. You will need to learn how to borrow her power."

"No need. I'll use my technology to defeat him."

"Don't be arrogant. Moorac is intelligent and powerful. He will figure out you don't have magic within you quickly."

"Perhaps it would be wise to learn what she can teach you," said Mehanna. "It wouldn't hurt to have a backup plan."

He wrapped an arm around her waist. "And what if you need that power?"

"She won't," replied Tosci. "We don't run out of power. Our energy is infinite. The more we use, the more we create."

"Is that why you've been pushing me?" asked Mehanna.

"Of course," the older woman replied. "You haven't used it in yepas. My brother knew what he was doing when he gave you amnesia and blocked your powers. He knew if you didn't know how to use it or how to make it stronger, he would be able to defeat you easily."

"Why didn't you tell me this before?"

"What would you have done if I did?"

"Practiced."

"But would you have pushed yourself? You mastered the lightning in one dura. Why?"

"Because you said to?" She wasn't sure what she was getting at.

Grinnell squeezed her waist. "I think Tosci is saying if you knew that your power could replenish itself, you wouldn't have tried your best. You would have expected your power to do what it should. And you need to continue to push yourself."

"As do you," Mehanna said.

"Promise." He looked at Tosci. "I'm ready to learn how to use her power."

"I hope you have a strong learning ethic, because this won't be easy for you. You're not used to having the power. For us, it's second nature, but not for you."

"Believe me, I know."

"Then let's begin."

Tosci pushed him. There were a few times when he wanted to snap at her, but he knew she was pushing him for a reason. Drawing Mehanna's power to him was hard. In the beginning, he couldn't figure out how to tap into it, but he kept trying. His head hurt and his nerves were fried, but he had been able to create a small spark.

"How do you do this?" he asked Mehanna as they headed back to the ship.

"It's natural for us." She took his hand. "It will become natural for you too."

He rubbed his head with his free hand. "You sure? Right now, I'm thinking it will never happen."

"Grinnell, you can do anything you put your mind to. You'll get this."

"When did you become such a supporter?"

"When we bonded. But I've always known this about you. You came to my home knowing what you wanted, and when you found a problem, you used it to your advantage."

"I wasn't that bad, was I?"

"I saw it as a good thing." She hugged him. "You are tenacious, and that is what you need to master what you have to."

"Are you going to make me work on this toduro?"

"Only if you want to." She smiled up at him. "Is there something you'd like to do instead?"

"I have a few things I'd like to do, and you would be involved." He picked her up in his arms. "Do you have a problem with that?"

"As long as you're focusing on me, I don't have a problem with it."

"Good, because that's what I'd like to do." He carried her up the gangplank and didn't put her down until they were inside the ship. "Are you hungry?"

"Only for you."

"Oh, good answer." He captured her lips with his as he backed her toward his chair, which he had converted into a bed for them. "I can't seem to get enough of you."

"What does that mean?" She stopped moving when her legs touched the frame of the chair. "I heard it in the stories, but never quite understood it."

"It means that no matter how many times we make love, I still want you."

"I'm glad to hear that." She wrapped her arms around his neck and pulled him back down for another kiss. "Because I feel the same way."

Grinnell lowered them to the soft mattress. "How did I get so lucky?"

"It wasn't luck. It was destiny."

He removed their clothes quickly. The desire to feel her body take him in was overwhelming. How fast could he arouse her? Grinnell pushed himself up and found Mehanna smiling up at him. "Everything okay?"

"Oh yes." She wrapped her arms around him and flipped them over. "I know you want to make sure I'm ready. Believe me, I am." Mehanna braced her hands on his chest as she eased herself down on his shaft.

Grinnell groaned as her heat surrounded him. That was what he wanted, too. He helped her set a pace that had them sucking in their breaths. They didn't talk, but they didn't have to. Each seemed to know what the other wanted. What felt good. They moved together, their pace picking up speed as they got closer to their releases.

Grinnell flipped them back over so he could take control. He drove into her, and she met him thrust for thrust. Quicker and quicker they moved, each reaching for that perfect moment of bliss.

"I…need…my stars…Grinnell…that…" A groan escaped her as her as her muscles clamped down on him.

Her body tightened around him, sealing him in an exquisite vise that sent him over the edge with her. The moment he could move again, he pressed kisses along her hairline. "That was wonderful."

"I didn't think it could get any better, but you just proved me wrong." Mehanna brushed a few strands of hair out of his face. "You made me see fireworks."

"Fireworks, huh?" He turned so he could take her into his arms. "I wish I could give you fireworks."

She settled in his arms, resting her head on his chest.

"That's a nice touch." He pointed above them.

"What?" She looked where he was pointing. Above them, fireworks exploded. "Oh, my. Um, I didn't do that."

"You didn't?" he brushed his fingers along her arm. "Then who did?"

"I think you did."

"What?"

"You tapped into my power."

"I don't know how I did that. I was just thinking that I wish I could give you fireworks all the time."

"Try something else."

"Like what?" He pushed himself up on one elbow so he could look at her.

"I don't know."

"I don't either." He looked up at the fireworks. "I guess I should think about something else I could give you."

She turned her head and looked at him. "When you need to use this ability, it won't be to please me."

"I always want to please you." He brushed his fingers along her jaw. "I also want to protect you from Moorac. Something I'm not sure how to do."

"I have faith in you, Grinnell. You have proven to be quite resourceful when you need to be."

They walked back to Tosci's house hand in hand the next dura. Grinnell hadn't been able to recreate anything except for the fireworks. Hopefully, Tosci will be able to help him do it again.

The two ladies were busying themselves getting the morning meal ready for them.

"How did we alert you we were coming?" asked Grinnell.

"Oh, you didn't. But you have arrived about the same time very dura. I watch the sun and I knew you would be arriving soon." Tosci set a bowl of fruit on the table. "There is still a lot of training to do."

"Grinnell manifested something last duro."

"Way to ease into the conversation," mumbled Grinnell.

She laughed as she tugged on his arm. "He's not sure how he did it, and we were hoping you could help him do it again."

"How did you do it the first time?" She gestured for everyone to take a seat at the table.

"Um, I wanted her to see fireworks."

"Oh." She was quiet for a secur. "I'm assuming you two were having sex?"

"It was more than that, but yes." Grinnell accepted the bowl Lawaya handed him.

"Then it is your love for Mehanna that allows you to tap into her power." She handed him the fruit bowl. "You need to think about your love for her, then think of something you want or need."

"Like what?" He spooned some of the fruit onto his plate and then passed the bowl to Mehanna. "That was one of the problems I had. I did the first one accidentally. When I tried to do it on purpose, I couldn't do it again."

"How long did the fireworks last?"

"Um, about half an hora?" said Mehanna. "It was quite beautiful."

"Thank you." Grinnell popped a piece of fruit into his mouth. "I wish I could do that again for you."

They ate for a few securs before Lawaya moved. She didn't say anything, just pointed up. Fireworks were going off above their heads.

"You did it again," said Mehanna as she wrapped a hand around his arm.

"How far away can that be seen?"

"Don't worry," Tosci held a piece of fruit. "I've kept it from being detected. But we're pretty far out from any village. This is good progress. When you learn to tap into it all the time, my brother will think you have your own power."

"I don't feel right about this." Grinnell looked at Mehanna. "I didn't bond with you to use your powers, and I've created some weapons that I could pass as magic, rather than borrow from yours."

"And you should use them. I believe if you do, my brother will dismiss you as a normal. Then when you do use magic, he will be caught off guard."

Once Grinnell figured out how to tap into Mehanna's power and control it, he spent horas learning to manipulate it. His head hurt and his body ached, but he made headway.

For the next few cycles, he and Mehanna worked hard at mastering anything Tosci gave them. She pushed them as hard as she could, making each task more elaborate than the one they had just learned.

"You two are a good pair," said Lawaya as she laid out another wonderful meal. She had found a love for cooking while there. It was her contribution, and she clearly had fun doing it.

"Thanks." Grinnell was the first to join her. "What delectable dish have you created this time?"

"A hearty stew that will put some meat on those bones of yours."

"There is nothing wrong with the amount of meat on my bones."

"You are thin, like a young pumat."

"I don't see that as an insult. A pumat is quite regal, with its large antlers and long legs."

"That is, after it is full grown," Lawaya teased. "The young one is not sure on its legs and has no antlers."

Mehanna laughed as she joined them. "Grinnell can't be a pumat. He is quite sure of himself."

"Hey!" He wrapped his arms around her. "Are you teasing me too?"

"Maybe." She wrapped her arms around him as well.

"Then what animal do you think I am?"

"Hm, that is a good question. I'm not sure. You are proud. Strong. Like a sorki. They fly high in the skies of a dozen planets. I saw them in the feeds. You are like them."

"I hate to tell you this, but the reason sorkis are on so many planets is because they are pets."

"Oh." Mehanna smiled. "Then they obey their masters."

He narrowed his eyes at her in mock anger. "What are you getting at?"

"Nothing." She paused for a moment. "My pet."

"Your pet?" A gleam entered his eyes just as he moved toward her. A squeal escaped her as she took off.

"You disagree?" she shouted behind her.

"Do you think you are my master?" he asked as he chased her.

"Do you think you're mine?" she questioned back.

"I think we have an equal relationship," he responded. "But if you wish for me to dominate you, I can."

She stopped in front of a tree away from prying eyes. "And what if *I* want to dominate *you*?"

He stopped in front of her. "I don't have a problem with that. As long as we're both happy afterwards."

"Are you happy, Grinnell?"

"With you?" He braced his hands against the tree on either side of her. "Yes. With us? More than I thought I would be."

"And our bonding?"

"Never been happier." He leaned in and pressed a kiss against her cheek. "You?"

"The same." She wrapped her arms around his neck. "I wish we didn't have to face Moorac. I'm excited to start our lives together now."

"Me too." He wrapped his arms around her and led her back to the clearing where the other two ladies were waiting. "But we have a lot more training to do."

"And we do need to master that before we master each other, don't we?" Mehanna teased.

"Exactly."

CHAPTER TWELVE

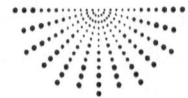

"**D**o you think we're ready?" Grinnell asked Tosci. They had been pushing themselves for several cycles, knowing they needed to get back to Emori.

"Why?"

"Because we need to get back to Emori before your brother gets impatient and harms one of my friends."

"It would take yepas for me to make you masters of your craft. But have I taught you enough to face my brother? I hope so. There's no way to test it. I don't know how strong my brother has gotten. You have passed my ability in the few cycles you've been here, and that is all I have to go on."

Grinnell took Mehanna's hand in his. "Then let's get ready and go."

Lawaya demanded that they bring fresh vegetables, and a few dried meats with them so she could continue to cook for them. Grinnell promised she could use the food sources on the ship to help her with her meals.

It would take them about a cycle to get to Emori. Tosci used that time to work on their finesse. Each duro they went to bed exhausted.

When they were only a few duras out, everyone was feeling the tension of what they had to face.

Grinnell planned a surprise for Mehanna. They had worked so hard, even though they didn't know if it was worth it. The two other ladies had settled into their rooms, and he and Mehanna reclined in the sleeping area he had created for them.

They had gotten comfortable. Mehanna was snuggled up against him, her head on his shoulders. He pulled a sheet over them.

"Everyone seems so tense," said Mehanna.

"We're scared." He brushed his knuckles against her cheek. "We have no idea what is happening on Emori. Everything could be fine, or Moorac could be causing trouble for our friends. We won't know until we get there."

She shifted so she could brush her hands across his forehead. "I wish I could wipe that worry from your brow."

"I am fine." He took her hand and kissed her palm. "My goal is to keep you safe."

"Funny, that is my goal as well. If he harms you, I will kill him."

He kissed her. It was soft, deep, and took her breath away. "I have something I want to show you."

"A little more magic?" She settled against him again, resting a hand and her head on his chest.

"Something like that." He hit a button on the seat and held her close as the bulkhead cleared and became transparent. Her breath caught in her throat when she realized that she was looking at the stars surrounding the ship.

"How are some of the stars standing still while others streak past like meteors?"

"The ones that stand still are very far away. You'll see some that oscillate, and a few that will move so slow you might not realize they're moving, but then you'll suddenly realize they're no longer visible. Those that are the closest are the ones you see streaking by."

"This is beautiful."

"I had hoped you would like it. Every time I look at this, it calms me. It also puts things into perspective. I am one person in the cosmos." His voice came out soft and low. "It humbles you."

"I remember sitting at the mouth of my cave looking up at the stars. They were so pretty. Like perfect crystals on a black cloth." She linked her fingers with his. "You're right. It is humbling."

"It puts things into perspective."

She looked up at him. "Does Moorac frighten you, Grinnell?"

"I'm not sure how to answer that question." He brushed his fingers through her hair. "Of what he could do to you? Yes, that frightens me a lot. Of what he could do to me? I don't care, as long as you are safe."

"But I care what happens to you. I won't let him harm you."

She said it with such conviction it worried him a little.

"I can take care of myself. It's you that I worry about." He touched her face with his fingers. "I am a warrior. I know what to expect from someone like him. I have dealt with too many like him. You haven't."

"I am strong."

"Of that I have no doubt." He smiled at her. "But this was the man who raised you. He knows you and could use that against you."

"Really? How?"

"He could make you believe that he is only trying to protect you. That I'm a bad influence on you."

"He won't be successful." She rested her head on his chest once again. "You and I are bonded. That bond is stronger than any mind control he could try on me."

"That's good to know." He rested his chin on top of her head. "I just know that people like him can be quite devious. I want to be sure he doesn't make you believe something that isn't true."

"Grinnell, you worry too much. He is just a man, like you. He bleeds like you, too."

"True, but he thinks he's a god." Grinnell watched the stars fly by. "He would never expect normal people to even try to best him, would he?"

"No." She pushed herself up so she could look him in the eyes. "He would expect you to be in awe of him."

"And if no one showed him the respect he is expecting?"

"I believe that would make him very angry."

"But if we bowed and scraped at his feet?"

"Then he should be all smiles and sweet. At least until he tries to take me with him. Or when he sees his sister."

"Do you think he'd believe me if I were to tell him I don't know what happened to you?"

"That's something I don't know. I don't think anyone has ever tried to cross him. His anger is the worst." She looked at him. "Why?"

"I'm just trying to figure out how to deal with him. I want to put as much as I can in our favor."

———

Once they were close enough to send a private message to Orla, he let them know to land at the palace retreat in the mountains. It was where the royal family would go to meditate or mourn the loss of family members. Astrid had gone there when her father passed, and that was how she had been able to escape from Varal's clutches.

May was still out learning the planet, and they needed to find her before they returned to the main palace. Moorac was still Orla and Astrid's guest, but he didn't know that May was on the planet. She had stayed far enough away that he couldn't detect her magic. Or if he did, Orla said, he was very good at pretending.

Once they reached the retreat, Orla would send one of the private transports for them to fly where he believed May and Grenta were, the main center on the other side of the planet.

Grinnell followed the route Orla gave him to keep them undetected and landed the ship on the private landing pad. Using the combination Orla gave him, the walls of the hangar opened and he moved his ship inside.

"So what do we do now?" asked Lawaya.

"We wait until the transport arrives."

———

Orla worked on the controls of the transport. He uploaded as much information as he could to give Grinnell everything he needed. As he was reattaching the panel, he heard a voice.

"What are you doing, Orla?"

"Moorac?" He stepped out of the shadow of the ship, cleaning his hands with a sonic cleaner. "I didn't expect you to show up here."

But he did. The man might be behaving as a proper guest, but Orla knew better. He had searched the palace for the girls. He must have sensed their magic but knew it was old. What Orla didn't understand was why he didn't go looking for them. It was like he was expecting Orla to hand them over on a silver platter.

Two could play at that game. The moment he got this ship to Grinnell, they would have a plan to save these girls from him.

"Since you're here, do you want to help me finish up?" Orla asked. "I have a few more things to check out before I send it back to the retreat."

"Oh no. I'm not very technical. My talents lie elsewhere."

"I see." Orla went to a small panel on the outside of the ship. He removed the cover and worked on the computer inside. "I love working with anything that can be considered technology."

"You said you were sending this back to the retreat? Where is that?"

"In the mountains. It's where my family can go when they need to reflect on anything bothering them. It's also where we can go to mourn. My mate went there after the death of her father. It's how we escaped Varal."

"Then you need to fly there to reach it."

"Yes." Orla smiled. He knew what the next question was and was ready for it. "Every craft we use has the royal seal. It's instantly recognized. I have this craft and several like it located all over the planet. If we ever need to escape again, we have vehicles to do it in."

"Which you didn't have the first time?"

"Exactly."

"You think what happened with Varal will happen again?"

"I don't know. That's why I need to be vigilant."

"And why he is such a good mate," said a feminine voice behind them.

"Astrid." Orla was beside her in securs.

"I'm fine." She rested her hand on her rounded belly. "Our child isn't ready to see us yet, but it will be soon."

"I thought you were supposed to be on bed rest."

"And I have been a good patient. The nurse recognized that I was restless and thought a walk would be good for me." She pointed to the private nurse assigned to her. "I have proof."

Her ever-present nurse waved at him.

"I don't mean to upset you." He put an arm around her waist and rested a hand on her womb as well. "I just know that we're two different races, so I worry."

"I do too." She put her hand on top of his. "But the doctors are quite happy with our progression and don't foresee any problems happening with the birth."

"That does make me feel better." He pressed a kiss against her forehead. "I can't wait to see our child."

"Me either. I would like to see my feet again as well."

He laughed as he hugged her.

"Do you wish to walk me back to our rooms?"

"I would love to." He looked at Moorac. "Hope you don't mind if we cut this short?"

"No. It's time for me to rest anyway."

Orla sent the ship on its way then took his mate's hand. Moorac hadn't moved. He just watched the ship shrink in size. "You coming Moorac? I need to lock this place up."

"Of course." He fell into step with them as they headed back to the palace.

———

Grinnell watched as the transport came into view.

"Is that what we're waiting for?" asked Mehanna, pointing.

"Yes." He grinned as the transport landed. "This will allow us to go to one of the major centers where we can blend in while we look for May and Grenta."

"Do we want to find them?"

"We need the strength in numbers. Grenta is a master Barou, like Lawaya. They can look like they have the same magic you do." He climbed on the small carrier and checked the vehicle out. He let out a joyful shout and then stepped out of the ship. "Orla has given us everything we need."

"What do you mean?" asked Mehanna.

"We have clothes and fake identities that will allow us to travel without suspicion." He'd also given them a chip to purchase anything they needed.

"Is the security tight here?" asked Lawaya.

"Every citizen is free to go anywhere they want, but we all are registered in the system."

"And you are famous."

"I don't like to think of me that way, but my name is well known because I helped Astrid and Orla take the planet back from Varal."

"What about your face?"

"There are a few pictures of me out there, but I asked Orla to keep my face out of any media that would go off world. I have enemies that could come looking if they wanted to."

"You worry too much," said Mehanna. "But this time it will help us, won't it?"

"Yes. Since few know what I look like, I can move about the people with this new identity and not worry that someone might recognize me. The chance someone would recognize me is small." He took her hand. "We also have information on Moorac since he arrived, as well as information on where we should find May."

"Then let's go."

Grinnell landed the small transport at the main port. Their fake identities said they were from a small town on one of the islands and had come to do a little sightseeing. Orla had left out some details so Grinnell could personalize. He made the changes, showing he and Mehanna were husband and wife. They had also created identities for Tosci and Lawaya. Tosci and Lawaya would be sisters, and Mehanna's aunts. They had kept their names for simplicity. Grinnell wasn't a very common name on Emori, but he knew how to play it off if someone were to say something. It would also make it easy for them to stay in character.

The ladies were excited like tourists should be. He had given them their files so they could memorize their personal information and backgrounds. Grinnell escorted them out of the port. They all stopped and stared when they saw the Crystal City for the first time.

"How beautiful," said Mehanna.

"It lives up to its name, doesn't it?" Grinnell looked around the city. It was beautiful with its crystalline skyscrapers. The buildings were made of a common crystal found on Emori. The qualities of the material made it perfect to use. It could retain heat during their cold season and stay cool during the warm season, maintaining perfect temperature without having to use any power. Light worked the same way: The building absorbed the sunlight, then glowed at duro.

"Are there living quarters in these buildings or are they for businesses only?" asked Mehanna.

"A little of both. The lower half is normally for businesses. Shops and restaurants on the bottom floor. Things like mechanics, servers, that kind of thing, are on the lower floors, then the housing starts. Those who work in the city live here so they don't have to travel far."

"Then we can live in one of these buildings?" asked Mehanna.

"Yes. We can live anywhere you want, but there are a lot of cities just as pretty as this one," said Grinnell.

"You want to leave our little island for this?" asked Tosci, trying to play the character of a concerned aunt.

"I know we're only here for vacation, but it's very tempting. We could start anew." She wrapped an arm around Grinnell's waist. "We're just starting our life together, and this would be a great place to begin that life."

"What would you do?" asked Tosci.

"I don't know. Let's see what's in some of the shops. Maybe they will inspire me."

Mehanna enjoyed the shops. She saw so many things that she had never seen before. Grinnell explained a lot to her in a soft voice, filling her in on things she should know as a member of the planet. They got to taste a lot of different foods she had never had before. Grinnell also bought her two new outfits, as well as a new outfit for everyone else.

"That was a lot of fun," said Mehanna.

"I'm glad." He escorted everyone to an inn where he had reserved rooms for them. "If you ladies would like to freshen up, we can go to our rooms for a while. Later, though, I'd like to take everyone to evening meal."

"Oh, that's so nice," said Lawaya. "I'll get to try a professional's meal that I can replicate."

That didn't surprise Mehanna. Every time they went into a spice shop, Lawaya would look at every spice and herb there. Grinnell picked up the herbs she spent the longest time with and made sure they were sent to her room. Mehanna wondered how she would react when she found them.

Grinnell took Mehanna to a separate room from the other two.

"Grinnell, this is wonderful." A large bed dominated the room. She sat on it and laughed. "This is so plush. I think I could crawl under the covers and sleep for duras."

"We're here to sightsee, not sleep the duras away." He sat down beside her. "Is that what you want to do? Sleep the dura away?"

"It is tempting." She rubbed her hand along the softcover. "Wouldn't you like to spend as much time as we want in bed?"

"With you? I'd love that." He pulled a small bag out of a pocket. "I bought this for you." He didn't say anything else, just sat it on the bed. "I'm going to shower."

Mehanna watched him step into the bathing area, then looked at the bag Grinnell sat on the bed. She picked it up but didn't open it right away. He had been with them all dura. How had he gotten this without her noticing? Her curiosity got the best of her, and she opened the bag and dropped the contents into her hand. The prettiest blue stone winked in the light.

"Where did he get this?" she wondered aloud. The setting was beautiful. Very delicate twists in the metal made it look like the stone floated in the center. She stared at it. It reminded her of the crystals she saw at the bazaar on the planet where Leabo lived.

Mehanna put the necklace on and removed her clothes. She stepped into the bathing area and waited for Grinnell to notice her.

"Do you need to shower now?"

"I just wanted to ask you where you picked up my beautiful gift." She had her hands clasped behind her.

"And the fact that you're naked?" He had the sonic shower on, but he turned that off and turned the water on.

"I thought it would be smart, or I would get my new dress wet."

"That was a good idea." He offered his hand to her, and she stepped in with him. "Do you like it?"

"Very much. Please tell me where you got this." She touched it with gentle fingers.

"You remember when we met Leabo?"

"I had wondered if that was where it came from." She touched the stone again. "You did spend some time at that crystal booth when I was having my first dress altered."

"I had to have it the moment I saw it." Water danced against his skin. "It's the exact color of your eyes."

"My eyes?"

Grinnell picked her up so they could look each other in the eyes. "Yes, your beautiful eyes."

She wrapped her legs around his waist to give her some stability. The moment she did, Grinnell could feel her moist heat against his erection. They moaned at the contact.

He wanted her with a passion only she could drive him to. Lifting her a little, he centered himself and let her slide down his shaft. They groaned again. Grinnell had her up against the wall of the shower. He started to move, driving in and out of her. His lips searched for hers. When he found them, he claimed them, drinking from them like they were his lifeline. He finally broke the kiss.

"I love the feel of your body as it hugs mine," Grinnell said in a soft voice.

"My stars, you make my body sing." Mehanna clung to him. "Every time is better than the last. Will it always be this way?"

"Gods, I hope so." He pressed his lips against her throat. "Making love to you is addictive."

Her muscles tightened against him, and he picked up the pace. Everything inside coiled like a snake ready to strike. He knew he was close. His concern was how close Mehanna was. He felt her tighten against him again, giving him an exquisite vice to move through. She sucked in her breath, and he knew she was close. The tight sheath made him pick up the pace once more. He couldn't stop now. He pounded into her. His release was so close. She clenched against him, sending him flying through his orgasm.

Mehanna made a soft noise, her body stiffened, then she gave him the most beautiful smile as she relaxed against him.

"I wish we could do this again," Grinnell said, "but I promised to take everyone to evening meal." Regretfully, he shifted them so she could put her feet on the floor.

"Then let's make that meal go by fast so we can come back here and do that again."

They sat around the table at one of the nicer restaurants. Mehanna and Grinnell tried to be attentive to their friends, but all they could think about was getting back to their room.

"You two seem preoccupied," commented Lawaya.

"No, we're not," countered Mehanna. She looked over at Grinnell, who sat at her side. He took her hand in silent support.

"Really? You two are all moons-eyed over each other."

"Grinnell gave me a gift."

"And that has made you two behave like moonbats?"

Mehanna smiled. Moonbats were well known for flying in pairs, doing intricate dances in the air while the moons on the planet they were on filled the sky.

"I don't know about moonbats, but I get the distinct impression that they would rather be in each other arms in their room than with us," commented Tosci. She took a bite of her food.

Mehanna wanted to retort, but something distracted her. She felt something. She looked at Tosci. "I feel someone searching for me. Could it be my sister?"

"Does May know you're here?"

She shook her head.

"You have your shields up?" asked Tosci.

"Of course."

"It has to be my brother."

"Don't you sense him?" asked Grinnell.

"No, but he doesn't know I'm here, so wouldn't think to look for me. But we know he's searching for you, and from what your friend Orla told Grinnell, somehow he knew you had been here."

"I have my shields up, but his pull is very strong."

"You must find a way to shield your magic," said Tosci. She looked at Grinnell. "Or make it look like someone else has the power instead of you."

"Make it look like Grinnell has the power? What if he comes after him?"

"I don't think he will. Moorac is looking for a female with powers. If he senses a male, he'd probably think it was someone on vacation and would assume he has touched the power of a mixed breed. We did have a few people who left our planet over the yepas, and he would likely assume the power he feels is from one of their descendants."

"Would a half-breed have the power I do?" asked Mehanna.

"It could come across that way." Tosci leaned forward. "Let me show you what to do."

It took only microns for them to prepare. As everyone enjoyed their meals, Mehanna felt Moorac searching for her. She grabbed Grinnell's hand and brought him into her magic.

"Can you feel him?"

"I can," said Grinnell. "He's quite arrogant, isn't he?"

Power filled him. He tightened his hold on her hand as he drew Moorac's attention to him. It was odd to work through Mehanna to reach the man.

"Now what?" he asked.

"Flex your power. Not a lot, but enough to make him believe you are the source," said Tosci.

He did what she told him, allowing the power to fill him then let it escape at different strengths. He made it look like he didn't know how to control his power. In fact, he made it look like he wasn't even aware of the power coursing through him.

Moorac stood on the balcony of his guest room. He looked out over the scenic view they gave him and focused. If his wards were on the planet, he would find them. His hosts have been good to him, and he was sure they didn't know who he was or what he was after.

He emptied his mind and focused. Magic called to him. He mentally followed a path to the source. He frowned when he found it. It was male. He'd been sure he had found one of the girls.

The power this male had was too strong for a half-breed. As he focused, he felt the man's power wane and then build back up again. He didn't know how to control it. Not what he was looking for, but he would like to know who had such power. He might be a good ally in the future.

Moorac tried to will the man's image to turn around, but he continued to ignore him. He probably wasn't aware someone with magic had found him. Moorac was using more power than he should to identify the man. If he kept this up, he could draw unwanted attention. He pulled back, dampening his power so no one would figure out the real reason he was there.

CHAPTER THIRTEEN

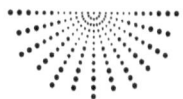

Grinnell released a pent-up breath when he felt Moorac's presence leave him. "I think we're safe for now. I don't feel him anymore."

"Thanks to the stars," said Mehanna. "I feared he would figure out we had tricked him and punish you."

"He wanted me to turn toward him, but I kept my face away."

"My brother is quite tenacious about things like that," said Tosci. "He might have thought he could use you if things didn't go his way. As long as he didn't see your face, you should be safe."

"So now what?" asked Lawaya.

"We go find my sister," said Mehanna.

The four of them got up early the next dura and decided they should break their fast before heading out. They were enjoying a morning beverage while they waited for the waitress to bring them the bill. The door to the restaurant they sat in opened, and people turned toward it.

Murmurs filled the air as people shielded their faces.

Grinnell was the one who caught a whiff first.

"What is that awful smell?" asked Mehanna. She must have been the second one.

"That is Tymin," murmured Grinnell.

The little man climbed up on their table and sat.

"Tymin had trouble finding you," he said.

"Why are you here, Tymin?" asked Grinnell. He signaled the waiter and ordered an ale for him.

"Orla sent me."

"Orla? He told us to stay out of sight. I don't see that happening with you here."

"I am to help you. Tymin is best tracker. I help."

Grinnell sat back. Tymin would be a great help for them. Other than the basic information Orla gave them, they had no idea where to start looking for May. However, he knew from experience the man's smell was not easy to overcome. It wasn't as bad as when he'd first met the man, but it still could make your eyes water. "I thought your wife was trying to help with the smell."

"This is Tymin now," he said. "No cure. Wife said so."

Too bad. He looked at the stricken faces of his tablemates. "I will leave this up to you, ladies. Tymin is the best, and he helped us when we needed him. The smell is something we need to deal with. If you can't, I understand, but if you can, we will find May and Grenta faster."

"Does he always smell like that?" asked Lawaya.

"Unfortunately, yes. I hate to tell you that it's much better than when we first met him."

"You're kidding," said Tosci. She pinched her nose.

He shook his head.

"Tymin will stay downwind." He downed the ale. "He learned that from princess."

"Princess?" asked Tosci.

"Astrid was the princess before her father was killed, although if you use that title around her, she will deny it. She gave up her royal status when we defeated Varal."

"But she lives in the palace," said Mehanna. "And the people still treat her as if she's still royalty."

"They love her. She stepped down as queen because she didn't want what happened with Varal to happen again. That just made them worship her more. She put her people first, and they found that showed how much she cared about them. She agreed to be the face of their world, but she has no power. That keeps everyone happy."

"You done?" Tymin climbed down off the table. "We go now."

"Now?" Mehanna echoed.

"Tymin, why don't you wait outside for us? We have to gather our things before we head out." Grinnell smiled at the little man.

"I understand."

Grinnell ushered the ladies up to their rooms.

"How do you feel about traveling with Tymin?"

Mehanna frowned. "Astrid traveled with him?"

"She did." He understood the frown. The smell was a hard thing to ignore. "She even helped him and his wife get back together, but that is a long story for another time."

"If Astrid could deal with the smell, I guess we can too."

"Good. He is the best."

Grinnell had secured them mounts for their trip. Although they could have used public transport, Grinnell knew Grenta. The only way she wanted to travel was on the ground. They could pass right over them in a transport and never know it. Besides, Tymin tracked best on land. Technology just got in his way.

Tymin had his own transportation. The small steed he sat on had been a gift from Orla. He was good on his word about staying downwind, something the ladies appreciated.

"So, what is the story with Tymin?" asked Lawaya. "He doesn't seem to fit with everyone else."

"Tymin knew all of us, except Astrid. He had gotten into trouble with a man over a trinket that had belonged to his wife. Tymin went to retrieve it but was caught by the man who had possession of it. He made Tymin's life a living hell, so he ran. Tymin couldn't go home, so he learned to track. If you wanted something, he could find it. Orla had met him during his travels. I knew him because he had helped others secure transport for items and people. When I met Orla, Tymin owed me for a transaction that had gone bad."

"He helped with the defeat of Varal?"

"Yes. He didn't want to, but he owed Orla his life and wanted to pay back the debt. I don't think he feels he has paid it back yet because he and his wife are still on Emori instead of their home planet."

"You done talking?" asked Tymin. "I found trail."

"Wow, he is good," said Mehanna.

"What did you find?" asked Grinnell.

"Here two animals." Tymin pointed to two sets of tracks. "This one carries Grenta."

"How do you know that?" asked Mehanna.

"Grenta fears truggars. The prints here are from the only animal she will ride. The second set are truggar. Both show light prints, which means women ride."

The three women turned to look at Grinnell for confirmation.

"He's right. Grenta would rather walk than ride anything if she could, but if she has to ride it's going to be the most gentle animal out there. The prints are from a merma. I can see her riding that. The gait of each animal is closer together and light. That normally means a female rider. A male rider makes their gait wider and deeper."

"They went this way a cycle ago," said Tymin.

"Then I doubt they will be at the next town we come across," said Grinnell.

"How are we going to catch up to them if they have that much of a head start?" asked Tosci.

"We know they're waiting for a signal from Orla that it's clear for them to return, so they're taking in the sights. We're going to continue through each town until we catch up to them."

"I hope we find them soon," said Mehanna.

"We will," said Grinnell.

The next town was much smaller than the Crystal City. It was well known for its heated spas.

"Can we take advantage of the spas?" asked Mehanna. "My butt doesn't care for the gait of my truggar."

"Sure." Grinnell smiled as he touched her face. "We can't have any part of that luscious body in pain. I'll get us rooms and find out how we can get appointments."

Mehanna smiled at him, making his heart skip a beat. How did she capture his heart so quickly?

He walked into one of the inns. "I am looking for two rooms. Do you have any available?"

"I do." The gentleman behind the counter answered him. "Just had two rooms open up. Do you need them next to each other? These two are near each other, down the same hall."

"That will be fine. My family would like to try the spas. How do I get that accomplished?"

"Well, it depends on what type of treatment you want." He pointed to the screen on one of the walls. "We have salt baths, mud baths, and hot springs. Which one do you want?"

"I have no idea." He laughed. "I think I better ask before I get in trouble."

"Smart move." The man took his chip and deducted the cost of the rooms. "We have a great room for you to dine in unless you'd like to eat in private."

"The dining hall should be fine."

The ladies came in behind him.

"Perfect." Grinnell signaled the ladies over to the desk. "They have three different types of spas. I had no idea what any of you ladies wanted, so now is the perfect time to pick your favorite."

Mehanna stepped up to him and wrapped a hand around his arm. "What types do they have?"

"My lady," greeted the innkeeper. He bowed. "We have several great spas for you to choose from. Do you prefer mud, salt, hot springs, or a combination?

"I'm not sure," said Mehanna.

"Here, you can look at what we have to offer." He guided her over to a holoscreen.

"So much to choose from." She read the list. Lawaya and Tosci joined her. They whispered amongst themselves as they pointed and nodded.

Grinnell would love to know what they were thinking. Even though they needed to find May, they had to look like tourists, and his companions were perfect. They all turned toward him at once and smiled. That couldn't be good.

"How long did you want to stay here?" asked Mehanna.

"I made plans for us at the Rainbow City in two duras, why?" Grinnell answered, wondering what they were up to.

"Well, we were hoping we could stay an extra dura. They have such a selection, we'd like to try them all."

"How about this: You ladies can try one this dura." He looked at the innkeeper to make sure they were still open. He gave him a slight nod. "Then, after we have our morning meal nesdura you may try another. Perhaps you can combine two nesdura so you can try them all."

"So no extra dura?"

"I'll see if I can move some of the plans I had set up. If I can, we'll stay an extra dura." He kissed Mehanna on the forehead. "How's that?"

"Thank you!" She gave him a beautiful smile as she pressed a kiss against his cheek before following the innkeeper to the spas.

He knew he was in trouble. She could get her way with him and he would let her if she smiled at him like that all the time.

He made a change to their meal plans, then brought their bags up to their rooms. Once he was done, he went to the local bar. Tymin, who had disappeared when they entered the town, stepped in right after him. "You know, the ladies want to know where you go at duro. They have noticed that you always try to keep your smell away from them, and they appreciate it."

"I remember Princess. She always nice to me. Explained how my smell bothered people. I try to be thoughtful." He climbed up on the table.

Grinnell ordered ales for them.

"New lady?" he asked. "You love?"

"I do, Tymin."

"Trouble."

"I know." He laughed. "I thought the same thing when she smiled at me. That smile is dangerous. She can get me to do whatever she wants with that smile."

Tymin just shook his head. He picked up the ale the innkeeper placed in front of them.

"I have something for you," said Grinnell.

"Me?"

"To give to your wife." He held out a small bag that held the other crystal he had bought on a pretty chain. "To thank her for letting you help us."

"I give." Tymin slipped it into a pocket. "Grenta is close."

"You've learned something?"

"I went to where you can house your animal." Tymin took a gulp of his ale. "Two women traveling alone left here two duras ago."

"And you think it's them?"

"Could be." Tymin shrugged. "Need more to be sure."

"Hopefully, we'll learn something that will support your theory."

Mehanna sighed. This was wonderful. She'd chosen the salt bath. She thought she'd be in very salty water, but instead, it was like she was lying in wet sand. They had helped her into a reclining chair in a single-person tank, then covered her body with warm, wet salt.

She had chosen this because she didn't want to have to be cleaning mud from every part of her body. Instead, she would be cleaning salt out for cycles. Lawaya and Tosci had both chosen the mud. They were on the left side of her, reclining in their tanks with their hair wrapped in linen and soft covers over their eyes.

"I could get really used to this," said Tosci.

"I know, I've never felt so relaxed," responded Lawaya.

Mehanna kept her thoughts to herself. Grinnell knew how to relax her so much she could fall fast asleep right away if she wanted, but she didn't want to talk about something so intimate. Her sex life was hers and Grinnell's, and no one else.

"You have a satisfied smile, Mehanna," said Tosci. "Thinking about Grinnell perhaps?"

That comment heated her cheeks. She removed her eye cover to look over at the other two. Both still had their covers on. How did they know she was smiling?

Tosci smiled. "You're looking at me right now, aren't you?"

"I am." But how did she know?

"And you want to know how I knew you were smiling and thinking about Grinnell without looking at you."

"Yes." Was she a mind reader too?

"I could drive you crazy and say magic," she said. She paused a little longer. "But it was your silence to our comments that told me all I needed to know."

"I don't see how." She laid her head back down and replaced her covers. "I just didn't see a reason to comment."

"Because you were thinking about your man."

The woman who had been caring for them came in.

"Ladies, it's time for me to drain your treatment and replace it with a bath. You will feel the floor beneath your feet drop, then the tank will fill with water. It might be a little uncomfortable at first. The water will sit on top of the treatment and replace it as everything drains away." She went to a control panel and pressed a few buttons. "Once the water replacement is complete, I will also treat your hair and face for the full-body experience."

Mehanna felt the floor fall from beneath her feet. The sloped seat made her feel like she was freefalling. The water filtered in, filling the tank higher than the salt bath. It did make her squirm a little.

As the salt disappeared, the water came in. The sensation of the water replacing the salt against her skin felt odd, but slowly she forgot as the water flowed around her. It was warm, like the hot spring of her bathing area. She felt like she was in a cocoon.

"I will do your hair first." She undid the wrapping on Mehanna's hair, allowing the wrap to fall against her headrest. Their caregiver gently rubbed a salt mixture onto her face. She spoke to Mehanna softly. "The salt I'm using now is a finer grain. It should feel like a paste instead of the sand-like mixture you felt on your body. The water will continue to move around you until there is no more salt detected in the water."

"That will tell you when there's no more salt anywhere?"

"Yes." She worked on her hair, combing a salt mixture into it. "Once I'm done combing this into your hair, I will use a special machine to help it melt properly. While that is happening, I will be applying the mud treatment to your friends."

Mehanna relaxed against the tank as she felt warm, gentle fingers brush through her hair. Warmth surrounded her face when the fingers were replaced with pulsing heat. It moved over her like waves.

She could hear the woman speaking softly to Tosci. The soft waves of warmth made her feel a little sleepy. It wasn't long before the woman moved to Lawaya.

That's when it got interesting.

"Oh." Still speaking softly, she murmured. "You are Barou."

Lawaya's hand shot out and grabbed the woman's wrist before she could back away. "You are not Barou, so how did you know?"

"Forgive me, mistress." She gave her a formal bow. "I meant no disrespect. Although I'm not Barou, I believe the child I carry is. She is the one who told me what you were, just like she did the last time."

"The last time?"

Mehanna turned her head so she could see the two women.

"Yes. About a cycle ago, we had travelers like you. Two women. My child reacted the same way. It was the first inkling that she has Barou power."

Lawaya released her wrist. "Does the power run in your family?"

"Yes, my husband's family as well. It has been several generations for my family, but my husband said his grandmother's sister was Barou. I didn't think my baby could have the power. She never showed any of the signs our parents told us to look for, but she knew when she was around anyone of power." She gestured to Tosci and Mehanna. "You two have some sort of power as well, she can sense it, but she only reacted when I touched your hair."

"How?" asked Lawaya.

"Burst of power. Not enough for anyone to notice, but I could feel it."

"May I?" Lawaya held her hand out toward the woman's womb.

"Of course."

Lawaya laid her hand on the woman's womb. A smile spread across

163

her face as she moved her hand into another position. She outright laughed as she pulled her hand back. "Your child definitely has Barou blood. You keep calling the child she. How do you know it's a girl? Did you use the program to tell you the sex?"

"No. My husband and I decided not to. We want the joy of knowing to be from the joy of birth." She smiled. "But when I met the other lady, I got the distinct impression I carry a female."

"I see." Lawaya removed her hand.

"Is it true?" the young mother-to-be asked hesitantly, "that if she is Barou she will have white hair like Queen Astrid?"

"Yes."

The young woman nodded. She looked at Lawaya's hair but remained quiet.

"You want to know why my hair isn't white."

She nodded again.

"People sometimes fear the Barou. Others want to take advantage of our abilities. When I am home where I feel safe, my hair is white, but when I travel I always disguise my hair. Most of us do." Lawaya sat up and allowed the white of her hair to show to the young woman.

"Thank you for trusting me, mistress." The young woman bowed. "That explains a lot. The other lady disguised her hair as well. I was too surprised to ask her the questions I'm asking you. I hope I'm not overstepping my boundaries."

"No." Lawaya smiled. "We're trying to catch up to our friends, but I would like to come back when you're close to giving birth. Help you prepare."

"I would like that." The woman bowed again.

"How long ago did the other Barou leave?" asked Tosci.

"She and her friend left two duras ago. Why?"

"I just thought that Lawaya might want to meet the other Barou. They might know each other."

"They said they were going to the Rainbow City."

"Perhaps we'll run into them. Didn't your husband say we were going the same way, Mehanna?"

"I think so. I'm pretty sure he named that city when I asked if we could stay an extra dura." The machine warming her turned off and lifted so she could sit up. She was handed a warm cloth to wipe her face.

"You ladies are finished. Would you like a robe to wear to your rooms, or do you want to get dressed?"

"I'd love a robe," said Mehanna. She was far too relaxed to want to put her clothes back on. Her friends did the same thing.

They came out of the spa with happy smiles. Mehanna went to their room and opened the door. Grinnell was nowhere to be seen. She did find a wonderful wine waiting for her as well as two glasses. There was a soft knock on the door. Should she answer it?

Before she could make the decision, she heard voices and watched the door open. Grinnell came in with an antigrav tray. She looked at it curiously.

"I thought you'd be hungry after going to the spa," he said.

"I am a little famished."

He rested the tray in front of the bed and gestured for her to sit down.

"I'm sorry I wasn't here when you got back. I went to the tavern to meet Tymin. He said your sister and Grenta was here until two duras ago."

"I know. We learned that as well." She uncovered several dishes and smiled as the wonderful aromas filled her nose.

"How?"

"The wife of the innkeeper said they were here a few duras ago and are heading to Rainbow City." She filled a plate and offered it to him.

"Tymin said the same thing." He took the plate as he sat next to her on the bed. "We could catch up to them before they reach the city if we leave first thing nesdura."

She nodded as she took a bite of food.

"Did you talk to the others?"

"I think we were all thinking the same thing. We exchanged looks, but we didn't say anything to each other."

"And you feel this nonverbal exchange is all you need to do to know what they're thinking?"

"I do." She smiled and pointed to words floating in the air.

Grinnell read the words out loud. "'Are we leaving first thing? We know we should.' Tosci sent this?"

"What do you think?"

"I should know better than to question my bond-mate. You might as well answer them."

"And what should I say?"

"Yes. We will leave after we break our fast."

The next dura they met in the common area, their items packed and ready to go. Grinnell had a hearty meal ready for them, plus a basket packed for them to eat later.

"Are you trying to make us fat?" asked Tosci. "I have never had so much food."

"We could travel horas before we can stop to eat. I want to be sure you ladies don't feel faint or get sick from traveling too far without a full stomach. Eat as much as you can. You need to be as strong as you can be to travel todura."

"Why?"

"Because I know a shortcut through the mountains nearby." Grinnell sat back in his chair. "We don't need to climb the larger mountains, just the foothills, but we still might have places where we might have to lead our animals instead of riding them."

"And you're not sure if we'll find a place to rest and eat while we're on the trail through them," said Lawaya.

He nodded.

"We will do our best to eat our fill," said Lawaya as she took more food. "But if I heave this all back up, you must hold my hair."

"Don't eat so much it makes you feel ill, but make sure you fill yourself enough to face the dura." Grinnell filled his plate a second time. "Pretend you're going to be working in your garden all dura and don't have time to stop for a meal."

The breads, fruits, and sweets that were leftover were loaded into a satchel they could nibble from as they moved. Once they loaded their animals, they headed off. Tymin met them at the city's limit.

The beginning of their trip was easy. The ladies chatted amongst themselves as they headed to the mountains. Tymin went ahead to scout out the path Grinnell wanted to take. He came back when they were halfway there.

"Path still there."

"Did you see any evidence of Varal? I don't want to find one of his minefields while we're using that path."

"It not used in several yepas. It safe."

"I hope so. I don't want anything to happen to these ladies."

CHAPTER FOURTEEN

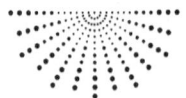

They followed the path for several horas. Tymin was first, while Grinnell pulled up the rear. He was making sure everyone was cautious. As they went around one turn on their way down, Grinnell called a halt to their climb.

"Tymin, is that what I think it is?" The mark was obscured by vines, but he recognized enough of it.

Tymin went up to it and pulled the vines down. There, clear as dura, was Varal's crest.

"Damn. I was hoping we wouldn't see anything like that." Grinnell got off his truggar and went through a few satchels strapped to its side. "Tymin, do you know how to use the scanner?"

"No, but this?" Tymin held up a small contraption Grinnell had exposed while looking for the scanner. "Yes."

"You sure?"

Tymin nodded as he assembled the machine. It was designed to detonate any mine they might find without anyone being harmed.

Grinnell handed the lead to his truggar to Mehanna, and he and Tymin led the group on foot. Grinnell used the scanner to find any mine that might be on their path. He had wanted to give them a shortcut but having to move as slowly as they had to would remove any horas they might have saved.

Whenever Grinnell found something, Tymin was on it. They were making better time than Grinnell expected. They cleared the area where the mark was, and as they continued up the path, they didn't run into anymore. They crested the foothills and started down. Grinnell found a few more, but Tymin made short work of them. They cleared the hills ahead of schedule.

"That didn't quite work out the way you wanted, did it?" asked Mehanna as she climbed off her truggar.

"No, but we didn't lose as much time as I feared." He tethered her truggar with his.

"I was afraid you'd ask us to eat and ride." Tosci rubbed her butt. "My tushy thanks you."

"We all need a break." He pulled the basket off of the animal they had to carry their cargo and set it on the ground. "I can pull out a blanket if you wish to sit while you eat, but I have a feeling you would rather stand."

"Yes, please," said all three at the same time. They grinned at each other.

He chuckled as he pulled out fruits, cheeses, and bread. Grinnell put a little of each item on a plate and handed one to everyone.

They ate quietly. Mehanna created a small, tall table for her to rest her plate on. As she picked up a piece of cheese, a multi-petaled flower appeared next to her plate. She picked it up and looked at Grinnell. The smile she gave him made it all worthwhile.

"I'm happy to see you two are still training."

Grinnell came to her side and slipped an arm around her. "We do try."

They finished eating and wandered down the path a little.

"Sorry about Tosci's comment," Mehanna said softly after she hoped they were out of earshot.

"She cares."

"I know, but she's also extremely hyper-focused, and at times that can be annoying." She looked around at the great expanse of land. "This is amazing."

"I haven't heard you complain too much when I become hyper-focused," he murmured. He smiled when her cheeks turned a pretty shade of lavender. "In fact, I'm pretty sure you enjoyed it."

"Oh, I did, but that is a little different." She pressed her hands against her cheeks. "We're talking about something both of us enjoyed, whereas Tosci is making sure we are constantly working, perfecting the magic we have access to."

"And we should." Grinnell took her by the hand and pulled her close. "We have to face someone who has had yepas to master what we've been working on for a few cycles. Anyone else would think this whole thing is crazy."

She looked up at him. "We will defeat him."

"I like your attitude."

"I hope so, because you are going to be living with it for the rest of your life."

He pressed a kiss to her cheek, but she wanted more than that. She slipped her hand around his neck and pulled him down. She tilted her head up, offering her lips to him. Grinnell claimed them, drawing a sigh out of her. He wrapped his arms around her. When she opened her mouth for him, he deepened the kiss. His grip on her tightened.

"I'm happy to see you two are true bonds mates, but you do have company," said Tosci as she drew close. "Do you want an audience?"

That broke them apart.

"Not particularly, but we do have the right to show affection for each other," Mehanna defended.

"You do. I just want to be sure that it's not going to lead into something that should be private."

"Do you think we lack control?" asked Mehanna, whose voice showed she was getting angry. "That we would throw caution to the wind to satisfy ourselves? Do you think so little of us?"

"Mehanna, it's okay," said Grinnell.

"No, it's not. Tosci has been against our mating from the beginning."

"Not true, Mehanna, but my job is to make sure you're focused on the right things. My brother will not care if you two are in love. He will try to take what he wants."

"And you try to anger us because you fear the way we care for each other will be our downfall?" Mehanna jammed her hands on her hips. "How do you know it won't be our strength?"

"I don't, that is something you need to figure out. And you need to do this before you face my brother."

They rode along with Tymin in the lead. Grinnell and Mehanna hung back a little.

"She's right, you know. Moorac will try to use our relationship against us. He could try to drive a wedge between us by telling you that I don't love you and I only want your power."

"We both know that's not true." She pulled on the reins of her truggar to move it a little closer to Grinnell's. "You fought me on bonding because you didn't want me to make a mistake."

"And I'm sure he has a way of swaying you. He could paint a really ugly picture if he wants to. I can think of several. Like he might say that I acted like I didn't want to bond so you would force me."

She looked at him.

"He could also say I drugged you to get what I wanted."

"Drugged me? With what? Kisses?"

"I must say your kisses are quite intoxicating for me." Grinnell smiled as he looked at her. "So is that beautiful body. It's a drug that I'm addicted to."

Mehanna couldn't help but smile and was quiet for a moment. "I feel the same way."

"We need to come up with something that will help us stay grounded. Keep our trust and love for each other pure."

"What do you suggest?" asked Mehanna.

"We are closest when we make love, but I don't think that will work while facing Moorac. But we can touch."

"How about holding hands?" She held out her hand to him, which he took. "This would be something we could do without much thought."

"We do hold hands all the time."

"And we can build our defenses around it."

He squeezed her fingers. "Then let's start."

They ended up having to camp for the duro. The sky darkened as they ate. Once finished, they set up tents for them to use. Grinnell built a large fire. After they ate, they all sat around the fire talking.

"I hope you understand that I only have your best interests at heart," said Tosci.

"I do." She put her hand out for Grinnell to take. "It's made us realize we need to be a united front against Moorac so he can't use what we have together against us."

"He will try." Tosci picked up a rock from the dirt and hefted it in her hand. "My brother was very good at manipulating you two girls. He always pitted the two of you against each other."

"No. I love my sister."

"I know you do, and you probably don't remember how he would make you two reach the same goals to see which one could do it faster. Knowing my brother, he altered your mind so you wouldn't realize what he was doing."

"What else has he done to us?"

"He kept you two apart as much as he could."

"No." Mehanna shook her head. "I remember playing with my sister."

"Something he planted in your head."

Mehanna shook her head, not wanting to believe her. "No, that can't be true."

"You only remember what he wanted you to remember." Tosci rolled the rock in her hand. "What I worry about is what else he might have put in your head when he planted those memories."

"Then I need to meditate to see what he has done to me and my sister."

"Do you think you can find anything he has left behind?" asked Grinnell.

She looked up into his eyes. "I have to."

Grinnell sat on the bed in their tent. Mehanna sat beside him. "Do you want me to leave so you can focus?"

"As long as you keep your hands to yourself, you can stay."

"I can't promise that."

"Then maybe you should go out and make sure everyone has settled down properly. This shouldn't take long."

He gave her a quick kiss and headed out.

She closed her eyes and worked on her breathing. Her focus went inward. Memories of her sister were a good place to start, but how could she figure out if Moorac tampered with her memories? She started with one that Moorac was in. The dinners where he would bring male guests should be a good place.

A memory floated to the surface.

Mehanna and May sat beside each other, opposite the man Moorac had invited over. He didn't pay a whole lot of attention to them, giving the girls a few rare moments together.

May set something on her leg. Mehanna slipped it into her pocket. They knew not to bring attention to themselves. Moorac might seem to be focused on his guest, but they knew he was always watching them.

This had to be a real memory.

So, what was a fake one?

She went back to the one where she and May were playing. As she examined it, there was something odd about it. The laughter sounded hollow. The image was unfocused. Like a dream. She took the memory and broke it down. Mehanna looked for hints of Moorac. At first, she didn't see anything.

Then another memory floated up.

"Shh. He can't know," said May in a young voice.

She couldn't see and bumped her head against a low beam. "I can't help it," she whispered. "This crawl space is smaller than me."

May giggled. "Then use your magic."

Mehanna shook her head. "That he will definitely detect. I'll suffer through to spend time with you."

BARBARA DONLON BRADLEY

"We were together nodura."

"No, we weren't," corrected Mehanna. "It was the dura before."

"No, we weren't."

They looked at each other.

"Moorac."

"What can we do?" asked May.

"We need to protect ourselves." Mehanna took her sister's hand. "He might be powerful, but together we are stronger."

Grinnell sat near the fire, listening to it snap and pop. He wanted to go back into the tent, but he didn't want to interfere with Mehanna's work. The door to their shelter opened and Mehanna stepped out.

"How did it go?" he asked as he stood up.

"There will be no trouble from buried commands made by Moorac." She offered her hand to him. "Now come to bed."

She didn't have to tell him twice.

They reached the inn early the next dura. They checked in and deposited their belongings, then went out to explore the city.

"I see why it's called the Rainbow City. Mehanna looked around. "This is beautiful."

Grinnell grinned. The silver material used on the buildings shimmered in the sunlight, revealing hundreds of colors as the rays danced across his skin. "At duro, they use spotlights to cause the same effect."

"Can we explore a little before we meet up with our family?"

"I don't see why not. We all wanted to have a few horas to ourselves before we meet to have our meal." He brushed his fingers along her cheek. "Where would you like to start?"

"Um, I'm not sure."

"Then let me show you something I have always made time for when I come here."

"Then you've been here before."

"This is where my apartment is," he said quietly.

She looked at him. "You live here?"

"When I'm not working at the palace, I have been known to stay at my apartment, but that is extremely rare." He slipped an arm around her waist. "I seem to stay at the palace most of the time. But there is a park nearby that I think you might like."

"Is your apartment near?" Mehanna looked around at the different buildings, trying to figure out which one held it.

"Oh, I see I piqued your curiosity." He gave her waist a playful squeeze.

"A little." She smiled up at him, placing a hand on his chest. "I mean, I have never seen a real apartment."

"Ah." He smiled down at her. "And you want to see what all the fuss is about. Or do you want to mark your territory? Make sure wherever I turn, I see you. I hate to disappoint you, but I see you everywhere I look now. Can't see my life without you."

His words affected her. She rested her head against his chest.

"You okay?"

She looked up at him with tear-filled eyes. "You make my heart sing."

He captured her lips with his. The salt from her tears mingled with the sweetness of her mouth. She sighed when he released her.

"You make my heart sing too." He touched her face, then took her hand. "Come on. You're going to love the park."

He led her past several buildings. They turned a corner, and he stopped and pointed.

The park wasn't the average patch of flowers and trees. The small area had pieces of the material in the buildings arranged in different shapes throughout the space. All different shapes and sizes jutted up to the sky. Colors danced in the air as sunlight moved across the surface of the pieces.

"How beautiful."

"Wait." Grinnell touched a few of the shapes, and a musical sound filled the air. It didn't take long before he was creating a melody.

"I'm amazed this place isn't crowded." Mehanna touched a few and smiled when she heard some of the same notes Grinnell had created.

"There are many throughout the city. I just know this one the best because my apartment is in that building." He pointed to one nearby.

"And I get to see it?" she asked.

"Of course." He took her hand and led the way. They entered the door and then climbed into the elevator. The car moved quickly to his floor then opened and allowed them to exit. His apartment was down the hall on the left. When he opened the door to his corner apartment, he stepped back and let her enter first.

Mehanna walked around, touching items here and there. She looked up at him. "This could be anyone's apartment."

"I know. It came with the job, but like I said, I spend more time at the palace than here." He went to the window and gestured. "There's the park we were in."

She stepped up beside him. Colors filled the air. "It's just as pretty up here."

"You should see it as the sun sets. Each of these parks lights up."

"That must be very pretty."

"It is, but not as pretty as you." He took her in his arms. "We still have time."

"We do, don't we?" She smiled up at him. "Would you like to show me your bedroom?"

"I'd love to." He scooped her up in his arms and carried her to the large bed in an adjoining room. "Perhaps when this is all over, you can help me make this place look lived in."

"Or perhaps we can get a new place that we both pick out to create memories in?"

"That sounds good too." He helped her out of her clothing as she helped him out of his. They fell on the bed together. "But right now, I'd like to make a few memories right here."

"Since I'm the one marking my territory, do I get to be in control?" She climbed up on top.

"Whatever you wish." He looked up at her. "Consider this your fantasy."

"Fantasy?" She smiled. "I can work with that."

With the wave of her hand, she changed the scenery around them.

The walls were replaced with bright colored canvas. The bed became a sea of pillows. Although she was still naked, she wore gold bangles on her wrists and upper arms. Around her waist was a thin gold chain.

"Where did you get this from?" He touched the bangles on her arm.

"One of the stories. The romances are my favorite, and I thought this would be fun."

"Douinar tents? Are you thinking that you're my slave?"

"Or you're mine." She gave him a sexy smile.

"Really?" He grinned up at her as he cupped her breasts. "Oh, my great queen, what do you wish from me?"

"Right now? I need you to make love to me. Let me feel you inside me."

"And later?"

"Well, it depends on how good a job you do."

"Good a job?" he wrapped his arms around her and flipped them over. "Have I ever displeased you, my queen?"

"Hm, let me think." She tapped her chin.

He started tickling her, causing her to laugh hard. "Tell me when I have displeased you, my queen. I've seen that smile of yours that says you love your life."

"I do, and I love you in it."

The tickling turned into petting. "Shall I make you see stars again? I know just the thing."

"Yes, please," she sighed.

Grinnell kissed her mouth, her cheek, her throat. He moved down to her collarbone and then a breast. He paid homage to one, then the other, drawing more sighs out of her. His tongue dipped into her belly button for a moment before he worked his way further down her body.

"You taste so good." He pressed a kiss against her pelvic bone, then moved to her core. "Open for me."

She shifted her legs so he could have full access, and she cried out when he latched onto her.

Grinnell lifted his head. "Did I hurt you?"

"No," her words were soft. "I guess I was anticipating it so much, I think I made myself hypersensitive."

"Then you're going to be in trouble, because I'm just getting started." He went back to paying homage to her body. Bringing her to heights only he could bring her to. There were signs he looked for. First, she needed to start moving, like she wanted something, or was reaching for something just out of her grasp. He pressed a kiss against her thigh when her legs shifted.

CHAPTER FIFTEEN

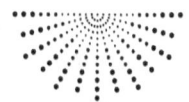

Mehanna had wanted a fantasy, and Grinnell gave her one. Her body wanted to explode, but he only brought her to the brink then allowed her to step back. It was driving her crazy. She wanted her release, and he wasn't giving it to her.

Her legs started moving. She felt him kiss her thigh before he started to move back up her body, planting more kisses along the way. If he didn't enter her soon, she was going to scream. As if he read her mind, he climbed until they were face to face. He touched her cheek softly.

"Ready?"

All she could do was nod. He drove into her, making her arch her back and suck in her breath. That was all it took to send her over the edge. Wonderful waves of euphoria filled her. She tightened her grip on him as she floated along.

Grinnell gave her a few moments before he started moving inside her. Each time he filled her he pushed her closer to that elusive orgasm once again. He set a strong tempo that she met stroke for stroke. Her body shook as delicious tendrils of her climax teased her.

"Please, Grinnell."

"Are we begging, my queen?"

"If it gets me what I want? Yes!"

He pressed a kiss against her throat. He picked up his tempo, causing her to do the same. They raced each other to reach the release they both wanted. Grinnell moved faster and faster, and Mehanna kept up with him. Her body hummed as he filled her again and again, but she wanted more. Her hands gripped him, trying to pull him in as close as she could.

Her body reacted each time he filled her. It wasn't long before she became a mass of feelings. Nothing mattered but the orgasm she wanted so badly.

Grinnell was now pumping into her, and she could only cling to him as he moved. Her body screamed for its release. She moved with him. Desire filled her. She wanted something only Grinnell had given her, and she knew she didn't want it from anyone else. Slowly, the fission of her release started to snake through her body. Little tendrils of her orgasm licked at her. Need filled her. Her body tightened; her muscles clenched. Securs later, her release flung her out to the stars. She floated along, every part of her totally relaxed.

"Have I satisfied you, my queen?"

"Very much." She stretched as she answered, her whole being happy. Something inside her shifted. She felt it but wasn't sure what it meant.

Grinnell pressed kisses against her cheeks, temples, and throat. He had experienced something just as profound as she did.

"That was wonderful," she said it softly, but she knew Grinnell heard her.

"My queen deserves only the best. I hope you feel that is what I gave you."

"Oh, I do." She kept her eyes closed. "I wish we could do that again."

"I agree, but we promised to meet everyone for the middura meal." He pressed a kiss against her stomach then offered her his hand.

"Perhaps we could come back after we eat." She sat up with his help.

"I sure would like to try."

They met their friends in the lobby of the inn they were staying in about an hora later. Once everyone was seated, Grinnell asked them what they did for the few horas they had to themselves.

"Honestly, we fell asleep," said Lawaya. "I guess we're not use to climbing mountains."

"Didn't you sleep well last duro?" asked Mehanna. She nodded at the waitress as she placed a glass of water in front of her.

"I thought I did, but it didn't stop me from snoozing away when we stopped in our room for a secur," said Tosci. "What did you two do? You look very rested."

"I agree," said Lawaya. "To me they look satisfied and rested."

The two ladies watched them, waiting for some sort of reaction.

Grinnell looked over at Mehanna, who had a lovely shade of lavender blooming on her cheeks, but she looked back at them without flinching. He took her hand, then smiled at the ladies. "We had a wonderful time."

"You must see a park like the one Grinnell showed me."

Grinnell looked at the door when a familiar odor assailed his nose. Tymin stood in front of it, shifting his feet. Grinnell excused himself and headed to the door.

"They're here." He pointed toward the center of the city.

He had already found May? That was fast. "Where?"

"Come, I'll show." He led him away from the restaurant. They went down a back street, then to one of the parks. May sat on a bench, watching the colors fill the air.

"Pretty, isn't it?" Grinnell asked as he sat beside her.

"Grinnell!" she shrieked as she hugged him. "You don't know how happy I am to see you. We were warned to stay away from the palace so have been wandering around aimlessly. Are you here to tell us that we can go back now?"

"We did come to find you."

"We?" She let him go and looked at him. "Is my sister here too?"

"Yes, she's at a restaurant nearby."

"Then let's go." She jumped up and called to Grenta. Once she got her attention, she pointed to Grinnell. "Look who just showed up."

"Grinnell, good to see you." Grenta also looked relieved. It was probably hard for her to keep up with May.

"My sister is here, and Grinnell is going to bring us to her." She turned and looked at him. "Right? Or are we to go straight to the palace?"

181

"We're going to the restaurant." He gestured for them to follow him. He walked beside Grenta. "You've had your hands full, haven't you, Grenta?"

"Oh, my. Yes." She fell into step with him as May walked in front of them. "She is a very curious person, so has to know everything she can about whatever catches her attention."

"I have learned a lot." May trotted back to where they walked. "I watched and learned how to create the glass used in this city. I have learned to make the metal in the structures here. Oh, and I can make a wonderful fromage pie."

"Have you been practicing?"

"Every dura." She skipped ahead and spoke to a woman selling flowers. When they caught up with her, she had a bouquet in her hand.

"The restaurant is there." Grinnell pointed but found he didn't need to when Mehanna came racing out of the restaurant.

"May!" She ran to her sister and wrapped her arms around her. May squealed her name and did the same. The two women hugged until Grinnell reminded them that they were in the middle of the street, drawing attention. Everyone entered the restaurant.

"Lawaya!" Grenta bowed to her. "I'm so glad to see you out of the mirror."

"Let's sit," said Grinnell. "We're drawing far too much attention."

The wait staff brought two more chairs to the table. May sat between Mehanna and Lawaya while Grenta sat between Lawaya and Tosci.

May continued to chatter, telling her sister all she saw and learned while water was placed in front of her. She glanced over at Tosci and paused. "I know you."

"Yes, you do."

"You're Tosci. Moorac's sister. You were with us when we were younger."

"She's been training me," said Mehanna.

The waitress brought two more menus for the new guests, then gave them a few microns to decide. While there was a lull in the conversation, she came back. She took their orders, promising to bring their food as quickly as possible.

"You know he's here, don't you?" asked May.

"Yes," replied Mehanna. "How were you able to get out of the palace undetected? I have felt him searching for me since we arrived."

"I decided to travel a dura or two after you and Grinnell took off for our home planet. I can assume you didn't make it there?" May responded.

Mehanna shook her head.

"Well, it was maybe a dura or two later when we received the missive not to come back until either we got another missive to come to back or until someone came to get us." May smiled. "I'm assuming you are here to bring us home."

Grinnell got ready to answer her, but May continued to talk.

"How long have you been here, anyway?"

"We arrived on Emori about five duras ago," said Mehanna. "Where are you staying?"

"The hotel near one of the parks." The food started to arrive, but May still continued to talk as she ate. "Have you seen any of the parks? They are so beautiful."

"I love all the colors." Mehanna responded between bites.

"Oh good." May took a drink. "I had hoped you had seen one." She took a bite, then pointed her fork at Grinnell. "Do we need to head back right away?"

"We don't have a deadline, but I don't like leaving Orla and Astrid alone with that man." He took a bite. Once he swallowed it, he asked, "Was there somewhere you wanted to go?"

"The local museum. There is a wing on the royal family that I'd like to see." She gave him a bright smile.

"I don't see why not. Do you want to move your rooms to the hotel we're staying at?"

"Um, I sort of picked that hotel for a reason. The people here say the lights at sunset and sunrise are spectacular and the best place to see them is in our hotel."

Grinnell laughed.

"What?"

"I'm sure whoever told you that probably worked in that hotel." He finished his meal. "The colors can be seen from all over the city during those times."

"How do you know that?" May took another bite of her food.

"Grinnell is from here, May," said Mehanna.

"Oh." May took another bite. "Is that how you were able to get a table here? I didn't even realize that this was a restaurant."

"There are a few that don't advertise so the locals have a place to go, but it's not like they'd turn away anyone who was visiting. The proprietor is a friend, and I knew he would keep my presence quiet."

"Quiet?" She looked at her sister. "I don't understand."

"He is well known here on Emori, so we had to pretend we're other people."

"Oh, what fun!" May clapped her hands together.

"Keep your voice down," reminded Grenta.

"Sorry." She ate her last bite. "I forget how loud I get when I get excited."

"It's okay. If everyone is done, we can head to the museum." Grinnell signaled their waiter. "I'd be interested in what they have there."

"What if you're recognized?" asked Mehanna.

"This is where I live. Most who see me don't pay any attention to me because they know I don't want that kind of attention. They know what I did to protect Orla and Astrid, and they honor my wishes. We used other names because we didn't want my presence known before we found May. If Moorac got wind I was on the planet but not at the palace, he would become suspicious. Since May's now with us, I don't think it will cause a problem. We can even take public transport."

"Let's do our best to keep his true identity quiet," said Grenta as she stood up. "I'm enjoying traveling the old fashion way."

"You just don't like using modern transports," reminded Grinnell. He waited for everyone to stand and they headed out the door.

They headed to the museum with other groups of tourists and waited for their guide so they could start their tour.

"We get a tour guide?" asked May.

"All part of the package," said Grinnell.

Their guide stepped up to them and smiled. "Welcome to our museum. I'm here to help you navigate the place properly and to answer any question you might have."

Mehanna saw the look of recognition when their guide noticed her bond-mate. She took Grinnell's hand when she realized all it would take was this man saying something to ruin their trip.

May grabbed Mehanna's hand the moment she had a chance and pulled her back so they would be last in the group.

"What is going on between you and Grinnell?" May asked quietly.

"Why?" asked Mehanna.

"It's the way you two behave around each other. There's something there, like you. . . you bonded with him?"

Mehanna nodded.

"Oh, my stars. I knew you were attracted to each other, but I never thought you'd bond this fast." She squeezed her sister's hand. "Are you happy?"

"Very much."

"And him?"

"Has been wonderful. I didn't go into this blind, May. He fought me because he was afraid I only wanted to bond with him to beat Moorac. I wanted to bond because it just felt right, and it took a lot to convince him of that."

"I'm so happy for you." She gave her a one-armed hug. "Has he learned to tap into your power?"

Mehanna nodded.

"Should I use the family technique to bond with him too? Give him access to my power as well?"

"That is up to you, May." Mehanna looked at her. "I can't make that decision for you."

Grinnell walked with the guide, Narfa. He had been heavily involved with the creation of this wing, and the guide was the curator he worked with. Since he was the one picked as his guide, the museum must have recognized him and wanted him to feel comfortable while visiting. This was the first time he had been back since the wing opened.

"Sir, do your friends know?" asked Narfa.

"They do, but we'd like to see the exhibit without a bunch of strangers recognizing me." He paused for a moment. "I thank you for helping keep my presence quiet. I know another guide would have reacted when they realized who I was."

"I remember how you tried to avoid anyone who recognized you when we worked together. You weren't a big fan of people fawning over you, and I assumed you didn't want a spectacle with your friends around you."

"And I'd like to keep my presence from the palace as well. My guests are friends of the queen and are a surprise. The smallest lady doesn't like using the transports, so we will be traveling the old-fashioned way. I'd hate to have someone leak that they saw us before we can surprise our queen."

"Of course, sir." He gave him a slight bow. One of the other guides stepped out to where he could see them holding a pile of clothing.

"Ladies and gentleman, we need to put these on." He handed each person a long cloak.

They each took the cloak handed to them and put it on.

"We will be going through interactive sections where you will see and feel major events that impacted the planet. These cloaks will protect you from the environments you will pass through. I hope you enjoy this segment of your tour."

They saw the creation of the planet, how it became terraformed, and when life first began. Next came the ancient animals and plant life. This was when they needed the cloaks; rain fell constantly, and they had to walk through muddy terrain, tall plants, and deep forests. Then technology started to show up as they saw the beginnings of towns develop. Old tools became more modern, and the creation of engines moved things faster.

"Everything will move so much faster now. It can cause a little disorientation, so if you have a weak stomach I recommend we move on."

"I think we'll be fine," said Grinnell when no one said anything.

Once they caught up with technology, they were brought into another section where art hung. Portraits, scenes, still life paintings filled the walls. They showed history, moments in time. Some were beautiful, others were scary. Any other tour groups they happened to run into were cloaked like they were.

Grinnell was happy when no one paid attention to who wore the cloaks. He didn't want any unwanted attention and each time they came across another tour group, he worried.

Narfa brought them into the next wing, which had the history of the royal family.

"The royal family has been in power for hundreds of yepas. After the fourth world war, the people of Emori were tired of the fighting because the different governments didn't see eye to eye. These wars had destroyed major cities as well as farms and factories. People had no money, no food, and no shelter."

"That's awful," whispered Mehanna.

"War does that. They fought in the fields, destroying crops. They took animals for carrying gear and to feed the soldiers because their supplies had run out. If there were any crops, the governing bodies took those as well to feed their soldiers," Grinnell told her.

"Very true," said the guide. "They took metal and tech to make bullets and weapons from whatever they could get their hands on to continue to fight their enemy. The war didn't end because they signed a treaty. The war ended when both sides ran out of ammo. It was okay when they were pushing buttons to kill their adversaries, but then they had to do it face to face the soldiers realized they didn't want to have anything to do with fighting hand to hand. Records don't show how the war actually stopped. All we know is that they dropped their makeshift weapons and demanded that the elder of each town and village remaining go to a predetermined central location." He turned to a screen that lit up. "The people decided on the area where the palace now sits. It was one of the larger villages and a central location for most people to travel to.

"Before any of the elders were tested, rules were set. The goal was to find the one person who was a true elder. The one who could lead all."

"The true elder?" asked Lawaya. "How did they know they weren't lying?"

"That is a good question. They devised a series of tests. Mind games, really. Each elder had to go through them. Those that passed the first group had to go through more. The tests got harder, more intricate.

Slowly but surely, they thinned the group down to five. These elders were the best. They didn't care about what they could get for themselves. They had to want the best for the planet. Each test was designed so there were only two choices: themselves or the people on the planet. Those tests continued until only one person remained. She was the elder from a village close to here. She became our first queen."

"Um, I understand why they chose her, but how could they possibly believe that attitude would travel through the generations?" asked Tosci.

"Because anyone who wanted to marry our queen or king had to go through the same tests. In the beginning, they had to go through the test to court the queen. As the generations came and went, it became ingrained in the royal family. They became empathic in a way. They never married anyone who didn't fit this category. They seemed to know what they needed in the royal family, and they maintained the rule of "planet first.""

"It didn't work for us too well when Varal came, because he was able to trick the royal family in the beginning," commented Grinnell. "You would think the family would have seen right through him, but he had done his research before coming to Emori. He was good."

"Too good," said the guide. "He chose the perfect time to come here. Right after the queen had died. He was sympathetic and offered to help while the king mourned. It gave him the perfect chance to take control. Once Varal was defeated, our people researched the death of our queen, and it was confirmed that he was involved."

"Once he felt no one would question him, he killed our king," said Grinnell. "His goal was to leave Astrid alone and grieving. He wanted her as his bride so his progeny would have royal blood in their veins. What he didn't know, at least not at the beginning, was that the princess had already been betrothed."

"I thought Orla grew up with her," said Mehanna softly.

"He did, but that's not common knowledge," whispered Grinnell. "Most don't know he is Miran."

"Really?" Mehanna looked up at him. "How do they plan on explaining it when her firstborn turns out to be Miran?"

"That is a question for Orla and Astrid." He smiled down at her and squeezed her hand.

She nodded.

The guide continued to talk about the royal family as they saw three-dimensional images of Astrid as a child with her parents. She always stood with her pet; its tail wrapped around her waist. As the story went on, they watched her age into the beautiful woman they now knew.

Grinnell cringed when his three-dimensional image showed up. It was the only professional picture of him. He allowed the museum to use it, but there were no other copies. One of his stipulations. He looked younger, and thinner, but that was when he and Leabo were constantly fighting for their lives. Everything had been recreated according to his specs, but this was the first time he had seen the exhibit as a patron. It was a bit disconcerting.

A soft laugh escaped Mehanna.

"Not funny," he whispered in her ear.

"You hate this."

"It's just the first time I've seen it."

"It shows me a different side of you." She slid her arm around his waist. "The one who would do anything for those you care about."

"I care about you." He pressed his lips to hers.

"You better." She looped her arms around his neck. "Because I care about you. Very much."

"That makes me happy."

"You two want to focus on the exhibit? Or should we get you a room?" asked May.

Mehanna blushed, but Grinnell put an arm around her and stared May down. "We have a room. Are we free to go to it?"

"Stop," Mehanna said. She took her sister's hand as well as Grinnell's. "Let's finish the tour, then you two can squabble."

"Squabble?" May acted shocked. "We're having a healthy conversation."

Mehanna laughed as she tugged on her hand. They caught up with Lawaya and Grenta and fell into step with them as the tour continued. There wasn't much more to cover, just how the government was now run by the people and Astrid was their queen in name only. She was more their ambassador when visitors came to visit and when she visited other planets.

189

"That is such a good story," said Grenta as they left the museum. She loosened the tie of her cloak. "You did a great job getting the information right."

"Thank you," said Grinnell. He made sure his hood still shielded his face. "I worked hard to get it right. I drove Narfa crazy."

"Our guide? He was the one you worked with?"

"Yeah." Grinnell smiled. "I think he recognized me when we came in and took over our tour. I explained that we were traveling by animal and wanted to surprise Astrid." He touched the cloak he still wore. Other patrons had to turn in their cloaks when they finished the tour, but their group didn't. "I think he did a good job."

They headed toward the center of the city.

"Tymin will be waiting by the animals," said Grinnell. "Would you like to have our endura meal in town, or do you want me to have it packed and we can eat it later?"

"I think we should take it with us," said Mehanna. "We should get going, and the sooner we get you away from here, the better."

The rest agreed.

———

They rode for a few horas before they stopped to eat.

"I have a question for you, Grinnell," said May.

"Sure."

"I want to bond with you."

"What?" He looked at Mehanna. "I'm already bonded to your sister."

"This isn't the same kind of bond. Ours would be something family members have, but it would give you access to my power as well."

"Do I need that?" He looked at Tosci.

"It wouldn't hurt," said Tosci. "My brother will try to separate you two. He'll figure out there is something between you, even if he doesn't think you've bonded right away. Having access to May's magic as well will make him wonder if you really do have power."

"Mehanna?" He wanted to be sure she was okay with it.

She looked at him and smiled.

"May spoke to you before she suggested this, didn't she?" he asked.

"She did. I told her it was her decision. If you want to know if I'm okay with it, I am. May and I did this bond when we were children, and it's still strong. I think that was how May became aware of me on the planet. Our bond activated."

"Why weren't you aware of May, then?" asked Lawaya.

"I think it's because of the way Moorac wiped my memories. I must have buried mine very deep so he couldn't detect it."

"It won't supersede the bond you have with Mehanna, it will complement it," added May. "Most of the time you'll pull from her power, but if you need more, you'd be able to pull from mine as well. If you were cut off from her, you'd be able to use mine to break through any magic that is blocking you."

"When you put it that way, it makes sense that I bond with you too. We don't know what Moorac will do and we need to be prepared for anything." He looked at May. "What do I need to do?"

CHAPTER SIXTEEN

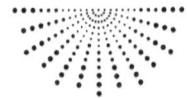

They waited until they stopped to camp for the duro. Once they had their sleeping areas set up and they had eaten, Tosci had Grinnell and May stand.

"This is rather simple to do." She took Grinnell's hand as well as May's. "This is a little different than the way you and your sister joined your powers. First, you need to hold hands."

Grinnell took her hand. Tosci then lifted their hands so they rested in hers. "May, repeat after me: We are family, we are joined. I share my powers with you."

Once May repeated the words, she looked at Grinnell. "Your turn. We are family."

Grinnell hesitated for a moment before he repeated the words. He also added, "You're my sister now."

"We are joined," said May. "I accept your desire to use my powers and promise to harm none."

Grinnell repeated his version of the words then added a little more again. "I promise to harm none unless they are trying to harm us. I will protect you and your sister at all costs."

Tosci murmured something over their hands before she let go.

"I'm assuming I need to learn how to draw power from her too?"

"Yes. Her power is going to be different from Mehanna's, so you need to see what works the best for you," said Tosci. "But since you have been through this once before, you should be able to do this quicker than with Mehanna."

"Now?" He knew the answer before she spoke.

"Whenever you're ready."

He nodded. The sky was darkening, but the fire they had going would light the area for them.

"You're probably drawing your power from my sister's heart because she's bonded with you," said May. "You will find you'll draw power from another part of my body. If I were to draw power from Mehanna, I'd draw from her stomach."

"You can also try drawing from her mind," said Tosci.

"Okay." He hoped the learning curve would be easier with May's power. How would he pick a spot to draw from, though?

Tosci maneuvered Mehanna away from where May, and Grinnell stood so he couldn't access her power. "Now try."

He cleared his mind as he had been taught and searched the area for the tingle he felt when he was around Mehanna now. He could feel her power brush up against him when they were together. How would May's feel? Something brushed against him. It reminded him of Mehanna, but it was a little different. Like the scent that animals pick up. They know family from enemy by a sniff. Grinnell focused on the thing he felt brush against him. He molded it in his mind and thought about flowers. May's flowers. She had created one for her sister, why not create some for her?

Laughter caught his attention first. Then May twirling in a shower of flowers.

"You are quite good at this." She smiled as she held out her hands. Soft petals fell against her fingers.

"Wow. I was just thinking of flowers."

"You do need to make sure you think everything through when working with our power. If you don't tell it every aspect, it will fill in the blanks." May caught several flowers. "Like this, which is beautiful. What were you thinking when you created this?"

"I remembered how you created that flower for your sister. I always try to show my devotion by leaving a flower for her. You deserve flowers as well."

"Thank you." She pressed a kiss against his cheek. She went to her sister and hugged her. "He's a keeper. Mehanna. Don't forget that."

"I won't."

Mehanna and Grinnell sat in front of the fire. The rest of the ladies had headed to bed; Grinnell always waited until they settled down before he retired as well. His goal was to make sure the perimeter was secure each duro before he went to bed.

"What you did for my sister was wonderful." She spread her hands out to the fire. "The smile on her face as she twirled in the flowers filled me with joy."

"Really?" He held a stick that he used to stir the fire. "I was afraid you'd be a little jealous. I've never done that for you before."

"I know, but you have always given me all I ever wanted. My sister doesn't have someone like you in her life, and the fact that you recognized that is why I love you." She took his hand in hers. "What were you thinking when you created that?"

"Really close to what I said. I remembered how she created that one flower for you, and you were very touched by it. I thought she deserved that. I'm not sure how I made the flower showers, though. That was a bit of a surprise."

"That could be because of May. I've found her power to be as bubbly as she is." She was quiet for a secur. The fire snapped and popped in the silence. "Do you think the only way to defeat Moorac is to kill him?"

He had been wondering the same thing. "What makes you ask that?"

"The things you added to the bonding you did with May." She shifted so she could look at him. "I know you will keep us safe. Why did you add what you did?"

"The 'harm none' could have tied my hands if I hadn't said something." He brushed his fingers from his free hand against her cheek. "You know he won't blink if he has to hurt one of us to win. I don't plan on using magic to defeat him, but if he does stop my weapons from working, I want to be sure he won't harm you or your sister to get at me."

"I don't want him to harm any of our friends."

"Is there a way to protect them?" asked Grinnell. "Do we have some sort of forcefield we can build to keep them safe even if we're in trouble?"

"I've never tried anything like that, but May and I were able to keep Moorac from knowing we had shared our powers. That's why he couldn't tell which one of us was the most powerful. We kept pulling from each other."

"Is there a way to bind his power, maybe block him from harming anyone?"

"I'll need to ask Tosci. She knows the most about this."

"I understand." He placed his other hand on top of their joined ones. "Are you scared?"

"Very." She looked up at him. "I fear what he will do to us, to you. I remember when May and I were children, he could manipulate people into giving him things they never wanted to part with. He'd make promises to them only to go back on them when it suited him. We'd meet people who would anger him. He would send us to our rooms, and we'd never see those people again. Now I wonder if he killed them."

"You can't think about the what-ifs." Grinnell tightened his hold on her hand. "He will look for your weaknesses and use them against you. You need to be strong, even when you're scared. Trust yourself and your family. We will be there for you."

She rested her head against his shoulder. She wished she could go back to her cave where they first explored each other and their relationship. Having to face someone who had controlled her all her life had her second guessing everything.

"You know I will be at your side. If I could fight for you, I would, but you need to face this man and make him realize that he's not the strongest anymore. He needs to know you're the strongest now. You and your sister."

She sighed.

He pressed a kiss against her head. "I know. I'd rather go back to the cave too. Back to when everything was simple. But we can't run from this."

"I know. I just wish I could blink and make everything the way we want."

"Why can't you? You have the power."

She leaned back to look at him. Could it be that easy?

If they pushed themselves, they could reach the palace the following duro, but they decided to spend one more duro in the wilderness. Tosci thought it would be good for them to practice one more time.

Grinnell hated putting everything off for another dura, but he saw the logic in working the magic one more time before they had to face Moorac. The better he was at what he had to do, the quicker that man would go down. That was all that mattered.

"Focus!"

"I am," growled Grinnell. Tosci was working with him to use May's power, and she wanted him to restrict her movements. She looked like she was walking through water, but she could still move.

He had tried everything he could think of, including weighing her feet down, but nothing worked. Grinnell knew he was missing something. What the hell was it? Too bad he couldn't tie her up. She wouldn't move then.

"What did you do?"

"Why?" Grinnell hadn't been looking at Tosci until she spoke to him. She was frozen in mid-stride.

"I can't move." She grinned at him. "Whatever you were thinking worked."

"I wished I could tie you up."

She laughed.

"I see a pattern, Grinnell. You always think about the other person to get the power to work for you. When you face my brother, how are you going to use that to your advantage?"

"That is a good question." He had to think. "When I realized I could slow you but not stop you, I felt like I was missing something. I knew if I could tie you up you wouldn't move."

"Then that is how you need to approach everything."

"I'm not sure I understand."

"You're pragmatic. When you think of how you would do something without power, it works. You need to keep thinking that way. Don't try to use the power, allow the power to flow through you to do what you need."

"So, you're saying that's how I create the things I do for Mehanna? The flowers for May? I did it by thinking about what I'd do if I were to buy them or make them with my hands?"

"In a way, yes. You create from the heart. You don't do things to make your life better, but to make everyone else's life better. My only concern is that when you are pushed, will you be able to fight back, or will it keep you from being to access the power you'll need to fight Moorac?"

"I will keep my focus. Always have."

"Even if my brother pushes all the right buttons and makes you so angry you could do something foolish?"

"That's not going to happen."

"You keep saying that, but you don't explain why," said Tosci.

"But he did explain to me," defended Mehanna. "I trust him to do what needs to be done."

He took her hand in his. "I told you about what Varal did to me," he told Tosci. "Do you want me to go into all the gory details?"

"I don't think you need to, Grinnell." Mehanna looked at him. "You have worked hard to move past that, and I don't want you to drag up old bad memories just to appease someone's curiosity." She then turned to stare at Tosci.

"Point taken." She smiled at Mehanna's protective nature of her bond-mate. "I just need to be sure that my brother can't drive a wedge between you two, because I know he will try."

"We expect that as well and are prepared," Mehanna said.

"You don't need to protect me, darling," said Grinnell. "I know Tosci is just trying to make sure we have everything in our favor, and that's what we all want." He squeezed her hand. "Like I told you before, I was a soldier for Varal. When I learned he had killed my family, I deserted him and stole one of his best ships in the process. I worked as a merchant for a while until I met up with Orla and Astrid. I worked with them to bring down Varal.

"That man told me my family would be safe as long as I worked for him, but he lied to me. He took everything from me. I don't see how Moorac could do worse. Mehanna and I are taking every precaution to keep him from tearing us apart. Our bond is strong."

Tosci nodded. "I hope so."

They arrived at the palace early the next dura, entering through a rarely used entrance so they could get in undetected. Once he made sure the ladies were safely in their rooms, he headed to Orla's workroom. He didn't get out of the sleeping quarters before someone grabbed him by the arm and dragged him into a nearby room.

"You are being careless, my friend."

"Not really." He smiled at Orla. "I expected you to meet me around here. The others are in their rooms. I made sure no one saw us. What has been happening?"

"Moorac is still here," said Orla. "He would leave for a few horas here and there but always came back."

"Does he still believe I will help him find Mehanna?"

"Yes. I know he grows weary of waiting, but he has not made demands or shown his hand in any way."

"It will take me a few horas to get everything ready," said Grinnell. "I will come to the throne room like I have come back from a long trip. Please tell Astrid that anything I say is a ploy and to go along with it."

"I will. Be safe, and I'll see you in a few horas."

Grinnell slipped up to the roof of the palace and took one of the small transports back to the mountain retreat. Once he had his ship, he programmed it to use autopilot to come to the main palace hanger. He rested it in its normal spot, and he came out of the hanger bay like he had just come back from space. He waved to friends and headed to the throne room. He entered the way he always did. No need to raise suspicion.

Astrid spotted him first. It took her a few microns before she could get to her feet.

"Grinnell!" She opened her arms, and he came to give her a big hug.

"Astrid." He was amazed at how much her womb had grown while he was gone. "The baby has grown!"

"I know." She rubbed her stomach. "And it makes Orla act a little crazy at times."

"Not crazy, just a little worried when she tries to do something she shouldn't." Orla walked up to him and they clasped arms. "Like trying to push herself too hard practicing. I don't want her to accidentally hurt herself."

"I won't do that, my love, but I can't just sit around either." She walked to Orla's side. "I get bored, and you know what happens when I get bored."

"You come to my office and interrupt me." He pressed a kiss against her temple. "And you know I love having you around, and I can't wait until this little bundle of joy comes into our lives."

"Good answer," she laughed. She saw Moorac come in. "Grinnell, I'd like you to meet our guest, Moorac."

"He's the one you want me to help?"

"Yes," said Orla. "He's looking for someone."

"Really?" He turned to Moorac. "Who is it I'm supposed to find?"

"My niece. She was doing some traveling and sent me a missive that she was heading back to our homeworld, but now she is overdue. I'm worried about what might have happened to her." He brought up a three-dimensional picture of Mehanna. She looked a lot younger, but Grinnell would know that face anywhere.

"She could have just found some man that caught her attention," offered Grinnell. "Maybe he delayed her a little but she's fine."

"She wouldn't dare." His voice held a sharp edge.

Everyone turned to look at him at his outburst.

Moorac must have realized he had reacted wrong, because then he smiled. "I mean she's been isolated all her life. I can't see her picking up with a stranger."

"I don't know about that," said Astrid. She looked up at her mate. "A handsome face can turn heads."

"So can a pretty one," reminded her mate.

She smiled as she leaned into his strength. "I am feeling a little tired and should lie down."

"I'll walk you to our room." Orla turned with her and headed out of the throne room.

That left Grinnell alone with Moorac.

"So, when was the last time you saw your niece?"

"I hate to say it's been a while. I was surprised when I heard she was on her way home, but it would be good to see family again. I prepared for her, but she never came. Now it's been too long, and I'm worried."

"Do you have the missive?"

"Excuse me?"

"The missive. It should give me a starting point to find your lovely niece. If she's lost that is."

"Oh." He didn't respond right away. "No. I didn't think to bring it."

The man was good at lying. Grinnell knew he could push a little more to see how he would react.

"That's not a problem. I can access any system on any planet. All I need is one of your devices and your password, and I can get the missive."

"Oh, no. I don't believe in technology."

"Then how did you get a missive? Orla said you didn't say much about where you're from. Is it someplace centrally located so that you could get something handwritten?"

"My planet isn't that well known, but we do get a lot of merchants coming to sell their wares. One of them brought me a handwritten missive from her. That's why I'm worried. She should have showed up within a couple of duras of receiving it."

Oh, he was good. To anyone else, he would come across as a caring relative. Too bad Grinnell knew the truth.

"Okay, so where was the merchant from? That could give me the information I need to figure out where to start."

"I don't know."

"You need to work with me here. I need something to give me a starting point. So far I have nothing."

Moorac stared at him. Grinnell wondered what was going through his mind. How far was he going to go to convince him to help.

"I believe the man told me he had come from the Hawa sector."

"I see." That was where he had found Mehanna.

"What is wrong?"

"That is in no man's land. Not a place I like to go. Are you sure that is where she is?"

"Probably not now, but it was where the merchant had been before."

"And where is your planet?"

"Why do you ask?"

"Really?" He frowned. "If I knew where she was going, then I could extrapolate her path. You know, if I have a starting place and an ending place, I can figure the most likely path she would take."

"Of course." Moorac hesitated for a moment more. "My homeworld is in the Meja sector."

"That is still not what I need but let me see what I can come up with." He walked over to a screen and started typing. He put the data Moorac gave him into what he was working on. Once the data was entered, he turned to Moorac.

"When do you think she started to travel?"

"Two cycles ago."

Just about the time they had left the palace. So what had probably happened was he went to check on the girls and found them gone. When he asked the village where they were, they probably told him they heard the women were headed home. They probably recognized the symbol on his ship when he landed, or someone watched as they left. Grinnell wondered why Moorac didn't mention May.

"How was she traveling?"

"I don't know, but I'm assuming ship. The planet she was on didn't have a spaceport."

At least he was giving him answers that resembled the truth. Now he had to figure out how long he should stretch this. "You haven't given me much to go on. It could take lunas for me to find her. She could have made it back to your planet by now."

"I check in with my holdings regularly and no one has seen her."

"I'll see what I can do, but I'm not making any promises." How was he checking when he didn't have technology? It dawned on him. He could feel their power. Did he have some sort of magical measure set up to let him know if they use their power anywhere? Good thing the girls used shields whenever they practiced.

Mehanna paced in the room Grinnell put her in. It wasn't the room Astrid had given her, so she could only assume that this was his room when he stayed at the palace. Here was where she saw the personal items missing from his apartment.

The first thing that drew her attention was a painting of a farmhouse. Was this the one he grew up in, or did it just remind him of home? There was also a picture of a couple. Although the man resembled Grinnell, she knew it wasn't her man. Perhaps his parents? There was also a wooden chair, two mismatched lamps, and of all things, a perfume bottle.

The door opened, startling her and making her dive for cover.

"Mehanna, it's me. You're safe." He closed the door behind him.

"What did you learn?" She came out from where she had tried to hide.

"He knows what you look like, and I surmise that he went to the planet right after we left. He must have had some sort of security set up so it would have alerted him to you leaving." Grinnell took her into his arms. "It's not inside you or he would have caught up with us a long time ago. I'm assuming there was some sort of device where you lived, and we triggered it by having May come to your cave. He knew it was time to come get you."

"But we had already left. How did he know to come here?"

"Of that, I'm not sure. I didn't ask, because I could have made him suspicious. The outfit I wore on your planet was an Emori uniform, so I'm thinking the people on the planet watched us leave. I didn't hide the seal on the ship. I saw no reason for that."

"Your ship stayed in orbit more than on the planet."

"I know, but it was visible when we were loading everything. They were so afraid of May they might have followed to make sure she left with us."

She nodded.

"Moorac gave me some information to find out where you went." He grinned as he wrapped his arms around her. "Now I have to find you."

"I am right here, my love." She looked up at him.

"Yes, you are." He ran his hands up her back. "And before I have to put our crazy plan in motion, I would like to spend some time with you."

"Oh? And what would you like to do?"

"Hm, how about we take advantage of that bed over there? I want to make us forget about everything but us for a few microns."

"Just a few microns?" She backed out of his arms and took his hands. "I think you're selling yourself short. Come with me. Make my world explode all around us."

He slipped one arm under her knees and lifted her. Grinnell sat her down next to the bed so they could undress before falling onto it. He captured her lips with his as his hands roamed her body, touching all the places that he knew made her need for him rise. Her hands did the same. They touched and caressed as they continued to kiss, heightening their desire for each other. If either moaned, it was into the other's mouth.

Grinnell broke the kiss and worked his way down to one of her breasts. He took the sweet tip into his mouth. Her soft sigh filled him with power. He moved to the other breast, focusing on it until he felt it pebble in his mouth. He started moving again. He pressed kisses along her ribcage. Dipped his tongue into her navel.

"Grinnell."

"You are so tense a slight wind could snap you in two." Grinnell moved back up her body so he could look her in the eyes. "Relax, nothing is going to happen to either of us."

"You don't know that man. I can sense him, and I fear he can sense me."

"You are being paranoid. You, May, and Tosci have put up protection to keep him from detecting any of you. You are a lot stronger than he is, you just don't believe it yet." He brushed his fingers along her jaw. "You are beautiful, strong, and powerful. Don't let him take that from you."

"I was fine until we came here. Maybe sneaking in and knowing he could find out we're here before we're ready has me questioning everything."

CHAPTER SEVENTEEN

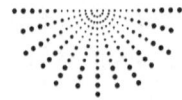

"Trust this. You are safe. Nothing is going to happen, because we have the upper hand. Moorac just doesn't know that. I'm your bond-mate, and I will protect you. I might be leaving, but you know it won't be for long, and I'll be in constant contact with Orla." He pressed a kiss against her collarbone. "Right now, I want to show you how much I love you. I want to make you see stars and make your body sing for me."

"I would like that very much."

He captured her lips once more, brushing his tongue against the seam of the mouth. She opened for him and another sigh escaped when he entered and started to brush his tongue against hers. Their tongues danced together as Grinnell's hands caressed her body. The soft touches made her blood race and her need grow.

She wanted to touch him as well, but he had her hands pinned down. He broke the kiss then started to press soft kisses down her neck and across her collarbone. Mehanna arched her back when she felt the heat of his mouth on her breast once again. He suckled her, making little tingles pool in her core. He released her hands, and she moved them across his back, her fingers gliding over and around his muscles. He was muscled, but not overly muscular. She loved that about him. His muscles were well defined, and she loved to outline them with her fingers.

Grinnell moved to her other breast, and she felt her heart start beating a little harder. She loved the way he paid homage to her body, but she wanted more. She wanted him deep inside her, bringing her to heights only he could bring her to. Her legs started moving.

Her bond-mate pressed a kiss to the tip of her breast and then looked up at her. The smile on his face told her he knew what she was trying to do. She didn't care.

"Please Grinnell."

He climbed back up her body and surged into her. She let out a gasp at the sweet invasion. She wanted to forget for a few microns, and this always worked.

Grinnell pushed himself up on his elbows and watched her face. He set a strong pace and watch her for the signs to pick it up or slow it down. She looked up at him until he hit her sweet spot, which had her closing her eyes and allowing it to wash over her. Everything tightened inside. He pressed a soft kiss against her forehead before picking up the pace. Her legs hiked up a little higher on his waist, changing the angle of his penetration.

Her breath caught in her throat as each time he filled her she felt it to her toes. Excitement filled her bones. Her body felt each stroke. Her toes curled. Her body clenched. Mehanna felt her orgasm race toward her, grab her, and fling her out into the stars.

She felt everything relax. She felt Grinnell press one more kiss against her forehead before he shifted his weight so he could take her in his arms. What she would give to keep him at her side instead of having to face Moorac.

Grinnell said goodbye to Mehanna, making her swear she would stay put. He then went to speak to the others. May and Tosci also had to stay out of sight, but Grenta and Lawaya could show up as if they had been seeing the planet. In the end, they decided to say in hiding as well, fearing they would give something away. He showed them how to order food through the computer and have it transported into their rooms.

He didn't plan on being gone for long, but he would have to disappear for several duras to make it look like he was looking for Moorac's niece. Cameras were already trained on every move Moorac made, but now the ladies could watch and let him know if Moorac was onto their scheme.

He walked out to his ship, powered it up, and took off. He then headed to the closest spaceport and landed. He went around, asking if anyone had seen the woman in the picture he carried. The picture was of May, not Mehanna, so he wasn't surprised when no one had seen her. A couple of people thought she looked familiar, but they couldn't remember where they might have seen her.

Astrid stood on the balcony off the throne room and stared out at the horizon. Moorac had been occupying this space a lot lately, so she was happy to have it to herself for a few microns. She sensed her mate just before he wrapped his arms around her.

"You okay?"

"Please stop worrying. I am fine, I promise." She leaned back against him. "I thought I'd take advantage of the balcony before Moorac takes it over again."

"Then what are you thinking?"

"Do you think we could be having twins?"

"Now what makes you ask that? I thought there was only one in there." He rubbed his hands on her womb.

"I told the doctor I didn't want to know." Astrid put her hands on top of his. "So although I'm pretty sure there is only one in here, I could be wrong. You were a twin."

"True, but I don't feel like I have a twin. I didn't grow up with him."

"And he tried to kill us. But do you think if you two had been raised together you would have been closer?" She tilted her head so she could look at him. "They say twins have a special bond that goes beyond normal sibling bonds."

"My brother and I had a horrible relationship." He shifted her so she turned in his arms. "But our children will love each other. They are coming into a loving family and a safe galaxy."

———

Astrid watched Moorac walk around the throne room. She touched Orla's hand. "I think I'll go lie down for a bit."

"Of course." He stood when she did. "Do you want me to walk you to our rooms?"

"No." She looked over at Moorac. "Entertain our guest."

Orla pressed a kiss against her cheek.

She walked to their section of the palace and opened the door to their room but didn't enter. With a smile, she disappeared from sight and created a false image of herself walking into the room and closing the door. She walked to May's room and opened the door. May looked up in shock.

"Okay, I know someone must have come in, but I don't see you." She had been sitting in a chair, staring out of the window. "Is that you, Grenta?"

"No." Astrid revealed herself. "I didn't mean to frighten you, but I thought you'd like to spend some time with your sister."

"Oh, I would love that, but I was told not to move. The security system would pick me up and ruin everything."

"I can help with that. I can block us from the system. I do it all the time when I need a little time to myself."

"Really?" May stood up. "That would be wonderful."

"Once I bring you there, you will have to wait for me to come back and get you."

"Of course. This will give Mehanna and me a chance to work out how to use our powers to defeat Moorac. And I have missed her."

"But you two didn't even know the other existed until recently." Astrid led the way.

"Moorac blocked our memories of each other. We were together for about ten yepas before he placed us on that planet."

They stopped in front of a door. Astrid smiled at her, then used her ability to open the door. Mehanna jerked around when she heard the door and darted into the bathroom.

"It's me, Mehanna."

"May?" she poked her head back out. "Are you crazy? We're supposed to stay put."

"Don't get mad at your sister, Mehanna." Astrid shimmered into view. "I brought her. I thought you two would like to be together while we wait for Grinnell."

"Thank you." Mehanna bowed. "It is a little lonely here by myself."

"I'll be back to get you when we know Grinnell is coming back. Try to make the best of your time." She watched as the sisters embraced before leaving them together.

After making sure he was extremely visible, Grinnell climbed into his ship and went to the next spaceport. He repeated this with all the major ports. If Moorac had any spies, they would tell him he was actively looking for his niece. After he left the last major port, he contacted Orla.

"How does it go, my friend?"

"No sign of the girl. Is Moorac there?"

"Why, yes he is." Orla looked off-screen to the person in question.

"Can you ask him how far out he wants me to look? She hasn't been through any of the major ports."

Orla continued to look off-screen for a few microns. "He wants to know how long it would take to cover the secondary space ports?"

"The secondary ones? If I travel to everyone between our home and his, it could take lunas."

"He made a face at that," said Orla. "Send a communique to all of them asking if they have seen her. Then give them one dura to respond."

"Sounds good," replied Grinnell. "I'm looking forward to a little downtime. By the way, tell Astrid that I have a little surprise for her."

"Really? What is it?" she asked.

"It wouldn't be much of a surprise if I told you, would it?"

"No," Astrid laughed. "But you can't blame me for asking."

Grinnell laughed at that. "I'll contact you in one dura with an update."

Grinnell set his ship down at the palace and went through his post-flight list. Once he did everything he needed to do, he climbed out and headed to his quarters. Mehanna waited for him. She had changed her hair and eye color even darkened the pigment of her skin and removed the blue tint.

"You ready?" He wasn't sure if he was ready.

"No, but we must do this anyway, right?"

"If you don't want to have to look over your shoulder for the rest of your life, yes. We could run, but how far and for how long?" He wrapped his arms around her.

"I know." She rested her head against his chest. "I missed you."

"I missed you too, and I wish I could show you how much, but we need to do this." He held her close and wasn't sure if he wanted to let go. "You ready to get everyone?"

She nodded.

He took her hand and led her to May's room first, then to the other three ladies' rooms. As a group, they headed to the throne room. He hoped they would catch Moorac off guard, even if it was for only a few microns.

He paused in front of the throne room doors to gather his thoughts. Once he was ready. he looked at his group, making sure they were ready too. Grinnell nodded to the guard, who opened the doors.

Astrid saw them the moment they entered. She rose from her chair and smiled. Orla saw her moving, then looked where she was headed. He smiled as well. Moorac was there, but out on the balcony. Since no one spoke, he ignored the royal couple as he stared out at the horizon.

Moorac leaned against the railing, outlining the balcony. He could feel magic in the air. Mehanna or May must be close. They were keeping their power under control so he couldn't track them. Something he didn't expect. Who could have trained them to do that?

He glanced over his shoulder and saw Astrid walking away from her throne. He turned back to the area surrounding the palace and focused on the power he could sense. No little girl was going to best him when he had gone through so much work to get what he wanted.

Closing his eyes, he opened his arms to reach out with his mind. This couldn't be right. All of a sudden, the power was behind him in the throne room. He looked in the room again but only saw Astrid hugging a man. Then he realized it was Grinnell. Maybe he had found Mehanna but Orla hadn't told him.

He walked in to see Astrid hug a young woman standing next to Grinnell. Magic, strong magic filled the room. Did Grinnell find her? Why didn't they tell him? Did they think it would be a great surprise? Someone came to stand beside him, but he was too busy trying to look at the young woman's face to figure out who had the magic to tell his intruder to go away.

"Hello, brother."

Brother? He whipped around to find his sister standing beside him. Was it her magic that he sensed?

"Tosci? What are you doing here?" His brow furrowed as he tried to put everything together.

"I've been traveling with a few friends."

"What friends?" He grumbled. "You ran and hid from me."

"You banned me from your home. What was I supposed to do?" She took him by the arm and brought him closer to the group. "Come meet my friends."

"If you insist." How did she get here, and why didn't he sense her long before this?

"I do." The hand that grasped his arm held small stones that Tosci had empowered with counterspells, so anything he tried should be easy to stop. Her only concern was how long the power on the stone would last. The more energy he used, the more the stones would be drained until it couldn't work anymore. She slipped them into a seam of his jacket.

———

"I am so happy for you." Astrid hugged Mehanna, but Tosci was sure her brother hadn't figured out who she was yet. He would soon enough. "I always wondered who would be able to capture Grinnell's heart."

"Me too," said Grinnell as he slipped an arm around Mehanna's waist. "She took my breath away the moment I met her."

"I feel the same way about you, love." She leaned her head against his chest.

"I think a celebration is in order." Astrid clapped her hands. Her aid came to her side. They spoke quietly for a few microns before the aid left. "This is so exciting!"

"Let's not get the baby so excited that it wants to come out before its time."

"Grinnell, you are as bad as Orla. I'm fine, the baby is fine, and we've been so bored that if you try to make me remain calm right now, I will punch you so hard you will see stars."

He gave her a look that had her ducking behind Orla.

"Now, Grinnell."

"What, my queen?"

Astrid made a face when he called her that. He knew she hated it, which is why he used it from time to time to tease her, especially when she threatened him with bodily harm. Astrid was like a sister to him. He might have lost his parents when Varal was in control, but he found people to whom he was just as close to. He knew his parents would be proud.

"You two are incorrigible," said Grenta. "Behave for a moment, please."

"Yes, ma'am," they both said. They looked at each other and laughed.

Grinnell could feel how tense Mehanna was. He was afraid she was going to break into a thousand pieces. He wanted to reassure her but knew better than to bring attention to them yet. May was still out of sight working on a few spells to restrict Moorac's power.

He hoped Tosci was able to place the stones she had charged. This had to work.

Mehanna was the anchor for everyone else. She focused on May and Tosci, waiting for them to signal her that they were successful. She saw the smile on Tosci's face and knew she had been able to place the inhibitors. Now they had to see how well they worked.

No one focused on her. Grinnell continued to tease Astrid, and like a mother hen, Grenta was chastising them. Lawaya was quiet, but so was Orla. He watched Astrid and Grinnell with a smile on his face, but he knew what was going to happen and was watching for signals as well.

Having Moorac so close made her blood run cold. Remembering what he put them through fueled her anger. She could sense when he came in from the balcony. Tosci kept him occupied so he wouldn't focus on anyone else until they were ready.

Mehanna could feel the inhibitors Tosci used coming from Moorac. At least that was in place. She felt relief from May and she knew her sister had finished what she needed. Now it was time to face the man who'd raised her.

She could sense him as he passed her. He was an outsider and didn't know how to act around the bond between Grinnell and Astrid. She had changed her hair, skin, and eye color so he wouldn't spot her right away, but she didn't alter her other features so he would know who stopped him.

May still stayed out of sight. He didn't need to know that the sisters had found each other right away. If he did, he could change his tactics. Mehanna wanted him to focus on her. Ignore everyone else. She waited until he was where they wanted him to stand. Once he was there, she spoke.

"Hello, uncle."

He spun at her words. "Mehanna."

"I hear you've been looking for me."

"I have." He looked at his hosts for a moment.

She bet he wanted to know if they had been lying to him this whole time.

He smiled and pretended to be the loving uncle. "It's time for you to come home."

"Sorry, I can't. In case you didn't hear, I found someone who loves me." She pointed to Grinnell.

"Don't be silly. He was hired to find you, that's all." He looked at Grinnell. "Thank you for your swift work."

"You don't understand." She smiled as she crossed to Grinnell's side. "We've completed the bond ritual. We are one now, and there can be no other."

"No!" he screamed.

Mehanna could feel him draw power to him, forming a ball of energy that he would use against them. She started doing the same thing.

"Yes." She smiled like she didn't have a care in the galaxy. She rested a hand on Grinnell's chest. "And I've never been so happy."

"How did this happen?" demanded Moorac.

"Honestly?" responded Grinnell. "I went looking for Lawaya. She also has power and looking for Lawaya brought me to Mehanna. Her beauty took my breath away." He placed his hand on hers. "I'm the one who took her off the planet you had abandoned her on. How dare you leave a child to the elements? She had no one to teach her or help her. Be glad she's brilliant, or she could have died."

"That wouldn't have happened. There were safety protocols put in place. She remembered how to use her magic to make food for herself."

"She was a child, Moorac." Grinnell removed Mehanna's hand and took a step toward him. "What sort of sick experiment were you putting her through?"

"No experiment," replied Moorac. He looked at Mehanna for a micron before focusing on Grinnell. "She needed to prove how strong her magic was."

"Well, I think you failed at that one. She didn't even know she had magic running through her veins when I met her."

"How did you meet her?" Moorac kept looking at Mehanna and then Grinnell.

Mehanna wondered what he was looking for.

"As I said, I went looking for Lawaya." Grinnell didn't volunteer anything else.

"And who is Lawaya?"

"One of my closest friends," replied Grinnell. After spending so much time with her, he wasn't lying. "So, I guess you can go now. I found your niece. She's safe and sound and happy."

"She needs to come home with me." He took a step toward Mehanna, which made her step next to Grinnell.

"I don't think so. She's with me now." Grinnell put an arm around Mehanna.

"Like you can stop me." He waved his hand. He growled when nothing happened. "What have you done?"

"Protected what is important to me," said Grinnell. "You're not going to take Mehanna from me. I won't allow it."

"How do you think you can stop me?" He started moving his hands.

"Do you think you're the only one who can wield magic?" Grinnell pulled power from Mehanna and made a glowing ball in his hand.

"I groomed her to be mine." Moorac worked his energy into the shape of a ball as well.

"Sorry." Grinnell played with the ball he had made, the soft blue sphere fit in the palm of his hand. "You destroyed that idea the moment you sent her away."

"And what about her sister?"

"I'm here." She stepped from behind the column she was hiding behind. "It took you long enough to acknowledge that I exist."

He ignored her little dig. "You look so much like your sister. Can I assume you came here with her?"

"It's still all about Mehanna, isn't it? I do look like her. Not something you expected? You should have. We're twins, after all." May glared at him. "I know you never thought I was strong enough, but you weren't sure about Mehanna either. Did you ever wonder why? You never thought it odd that we were equal in power? That one didn't excel over the other?"

"He won't tell you the real truth, so don't waste your breath. He didn't think you were pretty enough, May. Power didn't have anything to do with it." Mehanna stepped up to him just as her sister did the same thing. "He wanted the prettiest of us."

"I think we're about the same." May started to circle him, with Mehanna following suit. "Grinnell might argue, but he's allowed to be a little biased."

"My bond-mate sees beauty in both of us, Something I love about him. But most men?" She started weaving her magic. "They don't always use the brain."

"Is that why it took you a while to convince Grinnell to bond with you?" May was working in concert with her, creating a barrier around him.

"Yes. He didn't want me to make a rash decision."

"You wanted to bond with him?" asked Moorac. He looked from one girl to the other. "This wasn't his idea?"

"No. I love him and want to spend the rest of my life with him." She stopped in front of him. "I don't want to have anything to do with you."

"You'll change your mind." He brought his hands up and weaved them in front of her face.

"Oh, your magic won't work on me, Moorac." Mehanna smiled. She touched the air around him and activated the barrier she built.

"What makes you say that?" asked Moorac, as he smiled back. He moved his hands around his body then touched the same place she did. The barrier fell just as fast as she built it.

"Because I know you." Her smile widened. He might think he was shutting down something important, but the shield was simple and designed to measure his power. May was the one who thought of that. "You used to set my sister and me against each other all the time. You pushed us to see who would be superior. I don't care about that anymore. I only want to be happy. You won't make me happy."

Grinnell stepped up to her and took her hand. She shared her energy with him, filling him with as much as she could.

"You don't understand. I only wanted to make the both of you better." He continued to weave his hands, now building something new.

Mehanna recognized the movements from something Tosci taught her. She could feel the power he was building. If she didn't stop him, it would be too powerful to dissipate. She started to do the same thing. Once May figured out what she was doing, she joined in, building the shield they were creating and making it stronger so that it could withstand anything he threw at them.

Moorac had to laugh when he realized they could counteract what he was doing.

"What? You didn't expect us to know how to use our power?" asked Mehanna. "We're not stupid."

"I never thought you were," he responded. He stopped weaving his magic for a moment. "I'm assuming my sister had something to do with your training."

"Think what you want," replied May. She and Mehanna didn't stop building the shield they wanted to create to protect everyone.

"So, your friends. Are they from our race?" He looked at Lawaya, and Grenta. "Or are they like Astrid?"

"What do you mean by that?" asked Astrid.

"I'm sorry. I meant no disrespect. But you are Barou, right? Your power allows you to do what we can, but the moment people touch it, it dissipates."

"Really?" Astrid retorted. She stared at Moorac. A small surafic, a small bird like creature, well known for its pretty plumage, jumped up on Moorac's arm. Its sharp talons cut into his arm, drawing blood.

"Get this damn thing off of me." Moorac waved his arm around, trying to dislodge the creature. All that did was make it tighten its grip on his arm. The harder he flapped, the tighter it held on. Blood dripped from the wounds it inflicted.

Astrid walked up to him and ran her hand through the bird. It shattered into a thousand pieces.

"Was that real enough for you, Moorac?" Astrid walked back to her mate's side. "The only people who can see through my creations is someone from my race, and they have to be a master. To everyone else, it is very real."

"I stand corrected." He flexed his wounded arm. "But I can take the air from your lungs."

Astrid gaped for a moment, then smiled at him. "That's not going to work on me."

"Why not?" he dropped his hand.

"Because you need to know where I am." She rested a hand on his shoulder. Then she moved, but it was so quick he wasn't quite sure where. "You see, I can create an illusion where you think I'm in one place, but I'm really in another."

"I can do the same thing."

"Can you make yourself invisible?"

"Of course." And he vanished from sight.

"Ah, but I can see you."

He didn't respond.

"Okay, then let me prove it to you." Astrid vanished from sight. When she touched his shoulder, he jumped and became visible. She didn't.

"Did you see it?" she whispered in Mehanna's ear. "A slight rippling effect."

Mehanna smiled. She did see it. The hint of how he worked his magic.

Lawaya stepped up next, pushing until he questioned another ability. Then she showed him how she did it and challenged him to do the same thing. Mehanna watched so she could find the shimmer that showed it wasn't real. Grenta was next. Each time someone challenged him, Mehanna did see a weakness, and it allowed her to see a pattern. And it allowed her to anticipate what he would do next.

Tosci was the one who pushed him the hardest, but she was the one who felt she had something to prove. She needed to show her brother she was a force to be reckoned with. She made rain fall on him, forcing him to create a shield to stop the water from soaking him. Then she created a wind funnel that only focused on him, wanting to see if he could block a wind that was designed for only him. That was a little harder for him to block but he was able to do it.

"Mehanna, it's time to go," said Moorac. He smiled as he offered her his hand.

She smiled back. "I'm not going with you Moorac."

"But I came all this way to get you."

"Don't care." She faced him, not afraid anymore. "You send me to a planet to grow up on my own, and you do the same thing to my sister. Yet you ignore her. Like you never really cared about either of us. All we are is a vessel for you."

"What sort of trash has that man been filling your head with?"

"That man? You mean Grinnell? Nothing." She smiled. "Your sister told me what your plan was. That you wanted to be the most powerful, and you want your children to be the same. That all you want the two of us for is to be baby-makers so you can have your progeny. Your problem is any children I have will be with Grinnell, not you."

That comment angered Moorac. He shot a blast at Grinnell, who had to dive to get out of the way. He in turn blasted back. Moorac absorbed the energy. It didn't even phase him.

"Mehanna," Moorac dropped his voice. It came out like silk. It wrapped around her, drawing her attention to focus only on his words. "You belong with me. This man doesn't care about you."

"Grinnell, his name is Grinnell." Her voice came out soft. It took all her concentration to remember his name.

"Grinnell doesn't care about you. Only I care." He reached his hand toward her once again.

"You care."

"That's right." He smiled.

CHAPTER EIGHTEEN

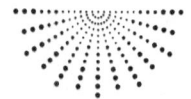

Grinnell watched Mehanna sway as Moorac spoke to her. He couldn't hear what he was saying, but he could feel the magic in his words. He had to stop this.

"Mehanna, don't listen to him." His words didn't penetrate.

She turned to face him. Mehanna looked right through him like he didn't exist. Grinnell could feel the hairs on his neck stand up. This couldn't be good.

"You don't care about me." Her voice sounded stilted.

"Mehanna, you know that is a lie." Grinnell faced her. Tosci had warned them about this. He just hoped what she taught them would work. He reached for her hand and was able to grasp it. "I love you. He will tell you I only wanted your power, but you know that's not true. Remember, Mehanna, remember what happened the first time you wanted to bond. What did I say?"

"You told me that I needed to be sure." She sighed. "That bonding to defeat Moorac wasn't a reason to bond. We could defeat him without doing that."

"Exactly." He took her other hand in his. "Then why did we bond?"

"Because I love you, and you love me." Her eyes cleared and she smiled at him. She squeezed his hand. "Thank you."

He pressed a kiss against her cheek, then turned to look at Moorac. So far, the man hadn't tried to use anything powerful. He must have wanted to get Mehanna to go with him without a fight. Did he suspect that she was more powerful than him?

"You are in my way, Grinnell." Moorac tightened his hand into a fist, and Grinnell felt something constrict his movements. He drew power from Mehanna and broke the hold, which surprised Moorac.

"Oh, come on," said Grinnell. "I know you can do better than that."

"You aren't worth my time." He continued to focus on Mehanna.

He should have paid attention to May, because she was working her magic up. Grinnell had seen her twirling her finger as she spoke softly to herself. He couldn't see the magic flow, but he could feel it when it brushed past him. Too bad he couldn't see it. It sure would make it so much easier to see attacks coming.

Looking back at May, he noticed a slight change in the air, then it filled with color. Holy stars, everyone was working some sort of magic. Colors filled the room around him. No one seemed to notice what he could see, though. If they did, they didn't show it. Each person had a different color. May's color was blue. Mehanna's was a beautiful purple. Tosci's was a soft shade of green. Even Astrid and Lawaya had colors. Moorac's, though, was almost black, with red bands. Grinnell had never seen anything like it. It flowed around him like it was alive. It would snake out every once in a while, only to curl back around him.

The man was testing the strength of the magic in the room, and they weren't even aware of it.

Grinnell pulled magic from Mehanna and May. He felt it fill him, then he started weaving as well. He created a wall. First, he laid the foundation he thought would protect everyone from whatever Moorac might throw at them, then he strengthened it layer by layer. He smiled when he saw those unknown attempts being blocked. He had done what he wanted to do.

Moorac turned his attention to him when he realized he was being blocked.

"Problem?" asked Grinnell. He was pretty sure Moorac didn't want anyone to know what he had been up to.

"You aren't from my race." Moorac focused on Grinnell. "How did you learn to do that?"

"You aren't the only one with a brain in their head. And I'm a quick study."

"Then you are the one I will take out first."

Grinnell saw colors flow toward him, wrapping around him and halting any movement he might have tried to make. It tightened around him, keeping him still.

"I don't think so," said Mehanna. She wrapped her magic around Grinnell as well, pushing off Moorac's magic and giving him his freedom again.

"Grinnell is family, and we protect our own," added May.

"Moorac, you should be proud," his sister said to him. "These two are strong and independent. They will be able to survive without either of us."

"No!" His hand shot out, and he released a flow of magic toward Mehanna.

Grinnell's magical wall stopped it from doing any damage. He had kept working on it to keep it strong.

When Moorac realized what Grinnell had done, he attacked, building his magic once again and shooting it toward Grinnell.

Grinnell didn't think, he just reacted, drawing power to him and forcing it out toward Moorac. His magic hit Moorac's, forcing it back onto its creator. Moorac stumbled back from the power of Grinnell's attack.

"How did you do that?" That seemed to be his favorite question. The shocked look showed he didn't think anyone could best him, let alone someone he didn't think had power.

"What? Stop you?" Grinnell wouldn't dare reveal he had no idea what Moorac was talking about. "You were aiming for my bond-mate, and no harm will come to her as long as I draw breath."

"I can fix that right now." He spread his hand wide.

"No." Mehanna stepped in front of Grinnell. "You cannot harm him. I won't allow it."

"How do you plan on stopping me?" He continued to mold the magic he was creating.

"I count six against one," Mehanna said as she felt Grinnell's hands on her shoulder. "We can keep you at bay if we attack one after the other, or we could stop you if we all attacked at once."

"Ah, but you can't. I made sure of that yepas ago."

"What do you mean?" She knew what he meant since she had removed his block while they were in the desert.

"A spell, my dear." He gave her a knowing smile. "You can't harm me."

"I don't plan on harming you." Mehanna smiled back at him. "I *do* plan on defeating you."

"Anything you try to use will be diminished."

"Hm, this spell didn't stop me before." Mehanna placed her hands on her hips. "I'm wondering if it has dissipated over the yepas."

A frown on his face showed he hadn't thought about that.

"And I have no qualm about harming you," said Grinnell. "Especially if you try to harm anyone I care about."

"So you're going to pick and choose who you deem worthy?"

"No." Grinnell looked at everyone. "All of these people are family to me, except you."

"You seem so confident. Why is that?" Moorac focused on Grinnell. He used his voice to get into his head. "You really aren't that confident, are you? There must be something that you hide from the others."

"Sorry, Moorac." Grinnell kept eye contact with him, showing his magic wasn't working on him. "I've already been through hell and back. Mehanna knows all my deep dark secrets. You can't use that against me."

Mehanna was glad she had pushed Grinnell the way she did. They didn't have any secrets, and right now that was keeping Grinnell safe. Something inside her shifted again. She tilted her head a little as a huge flow of energy filled her.

Grinnell stood beside her, but he didn't know. Mehanna wanted to jump for joy. She knew life just started inside her. Something wonderful was created by the two of them. She took his arm and hugged it. He placed his hand on hers.

He didn't look at her, keeping his attention on Moorac.

She leaned in and whispered her good news. When he realized what she was saying, he forgot all about Moorac and looked at her.

"Really?" He focused on her, totally ignoring everyone for a micron.

She nodded, smiling.

He pulled her close and gave her a quick kiss. Grinnell then turned his attention back to Moorac.

"You two going to share?" he asked.

"We will," said Mehanna. "With family."

Moorac growled and threw another powerful blast at them. The wall stopped most of it. Mehanna stopped the rest.

Grinnell went back to reinforcing that wall. Every blast weakened it, so he was always adding to it. It had become second nature, allowing him to focus on Moorac while he did.

"I'm not leaving here without Mehanna."

"Then you're never leaving, because she's not going anywhere with you," said Grinnell. He slipped an arm around her waist. He blinked when he felt extra power fill him.

"You can't stop me."

"Watch me. You might have mastered your power, but you only have anger to fuel it. I have love, passion, and the desire to protect to fuel mine."

"Let's see what you can do." He took a deep stance like he was going to do hand-to-hand combat.

Grinnell watched Moorac build power around him, so he did the same thing. He drew from Mehanna, and from May, until he couldn't hold anymore. Drawing from what he had been taught, he wrapped the power around him, shaping and molding it into a sharp point to throw at Moorac. He wouldn't be the first to attack, but he would make sure he was the last.

Moorac waited, holding his stance. When Grinnell just stood there, he groused, "Are you just going to stand there?"

"You are the one who is causing all the trouble. If you were to just turn around and leave, knowing you weren't going to win here, I wouldn't have to attack."

"You think you're better than me?"

"No, but our cause is just where yours isn't. You want to take my mate away from me so you can be the biggest, baddest warlock of our galaxy. That's for personal gain, and I can't allow that. That is what Varal did, and he made everyone else's life miserable."

"Who told you I wanted to do that?" he looked at his sister accusingly.

"Does it matter where I heard it?" said Grinnell. "You know it's true."

"I think I need to take you out of the equation."

"You said that before, yet I'm still standing. Did you lose your edge?"

Moorac growled in anger. He built a large ball of energy and shot his arm out toward Grinnell.

"No!" shouted Mehanna. She blasted her uncle with a volley of her own, hitting him square in the chest.

Moorac fired back at Mehanna. The magical wall absorbed as much as it could, but it didn't stop it and Mehanna took what was left in the chest.

"Moorac!" shouted Grinnell. He drew power to him to deflect as much of the attack on Mehanna as he could. Then he started to draw more when he found power he never used before fill him. The power was a little heady. He took aim and struck Moorac in the chest, this one driving him back.

"How did you do that?" Moorac rubbed his chest. It left a mark.

Grinnell had no answer, but he wasn't about to say anything to Moorac. He glanced around the room and saw Tosci smiling. Was it her power? She was part of the bond he and May made, but he didn't think he could access hers. At this point, he didn't care, as long as he kept Mehanna and their baby protected.

Moorac didn't allow anyone to break his focus this time. He attacked Grinnell once again. When Mehanna tried to hit him with her power, he blocked it with the flick of his wrist.

Grinnell poured more power into his shields as Moorac tried to tear them down. He took shots at him when he could, but it was getting to the point where all he could do was work on his shields. Another burst of energy filled him. Where did this one come from? With a wave of his hand, he had the wall reinforced. With a wave of his other hand, he shot Moorac with a ball of energy so strong it took the man off his feet.

"You can't have that kind of power." Moorac staggered back to his feet.

"Why not?" he asked. "Because you're supposed to be the strongest? Most powerful?"

"I have worked hard on mastering my craft." Moorac puffed his chest out. "I perfected it."

"But you have no love, and I've learned that's what powers anyone's ability is love. The purer the love, the more powerful the ability." He wasn't sure how he knew this, but something deep inside told him it was true. "Mehanna and I have that love. You won't win, and I wish you would see that."

"You are delusional." Moorac shook his head. "No one can beat me."

"You're wrong." Grinnell took his newly found power and wrapped it around Moorac, tightening it around his body, crushing the air out of him. Once the man's face started to turn an ugly shade of purple, he released the hold and allowed him to breathe again. "Why didn't you break my hold if you are that powerful?"

He had no answer. Moorac fought back with volleys of power instead. Like little balls of lightning, they soared through the air, straight toward Grinnell, who smacked some to the ground, ducked the higher ones and hit a few back.

Grinnell was very glad he could see the color of everyone's power. It helped him avoid everything Moorac threw at him.

"Go home, Moorac," said Tosci. "Mehanna belongs to another."

"No." He looked at his sister. "She is mine, and I will take her with me."

He shot his hand out toward his sister, hitting her hard and knocking her out. May was his next target.

Grinnell could see the blast as it left Moorac's hand. He wondered if he could take the man's power and turn it back on him so he took the damage. Focusing on the trajectory, he couldn't turn it around, but he could change it. That surprised everyone.

"What the hell did you just do?" demanded Moorac.

"Does it matter? I stopped you. That's all I care about." Grinnell wouldn't volunteer anything else.

"You shouldn't have been able to do that." Moorac looked at him in awe.

"Why?" asked Grinnell. "Because you don't see magic the way I do? You think there is only one way to use it?"

"You can't have any magic in you. I don't sense it. You're using Mehanna's, which means you shouldn't be this strong."

"You seem so sure of yourself." Grinnell tilted his head and watched him.

"I have trained every dura of my life to be the best." Moorac' sounded sure of himself. But his stance showed someone who was losing their confidence.

"That's what I heard," said Grinnell. "Something about some kid angering you so much you pushed yourself hard."

"Who told you that?"

"The woman who you tried to kill." He pointed to where Tosci had fallen. "She wanted me to understand what made you the way you are. Knowledge is power."

Moorac laughed.

"Okay." Grinnell nodded. "You don't agree, so I guess I'm going to have to show you."

Mehanna came to his side. They clasped hands and faced him. May came on the other side of Grinnell and took his hand as well.

"So the three of you think you can beat me by combining your power and channeling it through him?" He changed his stance so he could absorb any blast they threw at him.

Tosci moved, letting everyone know she was okay and alert again.

"You okay?" asked Mehanna.

She nodded as she got to her feet, stepped up to the three of them, and took Mehanna's free hand.

"Showing your moral support, sister?" asked Moorac snidely.

"Sharing my power, brother." She smiled brightly. "When I helped Grinnell and May bond so they could share their power, I added mine to the mix."

"You never shared your power with me." He frowned. "Why would you want to do that?"

"You never wanted my power, remember? You knew you'd have to share yours as well." She let her words sink in. "These three have such trust for each other they don't mind sharing their power."

He growled his frustration. Grinnell bet this wasn't something he expected.

"Now," said Grinnell. "Are you going to be smart and leave while you have your dignity intact or are you going to be a fool and make me beat you to make you leave?"

"I can throw him out of the palace if you'd like, Grinnell," said Orla.

"Thank you, but no. I don't want him trying to ambush us somewhere else." He watched Moorac. "What is your answer, Moorac?"

He refused to back down. "It is time for Mehanna to come home."

"I'm not going home with you, Moorac," said Mehanna. "Grinnell and I bonded, and I'm carrying his child."

That little bombshell got everyone's attention. Congratulations came from their friends, but not from Moorac. If anything, it angered him more.

Grinnell kept his gaze on Moorac. The moment the man tried something, he would be ready.

"And what would you do if I threatened the one thing you want safe, Mehanna?" He shot out his hand and wrapped his power around Grinnell, cutting off his air passage and lifting him off the ground.

Grinnell fought to breathe. He heard Mehanna scream as he dangled in the air and his ears started to buzz. Stars danced in front of him from the lack of oxygen. He felt energy start to fill him. He didn't know where it came from, but it felt good. Like soft feathers brushing against his skin. It filled him with love. He felt like he was being wrapped in a cocoon, working its way up his body.

Moorac's hold faltered and broke as the power flowing through him reached his throat and pushed back.

"How did you do that?" demanded Moorac once more.

"I don't know." Grinnell smiled. He still floated above the ground about three feet. "But I think you now understand that we, together, are more powerful than you. No matter what you try, you're going to lose."

"And I'm tired of hearing you say that over and over again."

"I'm saying that because I don't want to kill you. But I will if you push me to."

"I'm not leaving without Mehanna."

"So be it." Grinnell lowered to the ground. He didn't plan on using anyone's power, only the weapons he had created for this confrontation. He didn't start this, but he would finish it.

Moorac closed his eyes and stood quietly.

Grinnell bet he was centering himself to focus his power right at him. The energy that entered him before still filled him. He wanted to ask the others who the power belonged to, but he didn't want to give Moorac any information. He was ready. His new weapon hid under his clothing. Moorac shouldn't know he was using technology and not magic.

Moorac smiled, then flung his power out to attack Grinnell. The power he released reached Grinnell before he could move. The power wrapped around him then faded before it could do any damage.

Grinnell activated his device, then aimed and shot an energy beam right at Moorac.

Moorac laughed when he saw it. He held out his hand, expecting the blast to deflect up, but it continued on its trajectory and hit Moorac in the heart. He looked at Grinnell with shock before he dropped to his knees and fell over.

"Did you kill him?" asked Orla as the group approached Moorac's prone body.

"I don't know. I knew I needed to hit him hard enough to keep him from attacking any of us again, but I didn't create the beam to be deadly."

Lawaya touched Moorac's wrist. "He has a pulse."

Orla signaled for the guards to come and take Moorac. "Take him to the medical center, but do not let him leave that area. We will be there momentarily."

They bowed before picking up Moorac and carrying him out.

"So what just happened?" asked Astrid. "I couldn't see anything happening, but you four seemed to be able to see it."

"We can't see anything either, but we can feel the buildup of power and could tell when it was on the move," said May.

"I could see it," said Grinnell.

"How?" asked Tosci.

"I wished that I could see what was coming at us. I started seeing colors when Moorac was building his power." He looked at Mehanna. "I saw different colors for each of you. It was quite pretty."

"You have a wonderful talent, Grinnell. You might not have the magic we do, but you do have a special ability," said Tosci.

"And I want to thank you."

"Me?"

"Yes," said Grinnell. "Your power kept me safe."

"Not my power," said Tosci.

He looked at Mehanna and May, but they shook their heads. "Then where did the power come from?"

"You didn't use our power?"

"I did in the beginning. When Moorac had me that last time, I was pretty sure he was going to crush the air out of me. Power filled me, really strong power. I don't think it tried to hurt him, but it definitely protected me."

Mehanna went over and wrapped her arms around him. "I think I know where the power came from."

He looked at her as she took his hand and rested it on her stomach. "Really?"

"It's the only thing that makes sense." She touched his face.

"But how could something so small release so much power?" He rested his forehead against hers.

"Her father was in danger and she knew it."

"Oh? And what makes you think it's a girl?" He wrapped his arms around her.

"Because she was smart enough to protect you." She smiled at Grinnell. "I'll be able to prove it in about nine lunas."

"I can't wait," he laughed.

"What do you want to do with Moorac?" asked Orla.

"I'm not sure. I don't think he's going to leave us alone if we let him go free. I also don't think there is a cell that can hold him for long," said Grinnell.

"Let's go to the medical center and find out how he's doing first. Then we'll figure out what we have to do with him."

"You could maroon him someplace he can't escape," offered Tosci.

"That's true," responded Grinnell. "If we can find a place where we know he could survive but never escape."

They were greeted by the head doctor when they arrived.

"I'm not sure what happened to him, sir."

"Did he die?"

"No, sir. He regained consciousness quickly. But he doesn't remember anything."

"Nothing?" asked Tosci. She moved around everyone and went to her brother's side. "Moorac? How are you doing?"

"Tosci! Thank the gods. Where am I?" He took her hand like it was a lifeline.

"What do you remember?" She sat on his bed, holding his hand for moral support.

"I'm not sure. I remember going to school and working to be the best and I remember taking in two young girls when their parents disappeared, but I don't remember what they looked like. I don't know how I got here." He looked at her. "Can you answer these questions?"

"I can." She brushed a few stray hairs out of his face. "Let me speak to our friends first. They were worried about you too."

"Friends? Did I do something wrong?"

"Of course not, but you did get hurt and bumped your head." She touched his forehead, placing a scar so he would touch it and believe he had hurt himself. Tosci stood and gave his forehead a quick kiss. She went to the doctor. "Is his memory loss permanent or temporary?"

"It's a little early for me to say. I've done all the scans I could and still have a few out. From what I can see, his memory loss seems almost surgical. He remembers certain things, like your name, how old he is, where he's from, but it looks like anything dealing with the two ladies has been removed."

"If he doesn't remember us, then we shouldn't have to worry about him coming after us," said Mehanna.

"And if he gets his memory back?" asks Grinnell.

"Let me work with my brother. I'll know if he's lost the memories forever or not by asking the right questions." Tosci went back to her brother.

The rest headed back to the throne room.

"So what now?" asked May.

"I think we get to live our lives," said Mehanna.

Grinnell came up behind her and wrapped his arms around her. She leaned back into his strength. "That is something I'm looking forward to."

"What about you, May?"

"I don't know. I think I want to travel a bit. See what is out there." She looked at Mehanna. "Are you and Grinnell going to settle down here?"

"We haven't talked about it too much. We were so focused on facing Moorac, I couldn't think past that point."

"You know you are more than welcome to call Emori your home," said Astrid. "I've enjoyed having you around and having another woman here would be wonderful."

"Do you mind if Mehanna and I go for a walk?" asked Grinnell.

"Of course," said Astrid. "We'll be here when you come back."

Grinnell took Mehanna's hand and led her out into the warm sunshine. "What do you want to do?"

"Be with you."

He wrapped his arm around her. "I mean do you know where you want to live? Where we should raise our children?"

"Your job is here, working for Orla."

"I know, but if you want to go somewhere else, we will do that. I want you to be happy."

"I don't care where we live, as long as I'm with you." She leaned into him. "I know you love what you do for Orla, and I don't want to take you away from that. The room you have here is the one that shows your personality, and it would be nice to have a friend through my pregnancy."

"Are you going to be okay when I have to leave the planet?"

"Of course."

"You will?"

"Sure, because I'll travel with you."

He laughed at that. "Then let's go tell Astrid the good news. I know the first thing she's going to do is help you make my room less manly."

"Less manly?"

"Yeah." He escorted her back to the palace. "She'll show you how to add things you like to make it feel more like home."

"As long as you are with me, I am home."
"Good, because I feel the same way."

Don't miss out on your next favorite book!

Join the Satin Romance mailing list
www.satinromance.com/mail.html

THANK YOU FOR READING

Did you enjoy this book?

We invite you to leave a review at your favorite book site, such as Goodreads, Amazon, Barnes & Noble, etc.

DID YOU KNOW THAT LEAVING A REVIEW...

- Helps other readers find books they may enjoy.
- Gives you a chance to let your voice be heard.
- Gives authors recognition for their hard work.
- Doesn't have to be long. A sentence or two about why you liked the book will do.

ABOUT THE AUTHOR

Writing for Barbara Donlon Bradley started innocently enough, like most she kept diaries, journals, and wrote an occasional letter but she also had a vivid imagination and wrote scenes and short stories adding characters to her favorite shows and comic books. As time went on she found the passion for writing to be a strong drive for her. Humor is also very strong in her life. No matter how hard she tries to write something deep and dark, it will never happen. That humor bleeds into her writing. Since she can't beat it she has learned to use it to her advantage.

www.barbaradonlonbradley.com

ALSO AVAILABLE